THE HOUSTON ART CHRONICLES

A MARTIN TAYLOR CRIME MYSTERY

JOHN R. AARONS

Other books by this author. (Print & eBook)

    The Funicular

    The Docklands Mystery

    The Maltese Cross Mystery

    Author's memoirs. (eBook only)

    Fulfillment of my great Australian dream.

The Houston Art Chronicles
A Martin Taylor Mystery

Copyright © 2022 by John R. Aarons

ppbk: ISBN: 978-1-63812-429-0
ebook: ISBN: 978-1-63812-430-6

All rights reserved. No part in this book may be produced and transmitted in any form or by any means, electronic, or mechanical, including photocopying, recording, or by any information storage and retrieval system, without permission in writing from the copyright owner.

The views expressed in this work are solely those of the author and do not necessarily reflect the views of the publisher hereby disclaims any responsibility for them.
Published by Pen Culture Solutions 09/28/2022

Pen Culture Solutions
1-888-727-7204 (USA)
1-800-950-458 (Australia)
support@penculturesolutions.com

CHAPTERS

1.0	Setting the agenda.	1
2.0	A new day…. a new adventure.	20
3.0	Now for the serious stuff.	27
4.0	Being part of the Texan work ethic.	32
5.0	A happy reunion.	45
6.0	A culture filled day.	54
7.0	The Patron Saint of Lost and Stolen Articles.	62
8.0	Concentrating on the serious stuff ….again.	70
9.0	Let the Games begin! The Bidding War gets under way.	93
10.0	When art is more than just a pretty picture.	107
11.0	A "chilli" reception in Mexico!	127
12.0	Front page headlines.	153
13.0	Hitting the home run.	166
14.0	Many happy returns brings an unwanted birthday present.	178
15.0	It's a small, small world.	189
16.0	Bienvenido Martin!	198
17.0	Decision time.	213
18.0	Growing pains in Spain.	220
19.0	Martin's mini-war between Spain and France.	227
20.0	Peace in our time? Most unlikely!	241
21.0	A surprise ending.	252

THE HOUSTON ART CHRONICLES

CHAPTER 1

Setting the agenda

Martin was sitting in the lobby of the Marriott Marquis Hotel in downtown Houston, Texas, waiting to meet the Senior Editor of the Houston Chronicle newspaper. For the past ten days he had been in New York City attending a court case that had been delayed due to the Covid-19 pandemic. A man was on trial charged with the murder of a woman some eighteen months earlier. Martin was the main witness for the prosecution because he had been investigating the woman on behalf of the N.Y. Police Department at the time she was killed. She was suspected of being a member of a group of criminals responsible for the theft of an extremely valuable collection of religious objects belonging to a Maltese Cathedral that had been on exhibition in a Manhattan gallery. The jury had found the accused guilty of second degree murder and the judge had sentenced him to 15 years without parole in a maximum security prison. The killer had escaped a heavier sentence because the jury was satisfied that the murder was not premeditated. He was already in an upstate prison after being convicted and sentenced to six years in prison as a member of the team responsible for the robbery. He is to serve both sentences concurrently and would now be moved to the notorious Sing Sing Correctional Facility just north of the city along the Hudson River. Martin had been in New York to give evidence at the robbery trial also some six months earlier.

Subsequent to the murder trial, Martin spent a few days catching up with the N.Y. police officers he had worked with on that case. He had established a great rapport with the Police Commissioner and his associates and they were very appreciative of his work in bringing the case to a satisfactory conclusion. He had been wined and dined in expensive restaurants around the theatre district near Times Square and downtown close to the new

One World Trade Centre. He had an open airline ticket for his return to Australia and was about to call Qantas and fix the date for his flight when he received a text message on his mobile phone to contact a Mr. Robert Mason. The message stated that he was the Senior Editor of the Houston Chronicle newspaper and wished to discuss a potential assignment. He immediately called the number provided in the text message and following introductions Robert explained that the assignment was related to an auction of an exciting art collection to be held shortly in Houston. Martin agreed to fly down early the next day. Robert gave him his email address so he could send through his flight and accommodation details. He had the front desk at the New York hotel, where he had been staying during the trial reserve a business class seat on a non-stop flight to Houston with American Airlines arriving around mid-day.

The flying time was a little more than three and a half hours so he would have plenty of time to think about how the newspaper knew of his expertise in this field, and what they had in mind for him to do. He had also asked the hotel clerk reserve a suite in a good hotel in centre of Houston for two nights. She suggested a hotel that was part of the same group and told him the room rates were comparable with this one. He told her to continue with the reservation and confirm the details later.

He sent off a message to his office manager back in Melbourne briefly explaining the delay to his planned return, and a similar one to his fiancée in Bilbao, Spain, promising more details once he knew what the Houston Chronicle was proposing. Shortly after, the front desk clerk called with his flight and accommodation details. He then emailed Robert with his expected arrival time in Houston and the name of the hotel where he would be staying. Five minutes later he received a reply saying Robert would come to meet him at his hotel around 1.30 in the afternoon.

The next day, after a pleasant flight from New York, he arrived at Houston's George Bush Intercontinental Airport and took a taxi to the

Marriott Marquis Hotel which he was pleased to see was right in the heart of downtown. After settling in to his suite on the 12th floor, he unpacked his suitcase and went down to the lobby to wait for Robert. He picked up some tourist brochures from a display stand and was seated in the lounge browsing through them to see what was on offer for visitors to this thriving metropolis.

He was reading about the Houston Museum of Fine Arts when he realised someone was standing in front of him. He looked up to see a tall well-dressed person smiling as he introduced himself saying the clerk had pointed Martin out when he asked for him at the front desk. He briefly studied the man and guessed he was probably in his early fifties. He spoke well and was obviously well educated. Martin stood up and they shook hands. They moved to a quiet corner of the vast lounge and ordered refreshments. Robert told Martin that the trial in New York had made headline news around the country, and his newspaper had carried daily reports on its front page. He explained that the man charged with the murder had connections in Houston linked to a criminal organization that had been under investigation by the FBI for some time. This made it of particular interest to their readership. At this point, Martin asked, 'Was this criminal organization allied with the Houston chapter of a motorcycle gang?' Robert nodded adding, 'It certainly was, and the leading bikie is currently before the courts on a number of drug and firearms related charges.'

Coffees and a bowl with pretzels and nuts arrived. After the waiter had moved away, Robert began his explanation of why he had asked Martin to meet with him. Every now and then he referred to a notebook he had brought with him. Martin thought to himself that obviously this man had worked his way up from the rank of a reporter to being a senior editor. 'During the trial in New York, I had our team look into your background and we found it extremely fascinating. We learnt that a detective with the Victoria police force in Melbourne had earned a reputation as a leading expert on art crime and had been instrumental in solving a number of high profile cases not only in Australia, but in Europe and the USA as well.

At some point, you decided to resign from the police force and start your own private investigation firm. This led to the assignment in New York and the eventual solving of that case which made headlines around the world because of its European connection.' Feeling somewhat embarrassed, Martin sat quietly listening whilst Robert explained that they had looked into his background thoroughly.

'We have an excellent team of investigative journalists and I became interested in having your story published as a series of articles in our weekend magazine. I decided to dispatch one of our senior reporters, Janita Sullivan, to Melbourne to interview you. We sent a message via your company website a few days ago saying she would fly to Melbourne to meet with you later in the week. We were keen to get there before other media outlets beat us to the punch. Overnight, we received a reply saying that you were expected back in the next couple of days and on arrival in Melbourne she should telephone the Brighton office to make a formal appointment. Obviously, these arrangements took place at the same time you changed your plans to spend a few extra days in New York. This resulted in Janita being told when she arrived at your office that unfortunately you were still in New York. Because our reporter didn't want to have a completely wasted trip, she chatted a little with your office manager, Jessica Wainwright. I have to say she was very loyal and didn't want to divulge too much!' Martin smiled as he thought about Jess saying very little to the reporter and knew that she would have responded politely to the questions without giving much away.

Robert continued, 'Jessica did suggest that our reporter speak with the owner of a Melbourne art gallery for whom you had carried out a very special assignment a couple of years ago. She made arrangements for Janita to meet with the gallery owner and he generously picked her up in his car and drove her to his gallery. It seems he was full of praise for you. He allowed her to take some photos of his gallery which we may use later in the article should you agree. He also didn't want to tell her too much without your permission, so when she emailed me with this news, I decided the best thing would be to have her head back to Houston and I would try to track you down in New York and invite you here. We were fortunate that our New York office has connections with the NYPD and managed to speak with the Police Commissioner who agreed to provide us with your cell phone number.' The waiter came by just then and Martin ordered fresh drinks.

'Our newspaper is a member of the Hearst Publishing Group,' Robert continued, 'and we have an enormous combined readership with the group's other publications. Our management team has discussed how best to make our proposals of interest for you and we have come up with the following plan.'

The waiter returned with the refreshments and the discussion paused while they both took a break before Robert continued. 'Our plan is to run a series of articles about you in our weekend magazine which we believe our readers will find interesting. Texans have always shown great affection towards Australia as they believe your country is similar in many ways to their great state. You have huge cattle ranches, or stations as I understand you call them, and great open spaces.

Many of your movies feature cowboys and rodeos just like Texas and obviously there is a great love of horses.' He paused to refer to his notes before continuing.

'We were able to learn a little of your background thanks to Google and Wikipedia, but obviously we will need to expand considerably on their brief information. It will start with your early life growing up in Melbourne, and after graduating from college, you followed in your late father's footsteps as a member of the Victoria Police force. We saw on-line that the Victoria Police academy in Melbourne is one of the finest in the country and would like to write about your experiences when training there. Naturally we'll expand a little on your first years in the force as a rookie before moving to the art crime division. We'll need your input into what we can reveal about some of the cases you solved that led to your ultimate promotion as the head of the division.'

Martin spoke up at this point, 'I am flattered by your attention to my achievements but I have to point out that I have a reputation to maintain and clients' privacy is of the utmost importance. Should I agree to these articles being published, I would insist on reviewing the drafts before they go to print.'

Robert nodded his agreement and continued, 'Next, we'll write about your subsequent decision to resign from the police force and start your own private investigation firm in Melbourne. The series will cover some of the high-profile cases you have been involved with in this new role and we'll respect whatever privacy information you wish us to adhere to in describing these. We also discovered that you have recently expanded your business and opened a second office in Spain to handle assignments in Europe. It is important for us to provide a little background about your private life, family and relationships, but we'll only publish as much as you want us to.'

Martin stepped in saying, 'Robert, you will appreciate the work of a private investigator carries with it certain dangers, particularly when it involves stirring up notorious criminal organizations and outlaw motorcycle gangs. Certain details of family and close friends should not be disclosed in newspaper articles, particularly where they live or work.'

'That is absolutely clear Martin,' Robert responded, 'our articles can be vetted by you prior to going to print and I will personally guarantee that we will remove anything you find offensive or too revealing.' Martin thanked him concluding, 'Please ensure these conditions are included in the contract that your company draws up for our signatures.'

'Finally,' Robert added, 'apart from the articles about you we will run in our weekend magazine, the assignment we would like you to consider is to attend an art auction that is scheduled to take place here in Houston this month. The collection that is being auctioned had previously belonged to a Mexican drug baron named Miguel de Cristobal who lived here in one of our exclusive suburbs. He was assassinated a few months ago as he walked out of his front door one morning to pick up the newspaper from the lawn. The art was confiscated by the authorities because it had been purchased with the proceeds of crime so the money from the auction will go to the Government Treasury. He owed millions of dollars to the IRS for unpaid taxes.

The authorities have searched the Mexican's home from top to bottom but were unable to uncover any sales documents proving the authenticity of the paintings.

This means they will be auctioned on the basis that the buyer accepts the risk that the artists' signatures on the paintings may not be genuine. As you will see, it is an amazing collection and the Chronicle would like to acquire some of the paintings to hang in the company boardroom and top management offices. We would like you to inspect and suggest which paintings we should bid for. A total budget figure will be advised once you have agreed to take on this assignment and signed a confidentiality agreement. In this regard, we would then ask you to actually bid on our behalf once we have agreed to the paintings you select. I have brought with me a catalogue of the items being auctioned so you can study it before you actually go for a viewing prior to the auction date. As it happens, your choice of hotel is fortuitous as the auction will be held at the nearby George R. Brown Convention Center. It is right opposite the hotel and there is a sky bridge connecting the hotel to the convention centre.'

'I didn't know about the sky bridge,' said Martin, 'I haven't put on my detective's cap since arriving at the hotel. So far I've only seen this lobby and my suite.'

'Well, it will be extremely convenient,' continued Robert, 'and I hope you don't think this is too presumptuous of me, but I am keen to have you on board and would like you to seriously consider our offer. Following the auction, we'll ask you to write a story about each of the paintings we successfully bid for, describing their background and history. Your report will be called *The Houston Art Chronicles* which the board believes is a very fitting name for our new art collection. This assignment would also make an excellent conclusion to the weekend magazine series.'

Martin took some time before replying, 'I have to say Robert, that what you have just laid out before me has whetted my appetite for adventure in the art world which has always been a favourite topic of mine. I will certainly give it a lot of thought today. I need to check my schedule of appointments with my office and possibly delegate some work to others in both our offices, Melbourne and Bilbao. I will be speaking with Jessica Wainwright later today and have her email me a list of the work that is in progress or about to start. I should be able to respond to you by late tomorrow. Depending on the timing, I may have to fly back to Melbourne for a couple of days then return to Houston early in the week of the auction. The Australian national airline Qantas, has non-stop flights between Dallas and Sydney via Brisbane but the stopover in Brisbane and the change to a domestic flight in Sydney extends the total flight time by at least three hours making somewhere around seventeen hours. Qantas is starting direct Melbourne to Dallas flights at the end of the year and I would have found it quite an interesting experience to take such a long flight. In any case, there are multiple non-stop flights every day between Los Angeles and Melbourne which will be quicker and less fuss than flying Houston to Dallas then on to Melbourne.'

Robert nodded and replied, 'I didn't know about the Dallas to Sydney flight, our reporter flew with American Airlines to Los Angeles then changed to Qantas direct to Melbourne. She is on her way back as we speak so you will have an opportunity to meet her later this week.' Martin said he was looking forward to meeting her.

'The Houston Chronicle will cover all your expenses for accommodation plus business class flights from Australia should you need to go back to your office this week. We will also provide you with an office to work in when you are not at the convention centre and a rental car to get around in. Of course, your time will be covered by an agreed-upon daily rate. We'd like you to consider our proposal and respond to us as soon as possible.'

Martin looked at his watch and suggested they might have a quick lunch together at the hotel restaurant but Robert declined saying, 'Thanks Martin, I have to get back to the office but if it's OK with you, I'll pick you up this evening around seven o'clock and we'll go for dinner at my favourite steakhouse that is not far from this hotel. I will do my best to answer any questions you toss at me over dinner.' Martin responded, 'OK, thanks for the invitation, I'll make sure I'm ready at seven.'

Martin spent some time after Robert left taking a stroll around the CBD looking at a number of impressive office buildings and department stores such as Foley's and Sears. He came across a concert and performance venue called Jones Hall which had a poster on the front announcing it was the home of the Houston Symphony Orchestra. He stood across the street admiring the impressive modern architecture and was thinking he'd certainly like to attend a concert there if he does accept the proposal from the Houston Chronicle and spend some time in this bustling city.

It was a warm humid afternoon and he found that he was perspiring quite a lot by the time he returned to the hotel around 4 o'clock. He checked the time difference and found that Melbourne was 16 hours ahead of Houston so if he called now it would be 8am there. That should be a reasonable time to catch Jessica at home before she left for the office. She picked up on the second ring and said she was glad to hear from him. 'How are things going over there boss?' she asked. 'Great Jess, I've met the senior editor from the Houston Chronicle today, and apart from writing a serialized article about me which apparently you already know about, they have asked me to assess some paintings that are coming up for auction shortly. Please email through the current assignment status report for both the Melbourne and Bilbao offices so I can look through them before I go out in a few hours. I need to check the expected duration of each assignment and possibly re-allocate jobs to others because my absence will affect everyone's workload.' Jessica told him about the recent visit of the reporter from the newspaper and her subsequent chat with the owner of the Armadale gallery gathering information about Martin for the newspaper's article. 'I'm going out for dinner this evening with Robert Mason, the gentleman I met earlier, and we'll be discussing further the proposed art assessment job which at the moment I am keen to accept. If necessary, I'll fly back to Melbourne in a couple of days and will go through everything with you then.

Should I take on this assignment, I will have to return to Houston two to three days later. Meanwhile, I will mark up the work status list you'll send me tonight and return it to you first thing tomorrow.' Jessica told him that all the work on hand was proceeding well and the issues that had arisen while he was in New York had all been cleared up thanks to brain-storming sessions. 'That's great news Jess, I'll include details of my movements when I send back the work status list.'

He set up his laptop and logged onto the internet to send emails to his office and his fiancée Isabella who lives in Bilbao, Spain. He detailed the newspaper's proposal to Jessica and asked her to inform the company accountant, Paul Cohen. Martin attached copies of all his travel, accommodation and meals receipts for Paul to prepare a final invoice for the New York Mayor. His instructions for the accountant stated that the invoice must summarize the expenses incurred whilst he attended the recent murder trial in Manhattan. He is also to update his daily rate should he accept the Houston Chronicle offer.

He then emailed Isabella and told her about this unusual but potentially exciting proposal to spend some time in Houston and suggested that if he accepts, she might like to join him for a weekend if she can spare the time. He assumed that there would be regular flights from Spain to Houston. She had always managed to take a few days off from her busy schedule at the law firm where she was a senior partner and meet Martin somewhere in the world wherever he happened to be working on a case.

After a shower and a change of clothes, he went down to the hotel lounge to wait for Robert. It was early evening and he had plenty of time to consider the newspaper's offer before being picked up to go out for dinner. He sat with a pint of ice cold Lone Star beer whilst he read a copy of the Houston Chronicle he had picked up from the front desk. The page one stories consisted mostly about events that had taken place in and around Houston and Dallas with a couple of articles related to world issues. He found page two of particular interest because there were short stories of shootings that had occurred the night before! He knew that Texans in general have been gun lovers since the old cowboy days, and tucked this away at the back of his mind to ask Robert about later. He noticed an ad at the bottom of the page for the newspaper offering a guide to Houston's bars and BBQ joints. By the time he had finished reading most of the stories, he had decided it appeared to be a quality newspaper with well written articles. As far as he was concerned, this was an extremely important aspect for him when considering whether or not to accept their proposal.

He then started reading the art auction catalogue which was a glossy booklet that had clearly been an expensive production because the photos and colour printing were of the highest quality. It was obvious to Martin that the auction house had been instructed by the government to make it as eye-catching as possible to attract the attention of private galleries and cash-flush art collectors. The items were listed in alphabetical order of the artist whose name was attributed to the paintings although there was a disclaimer at the front of the catalogue stating that documents were unavailable to prove the authenticity of each art work. Although there was no question as to the quality of the artworks on offer, the buyer was to accept the risk that the paintings may not be genuine.

The auctioneers had employed international experts to examine them and their report stated that in a small number of instances, there was the possibility that they were produced by the artist whose name appeared thereon. Those paintings were marked in the catalogue with the letters PG indicating possibly genuine. The catalogue had been sent to museums and galleries around the world with an invitation to attend the auction although it is doubtful any reputable institution handling works of art would buy paintings without a provenance. The auctioneers anticipated that if any of the paintings had been stolen, claims would have been made by those institutions after they had studied the catalogue. Up till now, no such claims had been raised.

One of the first paintings in the catalogue was listed as a Canaletto and depicted a scene in Venice highlighting *The Bridge of Sighs*. Highly detailed, this painting looked magnificent in the photo and if genuine, Martin believed would fetch millions. There was no PG symbol against this item!

The next two in the catalogue were listed as possibly having been painted by El Greco. One was titled *Scenes of Toledo* and the other was called *Adoration of the Magi*. Toledo was one of the towns in Spain where he lived and Martin had read that for some reason, El Greco's paintings were not popular in other European countries in the 19th century. On the other hand, American museums bought quite a number of his works and finished up with more of this artist's paintings than any other country apart from Spain. The pictures shown in the catalogue looked to be fine examples but Martin would need to examine them closely at the pre-auction viewing.

He was surprised to find that the next painting was listed as a Thomas Gainsborough and it was a portrait of a beautiful woman. The colours were superb and the facial details of the woman looked almost like a photograph.

Martin was so engrossed in studying the catalogue that he didn't notice the time and nearly jumped out of his skin when the telephone on the desk rang loudly. It was the doorman saying a gentleman was waiting by the front desk to take him out for dinner. He quickly grabbed his coat and took the elevator down to the lobby.

Apologising to Robert, they went out to where a Cadillac Escalade SUV with a chauffeur was waiting. The motor was running with a powerful air conditioning system keeping the Houston humidity under control. A few minutes later, they pulled up outside a very smart looking restaurant with the name *Vic & Anthony's Steakhouse* in large letters on the front. The two men entered what was a most impressive large space with modern furnishings and a huge bar at one end. Everything about the restaurant appeared first class and Martin was immediately aware of its friendly atmosphere. They were led by the maître d' to a table on the opposite side to the bar where it would be quiet and enable them to talk without having to raise their voices.

Once they were settled comfortably, a waiter brought menus and asked if they would like a pre-dinner drink. Robert suggested to Martin that they should start with a Kentucky whiskey as bourbon was a favourite drink in the southern states.

'As it happens,' Martin answered, 'I was introduced to it when I was in New York working on that high profile robbery case and I did find it easy to drink. I am not a lover of Scotch whisky or vodka so I'm happy to go along with bourbon thanks.' Robert nodded to the waiter and asked for two glasses of Jim Beam Black Label on ice with bottles of 7-Up and Coke to choose for mixes.

The waiter headed for the bar to get their drinks whilst they began perusing the extensive menu. By the time the waiter returned, Martin had decided on a shrimp cocktail appetiser and an 18 ounce prime rib-eye with baked potato and asparagus. 'Great choice,' Robert proclaimed and ordered a dozen oysters to start, followed by a New York strip steak. 'We'll also have a bottle of Napa Valley Merlot please.' The waiter typed their orders into his iPad and moved away. The two men sat back relaxing and savouring their drinks. Martin started the conversation regarding the art auction. 'I noticed that there are no indicative price ranges for the paintings in the catalogue and I find this extremely unusual Robert.'

'Martin,' he replied, 'the Justice Department which is in charge of disposing of the artworks, apparently mulled over this issue for a long time. Finally, after long discussions with the auctioneer, it was decided that without documentary proof of the claimed artists, it would be better to let the market forces come up with prices they felt comfortable with. Art experts were called in to advise a range of prices and a secret list was drawn up showing the minimum amount the auctioneer would accept for each painting. If the minimum price is not reached for a particular painting, the auctioneer will pass it in and that item will be open for negotiations following the auction.'

Martin considered this for a couple of minutes before declaring, 'Obviously, the Houston Chronicle has allocated a certain amount of funds for the art auction and I would like to be accompanied by someone from the company with authority to agree to the bids as I raise our ID card for each painting. Once the total amount of our purchases approaches the budget figure, I assume that I am to immediately stop bidding for any more paintings even if the original aim was to acquire more paintings. Is that a correct assumption?'

At that moment, the waiter appeared with large bowls of green salad with a choice of thousand island or French dressings to cleanse their palates before their appetisers arrive. Martin had not been to the USA prior to the New York assignment so until then had been unfamiliar with the American custom of providing salads before the actual meal was served. He was now quite used to it and found he looked forward to it when out at fine restaurants such as the one he was at tonight.

'Restaurants in Australia certainly don't bring salads to the table unless ordered as sides,' he told Robert. As they munched on the crisp fresh iceberg lettuce, Martin looked around the dining room and saw that it was now almost full of smartly dressed men and women. He decided that the patrons were probably business people, particularly as there were no children accompanying them. A few minutes later, the appetisers arrived and their discussions were once again on hold while they enjoyed the food.

Robert had finished his oysters and began by answering Martin's question on monitoring and controlling the expenditure at the auction. 'Your assumption is absolutely correct Martin…. our finance director, Neville Montgomery, will accompany you at the auction. He has the authority to accept your bids and at any time during the auction he feels that the price for a particular painting is heading too high, he will ask you to stop. There are a large number of different types of items to be offered at the auction, not only paintings. There are sculptures and antiques as well, so three days have been allocated to clear them all. We will also be engaging the services of an experienced Houston art valuer named Darryn Smith to suggest some values for the paintings you select. By the way, we have decided to only bid for paintings so I have not provided you with the separate catalogue which covers the sculptures and antiques. I will be dropping by now and then whenever I can get away from my busy editorial schedule as I am interested to watch how things pan out. Incidentally, it might be useful if you visit our fabulous Museum of Fine Arts and speak with the head curator there about the forthcoming art auction. They will certainly have someone at the auction, not necessarily to buy, but to observe the outcome. I will arrange an introduction for you with the museum's head curator when you return to take up your post. She may be able to help you with some of the background of this collection as I'm sure they would have looked into it very carefully since the auction was announced. Coincidentally, they recently had an exhibition of French Impressionist paintings that were on loan from the Boston Museum of Fine Arts. This collection had been on show in your National Gallery of Victoria before coming to Houston. Did you happen to see it when you were home?'

'Unfortunately,' replied Martin, 'due to the Covid-19 situation in Melbourne, the gallery was closed due to lockdowns imposed by the state government for most of the scheduled exhibition period so I didn't get a chance to see it. They did video the exhibition and it could be viewed on-line but as you know that is nowhere as good as actually standing in front of the paintings and seeing them close up in all their glory.'

The impressively presented steaks arrived at that moment and the waiter poured glasses of the Californian Merlot before leaving them to enjoy their meal. As they ate, Robert explained, 'I have travelled extensively in Europe and South America but have never crossed the Pacific Ocean to explore *down under*.' He then asked Martin to tell him something about life in Australia and how it compares to what he had seen since arriving in the USA.

Martin grabbed the opportunity to brag about the fabulous beaches found along the coastlines of every state and the amazing red colour of the *outback*. 'During our training at the Police Academy, we were taught about the population spread throughout the country to better understand where police numbers need to be allocated. We are mostly city folk, with 45% of the total population of 26 million living in greater Sydney and Melbourne. With a land area similar to the United States, there are only five states and two territories with huge areas of uninhabited desert and scrubland. The original inhabitants of Australia are known as Aborigines and Torres Strait Islanders and comprise a very small percentage of the population. Recent carbon dating of artefacts and cave paintings confirm they have been living there for around 60,000 years whilst British colonialism only started in 1770 with the arrival of Captain Cook who planted the Union Jack flag at Botany Bay near today's Sydney.'

'We'll definitely incorporate some of these details in our articles about your life,' Robert commented.

'In that respect,' Martin continued, 'there are similarities between our two nations although we didn't have to have a war with Britain to become an independent nation. A legacy of British rule is that our *Head of State* is the King of England and he is represented by a Governor General based in the Capital, Canberra, as well as a Governor in each state. These governors were originally sent out from England but that changed quite some time ago. Nowadays they are always Australians appointed by the Federal and State governments and their duties are mostly ceremonial. They live in mini-palaces and some are driven around in lovely old Rolls Royce sedans. A referendum in 1999 failed to change the constitution to replace the British Queen with an Australian in the role of *Head of State*. Another British legacy is that we drive on the left hand side of the road! Many of our language differences concern cars. What you call the trunk is known by us as the boot, the hood is called the bonnet, the licence plate is called a number plate and we fill up with petrol not gasoline. Unlike the USA, our political leader is a Prime Minister and is the leader of the party or coalition that wins a majority of the national votes at the election. The party can change the leadership at any time so it's possible to have a number of different Prime Ministers during the 3 year term of the Federal Government. Another major difference in our political world is that voting at elections is mandatory for all registered voters between the age of 18 and 80. This rule covers all Federal, State and local council elections. Fines can be applied to people who fail to vote and don't have a legitimate excuse. This means we have a big turn-out at the polls on election day'

Coffees and liqueurs closed out the meal and Martin was driven back to the hotel where he thanked his host for an enjoyable evening and promised to telephone him tomorrow with a decision and a plan to move forward. He was about to step out of the car when he said, 'I've just remembered something I wanted to ask you related to a column I read in the paper this morning. On page two there were reports of shootings that had taken place in Houston the night before. We are well aware of Texans love of guns so I wondered if these shootings are daily events.' Robert replied, 'It's true that Texans love their guns and back in the 60's and 70's there were many arguments settled using guns rather than fists but thankfully the situation has improved greatly since then. It was so bad back then that Monday's newspaper began the custom of listing the weekend shootings on page two, many of which took place in beer joints that were located alongside suburban main roads. Thankfully those rough and ready places have long since disappeared and the alcohol laws have been updated to make drinking a much more civilized affair. Unfortunately the number of shootings hasn't reduced as much as we'd like and recently we have also had terrible mass shootings at schools.'

Once in his suite, he switched on his laptop and checked the emails that had arrived since he went out earlier. Jessica had sent the list of current assignments showing who was consigned to each. He studied it for some time and noted that there were two new jobs not yet allocated to anyone.

One was for the Art Gallery of Western Australia that had requested some assistance in assessing the price they should tender for three paintings that had been offered to them by a large mining company. He decided that this would be an ideal assignment for Phil Wilson, a colleague who lived in Perth. This fellow was an independent art expert and would be perfect for the job.

Back in the 1980's, many large corporations expanded their permanent art collections by buying paintings of Australian landscapes from well-known local artists including indigenous artists. These were usually very large paintings and were hung in head office entrance foyers and boardrooms. Since the beginning of the 21st century, the value of many of these paintings had skyrocketed. The organisation in question was a coal mining company and was moving its corporate head office offshore due to the recent unpopularity of fossil fuels. As the collection of paintings was predominantly Australian landscapes, the board had considered donating their collection to the State art gallery as a gift but their shareholders voted to sell them. He marked the list for Jessica to contact Phil Wilson in Perth and offer him the assignment. They had used him once previously and had a schedule of rates in the files for his services.

There was also a new assignment for a client in Northern Spain that Jessica had marked down as a possible job for Martin as it would present a welcome opportunity for him to catch up with his fiancée in Bilbao. He suggested that she check with the client if the work could be postponed for a couple of weeks in order for the company principal to carry out the assignment. She is to explain that he was currently in the United States but was planning a visit to the Bilbao office soon after he has completed his current assignment. If they responded that it was too urgent to accept a delay, then she was to have one of their operatives from the Bilbao office take care of it.

The location of this assignment was a private gallery in San Sebastian which is not far from Bilbao and a short drive from the border with France and the popular French resort of Biarritz where the protagonist in this case resided. Martin knew of this town from a book he had read recently about spies during the Second World War who used Biarritz as their base. From the author's description of Biarritz it sounded like a very nice place to be stationed whilst the war was raging a long way from there. If the Spanish client agreed to the extension, Martin would definitely have Isabella join him there for a weekend of sunning on lovely sandy beaches and exploring the historic sites in that area.

As usual, his mind veered away from the business at hand that required his attention whenever he thought about his beautiful Spanish fiancée.

CHAPTER 2

A NEW DAY…. A NEW ADVENTURE.

Martin ate a light breakfast in the hotel's self-service buffet and sat reading the auction catalogue. There certainly was a huge mix of painting styles in the collection… from French impressionist to American abstract modern. There were some which could be by Monet or Manet, and others which could be by Andy Warhol or Jackson Pollock. Further along he found two small paintings by Frida Kahlo and one by her husband Diego Rivera. He knew of these two famous Mexican artists but had never seen any of their works. As he studied the photos of their paintings that were to be auctioned, he noticed that they had shown the husband's full Spanish name which took up much of the page under the photo of his painting. Diego Maria de la Concepcion Juan Nepomucheno Estanislao de la Rivera y Barientos Acosta y Rodriguez. Martin assumed he probably came from some sort of Spanish nobility and decided it was no wonder he shortened his name to Diego Rivera! He smiled to himself as he conjured up a picture of the artist signing an official document with his full name. As he moved through the pages of the catalogue he suddenly spotted a painting that stopped him in his tracks. It was a painting purportedly by the late Australian artist, Robin Black! If it was genuine, he wondered how it came to be in the collection of a Mexican drug baron.

He was so engrossed in studying the catalogue that he hadn't noticed that it was now 10 o'clock and the breakfast buffet had been cleared away leaving him the only person sitting at a table. The café was reverting to a coffee and snack venue for the rest of the day. He hastily grabbed his things and walked out of the dining room. As he passed through the lobby, he picked up a copy of the Houston Chronicle from the stack of newspapers at the front desk and together with the auction catalogue headed up to his suite. He checked his emails and found Jessica's response to his instructions regarding re-allocation of new work. Phil Wilson in Perth had agreed to the assignment at the Art Gallery of Western Australia and a contract had been prepared for signature. The Spanish assignment could not be postponed so was allocated to Juan Lopez at the Bilbao office. He was to drive to the nearby town of San Sebastian the day after tomorrow where there was a dispute over ownership of a painting between a private gallery in the town and a prominent businessman in Biarritz just across the border in France.

He worked out that if he telephoned his fiancée Isabella in Bilbao now it would be around 9.00pm which should be a reasonable time to catch up. She was probably in bed watching television as she answered the phone almost immediately with the Spanish greeting *'Hola'* before he had a chance to speak! As soon as she recognised his voice, she changed immediately to English which she spoke perfectly with a gorgeous accent. After confirming that they were both in good health, he went on to tell her somewhat excitedly of the Houston Chronicle's proposal. Firstly about the series of articles they would like to run in their weekend magazine about Martin's career, and secondly about the potential assignment as their adviser at the upcoming art auction. 'Are you going to accept?' she wanted to know.

'Well,' he replied, 'I first wanted to discuss it with you as it means there will be short delay before I will be able to come to Bilbao to spend some time with you and also to see how you felt about a series of articles about me which would inevitably include mention of my engagement to you.'

There was silence for a minute or two whilst she considered what he had just told her. 'Martin my love, I am happy with you achieving fame following the success of your recent overseas cases and have no problem with our engagement being publicized in the newspaper series. As for the delay in us meeting up, I am of course disappointed, but hopefully it won't be long before we are together again. I could even fly to Houston for a couple of days as you had suggested earlier whilst you are working there, especially if I did this around a weekend.' Martin then explained that he had expected to fly back to Melbourne for a few days before returning to Houston to commence the preliminary work on the upcoming art auction but this now won't be necessary. 'I'll advise the newspaper today of my acceptance and will keep you informed of my every move. In fact, once I have their contract, I'll scan and send it through to you for your comments before I sign it. Having a smart lawyer for my fiancée is definitely a bonus!'

They signed off, she to rest up as she had to attend court the next morning to finalize a settlement for a big case that had dragged on for a few weeks, and he to call Robert to advise his acceptance of the proposed assignment. Mrs. Rogers. told him that he wasn't available right now but a car was being sent to collect him in an hour and bring him to the newspaper's office. Dressed in the suit he had brought to wear in the New York court, he went down to the lobby and waited for the chauffeur. There was an upmarket gift shop near the front door and he went in to browse around for a gift for Isabella. He saw a couple of things he liked and told the shop assistant that he would be back later to make a decision as at that moment he recognised the same Cadillac Escalade pull up at the entrance that had taken him out the night before. He greeted the driver who invited him to sit in the front so they could chat as they drove to the Chronicle's head office.

As they headed out of the CBD, Martin asked the driver for his name. 'Lonnie Macpherson,' he replied. 'Well Lonnie, please call me Martin. Are you a Texan, or have you moved here from another state?' Staring straight ahead as he navigated the large vehicle through the traffic, he replied, 'Although my grandparents migrated to the United States from Scotland, I was born and raised here in an area south of the city, about halfway between Houston and the coastal city of Galveston which is on the Gulf of Mexico. My father is an aeronautical engineer and works for NASA at the Space Centre. He and my mother live in a modern townhouse in a suburb called

Nassau Bay which is opposite the Space Centre and alongside a pretty lake where locals water ski. Lonnie is a very popular name in this *neck of the woods* and the Macpherson name belongs to a land on the other side of the world. I once had plans to visit my ancestor's country but got married instead so overseas travel will have to wait for a while.'

They were now moving fast along the southwest freeway and in what seemed no time at all, they turned off the freeway and into the entrance of a very imposing modern structure.

Lonnie parked by the front entrance and escorted Martin to the reception desk saying he would see him later to take him back to his hotel. The receptionist asked Martin to sign in and then called Mr. Mason's P.A. to say he had arrived. A few minutes later, a smartly attired woman appeared to take him to the senior editor's office. She introduced herself as Mrs. Rogers and led him to the nearby elevators. She pressed the button for the 4th floor and within seconds they arrived at the executive level. Martin followed her along a brightly lit corridor to Robert's office where he sat at an enormous desk piled with folders and papers. He stood up and came around the desk to shake Martin's hand and welcome him to the newspaper's Houston head office.

There was a table and four chairs along one side of the office and Robert suggested they sit there so they could run through the contract together.

She reappeared soon after the two men were seated at the table and handed a folder to Robert. 'Thanks Mrs. Rogers, please order some drinks when you are back at your desk.' She then asked Martin if he would prefer tea or coffee so she could order it from their in-house canteen. After she had taken the refreshment orders and departed, Robert opened the folder and handed Martin a copy of the contract. A short time later as the two men were quietly reading the first few pages, a young man from the canteen knocked and entered the office with a tray of refreshments which he placed carefully on the table before departing promptly without speaking. He obviously saw that the two men were deep in thought and didn't want to interrupt. For the next hour, they worked their way through the twenty page document making some comments on the way. After they reached the end, Robert enquired what Martin thought of the wording. 'I am basically happy with the document,' said Martin, 'but I'm going to pass it by my fiancée this evening and if she doesn't raise any issues I will sign it tomorrow. By the way, I have sorted out the workload at my two offices and have decided that there is no need for me to fly back to Australia at this time.' Robert then pointed out, 'As you can see Martin, the remuneration package has been left blank at this stage. We can fill these details in at the time of signing.'

'I have requested some information from my accountant regarding our charges and associated costs and expect to have that for you when I see you tomorrow Robert.' He then invited Martin for a short tour of the offices which would include being introduced to the executive editor, and the finance director. As they walked around, he explained that the Chronicle's old headquarters had been established in downtown in 1910 and continued operations there for more than one hundred years. 'In the early 2000's it was decided to move to a new complex with up-to-the-minute satellite communications equipment enabling them to instantly hook up with news outlets anywhere in the world. The result was this ultra-modern, stunningly attractive building which has been the newspaper's headquarters since April 2014.'

They went down to the floor below and walked past rows of desks each with the latest models of computers with large screen monitors.

Many of the staff were speaking on hands-free telephones as they speed typed their conversations into their computers. Some looked up and smiled a greeting at Martin as he passed and nodded to their editor. Robert told Martin that the paper was one of the oldest continuously published newspapers in the United States. It also had one of the highest circulations of a weekend edition in the country. At the end of this floor, there was a large meeting room that he explained was where the editors huddled around a large table with senior staff to thrash out which articles would finish up going to print and where they were to be located in the paper.

Returning to the upper floor, Martin was introduced to Emma Johnson. Her smartly furnished office was decorated with a number of ceramic objects that he guessed may have been Mayan, Inca or Aztec. The National Gallery of Victoria has a considerable collection of pottery from those ancient Central and South American civilizations and he had often admired them during his numerous visits. She greeted Martin and expressed her hope that their business relationship would be rewarding for both parties. 'We have allocated a spare office for you to use as your base when you need to spend time researching the paintings or writing reports about the art auction. It will also be a convenient place for interviews for the magazine article,' she told him. He thanked her and told her he was looking forward to working with the Houston Chronicle. They next went to the office of Neville Montgomery and following introductions, agreed to spend time together when he returned to sign the contract the next day. They needed to work out a strategy for the bidding process at the auction.

Martin declined an invitation to go out for dinner that night saying he had a lot of things to settle between now and when he returned tomorrow. Robert promised to email the details of the head curator at the Houston Museum of Fine Arts which will provide Martin with a worthwhile opportunity to visit in the next day or so. Mrs. Rogers then took him down to the lobby and called for the chauffeur to take him back to his hotel. Lonnie appeared like magic within moments, and as they walked out of the cool building to the car, the steamy Houston atmosphere immediately caused Martin's shirt to become clammy. The air conditioning in the Cadillac was so effective Martin was freezing before they had driven out of the car park and onto the freeway! 'Melbourne also has times of uncomfortable weather,' he told Lonnie, particularly when there are days of high temperatures and suddenly it turns cold and damp. People like to say it is the only city in the world that can have four seasons in one day! Despite living my whole life in that city, I'm not sure I he could ever get used to a climate like Houston's.'

They chatted like old buddies as Martin was driven back to his hotel. Lonnie told him that he and his wife had two children aged seven and eight. He said that being a chauffeur for a terrific company such as the Chronicle was for him a very satisfying job. Although he was a good student during his college years, he did not aspire to a professional career like his father. Instead, he chose to go out into the real world at a young age and start earning wages so he could save to eventually buy his own house. At the moment they were renting a large apartment but he hoped to be in a position to buy a house in the next year or so.

CHAPTER 3

NOW FOR THE SERIOUS STUFF.

Back at the hotel, Martin asked the clerk at the front desk to order a rental car to be delivered to the hotel tomorrow morning around 10.30. He had decided to do his bit for the environment and requested an electric vehicle assuming the car rental companies had one available. The clerk told him that Hertz had recently taken delivery of a large fleet of Tesla cars and the hotel has had charging stations installed in the underground garage. He could plug it in whenever he returned to the hotel during his stay and it would fully recharge overnight. As Martin figured he would not be making any long trips outside of Houston, the relatively limited range an electric vehicle should not be a problem. As he was now not interrupting his stay to return to Australia at this time, he advised the clerk that he expected to extend his stay at the hotel for an estimated ten days. He apologized for the uncertainty and promised to keep them informed every couple of days as he settled into his work in Houston.

Once inside his suite, he composed emails to Jessica at the Brighton office, and to Paul Cohen his accountant, telling them of his latest plans. He reminded Paul that he needed the updated daily rate and other costs overnight so they can be inserted into the contract with the Houston Chronicle tomorrow. All costs are to be in US dollars.

He went down to the hotel's business centre and scanned the 20 page contract and sent it off to Isabella in Bilbao for her review and comment. Back in his suite, he found an email from Robert with details of the contact at the Houston Museum of Fine Arts. As it was only mid-afternoon, he decided to call and make an appointment with the curator, Michelle Robinson. He had been given a direct phone number and introduced himself when she answered. He then told her that he was going to the newspaper's head office tomorrow to sign the assignment contract and hold some meetings with people he would be working with. As he was uncertain how long he would be there tomorrow, it would be better to head to the museum on Friday mid-morning to meet with her if that was convenient. She agreed that would be fine and said, 'Let's make it around 10am.' As he was not sure of the time needed to get between the different places, he asked if it would be acceptable if he telephoned her Friday when he was about to leave the hotel in the city. 'Tomorrow when I go to the Chronicle, it will be my first time driving a car on the right side of the road,' Martin told her, 'and to make things more uncertain, I have to find my way around a city I am totally unfamiliar with in an electric car that will also be a new experience for me. Thankfully, all modern cars now have built-in GPS systems so that should eliminate having to stop and ask directions.'

In the short time he had been in Houston he was struck by the vast freeway system and the number of lanes in each direction. Coming in from the airport on his first day, the taxi had driven over a complex system of multi-level overpasses with freeways extending in all directions. He hoped that he wouldn't have to navigate his way around that mind-boggling piece of crossover engineering that he'd seen from the taxi coming from the airport to the city.

Martin found the website details of the auction house in the catalogue and logged on to check opening times for viewing. It advised that the items to be auctioned will be on display at the Convention Center from this coming Saturday until the start of the auction one week later. Opening times are from 10am to 8pm each day. As it was Wednesday, this would give him enough time to finalise the contract, meet with Michelle Robinson, complete his study of the catalogue and discuss strategy with the finance director, Neville Montgomery.

Deciding he needed some exercise, he changed into light casual clothes and headed out onto the steamy sidewalks. As he slowly wandered the streets looking in store windows, he was struck by the diversity of clothing styles offered….. from screamingly modern to some shops specializing in recycled fashions from the 1970's. Getting into the swing of the city, he found that he was finding it exciting and thoroughly enjoyable despite the oppressive heat. Looking for a place to cool down, he spotted an eatery with a sign that read, AUSSIE STYLE CAFÉ and was flabbergasted to see that Australian eating and drinking habits had somehow found their way to Texas. The place was called Bluestone Lane. He Googled the name on his phone and saw that there were something like 50 of these establishments throughout the USA. They had been started in New York by a guy from Melbourne called Nicholas Stone. Martin entered this brightly decorated café and found a table near the front from where he could observe the passing parade of people. He ordered a smashed avocado on sourdough toast and an iced coffee. The menu stated that two of the café's most popular items were the avocado and a flat white coffee but right now what he wanted was a cold drink. The waitress who served him had a heavy southern belle accent so was definitely not an Aussie. He didn't attempt to strike up a conversation.

Later on as he continued his tour of the downtown area, he once again found himself outside the Jones Hall concert venue. The advertising banners on the front windows proclaimed the final week of a concert by the Houston Symphony Orchestra featuring the acclaimed Argentinian cellist, Sol Gabetta. She was to play the Haydn Cello Concerto which was one of Martin's favourite classical pieces. Martin decided to call Isabella to see whether she would be able to fly over for the weekend and if so he would buy two tickets for the concert. The box office was open so he went inside and asked if there were seats still available for Saturday night. He was told that there were a number of unsold seats in the balcony. He thanked the ticket clerk and told her that he would check how many seats he wanted and return shortly. He stepped outside and immediately telephoned Isabella who was at home reading through the contract. She was surprised to hear from him so soon after their last telephone call. 'Are you free to fly to Houston Friday and accompany me to a concert on Saturday night?' Without hesitation she replied, 'As it happens, I have just successfully finished that long drawn out court case and had decided to take a few days off to rest before the next one starts. I would love to join you for the weekend so when we hang up I'll book flights and let you know the details.

By the way, I have almost completed the review of your contract with the newspaper and apart from a couple of words I suggest should be added or changed, it is a very well written document. I'll email you shortly with my comments.'

Martin told her that he was outside the concert hall and would go in now and buy tickets. 'I'm looking forward to us having the weekend together as it's been such a long time mainly due to the restrictions on travel imposed during the pandemic. I'll have a car to use from tomorrow so will come to the airport to pick you up when you arrive. That's good news about the contract, I was certain this company knows what they are doing as it was obvious to me that they are extremely professional in the way they have presented themselves to me.' He said they would speak again once all arrangements for her visit were finalised and bid her goodnight. Returning to the box office, the ticket clerk showed him the seating plan for the balcony and he selected two seats that she said would give them an excellent view of the stage and the soloist. Leaving the building, Martin referred to his city map to navigate his way back to the hotel.

Twenty minutes later he was back in his suite and looking at the emails that had come in since he last had his laptop switched on. There was one from his accountant, showing the charges to be added to the contract with a note at the end wishing him all the best for the new American assignment. Another email was from Jessica telling him that operations at both their offices were running smoothly. After thanking both Paul and Jessica, he called Robert. 'Good afternoon Robert, I would like to come to your office tomorrow morning to finalize the contract. There's no need to send Lonnie as I will take delivery of a rental car at the hotel tomorrow. I expect it will be late morning when I arrive at your office if that is acceptable. My fiancée will return the contract tonight basically unchanged and I'll also have the details of my charges to be included in the contract which I have just received from my accountant.' Robert replied that if he was tied up in an editorial meeting when Martin arrived, he would be taken to Neville's office to discuss financial matters until he is back from his meeting.

CHAPTER 4

BEING PART OF THE TEXAN WORK ETHIC.

Martin was studying the auction catalogue at the desk in his suite that evening when the hotel telephone rang. He answered and was surprised to find that it was Lonnie the chauffeur. 'Hello Mr. Taylor, oops, Martin, I hope I am not disturbing you but I would like to invite you to come to dinner tomorrow night to meet my family. My wife suggested that as you are a visitor from the other side of the world, and possibly not knowing anyone here apart from the newspaper's *top brass*, you might like to experience a Texan home-cooked meal.' Martin was taken aback by the invitation and without hesitation thanked him and agreed to meet his family for dinner. Lonnie asked for Martin's email details so he could send through his address and cell phone number should he have trouble finding their place or be running late. 'We live in an apartment complex in Clear Lake City which is south of Houston off highway 45 to Galveston.'

After saying goodbye, Martin resumed his study of the catalogue. He made some notes regarding paintings that he thought might be suitable and decided he would ask to see the boardroom when he was at the office tomorrow. In fact, it would be advisable to take some photos on his phone not only of the boardroom but also other places they intended to display the paintings they successfully bid for. Measurements of the walls would also be useful.

Suddenly, he noticed it was now after 8 o'clock and realized he was peckish so picked up the phone and called room service. He ordered a snack and while he waited checked his emails. Isabella's comments on the contract had come in as well as Paul Cohen's details of the charges to be added to the contract. There was also the email from Lonnie with his address and cell phone number. He ate while he read the catalogue and continued to be amazed by the size and scope of the art on offer. Looking again at the description of the Robin Black painting, he decided to send an email about it to his friend Henk van den Haag. He is the owner of a successful art gallery in Melbourne that was referred to by Robert when his reporter was in Melbourne a few days ago. As the business centre was closed at this time he took a photo of the page in the catalogue with his iPhone and then forwarded it to his laptop. Martin's email asked Henk if he could find out if the attached catalogue photo of a supposed Robin Black painting could possibly be genuine. He had once told Martin that he had met the late painter's wife Sheila at art shows and had even discussed the possibility of selling paintings for her. She would be able to answer if such a painting existed and if so, who had bought it. Genuine paintings by Robin Black can attract excellent prices when they are occasionally offered for sale. He continued studying the catalogue until almost midnight before he decided to call it quits for the night.

He was about to shut down his laptop when he noticed an email had come in from Isabella. She had booked flights departing early Friday morning from Bilbao to Houston with Iberia Airlines. After a change of planes at Madrid, she would then fly non-stop to Dallas and on to Houston arriving around 6.30pm.

The timing should work out well enabling him to fulfil his meetings at the Museum of Fine Arts and the newspaper. He replied immediately telling her that he was looking forward to seeing her at the airport Friday evening.

Next morning, Martin went down to the business centre and connected his mobile phone to the printer, opened up his emails and printed out the contract which Isabella had marked up with her comments. He also printed out his accountant's list of charges. After a light breakfast in the buffet, he returned to his suite to prepare for the big day ahead. Although this was only his third day in Houston, he felt quite at home here and that he was already slotting comfortably into the Texan way of doing things.

Dropping the documents into his brief case that he needed to take to the Chronicle later this morning, he decided to explore the facilities of the hotel that he hadn't yet had time to see. Firstly, he took the elevator to the second floor where the sky bridge to the Convention Center is located and wandered across to familiarize with this very convenient feature. Signs advised patrons where various exhibitions were being staged and Martin saw the poster for the forthcoming art auction on the doors of one area that was close to where he stepped off the sky bridge. Walking back into the hotel, he spotted a sign pointing to an outdoor recreation area. This turned out to be a huge open space with a large swimming pool and bar where a number of patrons were enjoying themselves. There was also what appeared to be a water fun-park for children. He asked a passing waiter what this snaking water feature was. 'Well sir,' the waiter replied, 'it is for the amusement of the guests of all ages and we call it the *Lazy River*. If you are lucky enough to have a suite that looks down on this recreation area, you may be able to understand better the special layout.' Martin thanked the waiter and said, 'I do have a suite above this area but until now haven't spent time admiring the view. I promise to check it out when I return to my suite shortly.' He decided to take a swim in the pool when Isabella was here with him.

He went down to the lobby to enquire if the rental car had arrived as it was now almost 10.30. The desk clerk replied that Hertz had called a short time ago to say the car was on its way and just as if on cue, a woman in a Hertz uniform walked up to the desk and asked for Martin. He smiled and introduced himself and she led him out to a shiny white Tesla parked at the entrance. Martin was given a ten minute lesson on the unusual driving features of the car, handed the keys and told there was a booklet in the glove box that he should study before heading out into the traffic. He thanked the Hertz representative and taking the instruction book with him, went back inside the hotel telling the doorman that he would be back shortly to move the car from the entrance. 'No problem sir, I'll keep an eye on it for you. It's OK to leave the car there for a short while and your room key-card will also give you access to the hotel car park.'

Back in his suite he went to the window and looked down onto the recreation area. He studied the layout of the *Lazy River* but the shape didn't register with him. He gathered together the things he needed to take with him and sat for ten minutes speed reading the Tesla instruction book before heading back down to the lobby. He advised the desk clerk that his fiancée would be arriving tomorrow evening and would be staying with him for three nights. 'Yes, she has been fully vaccinated and has had two booster shots as well,' he answered when questioned about her Covid-19 vaccination status. On the way out of the lobby, Martin saw a stand that had free maps and picked up one of Texas.

Unlocking the driver's side door, he was struck by the strong smell of new leather. He turned on the ignition and on the touch screen opened the GPS. He took out the business card he had received from Robert Mason and punched in the address of the Houston Chronicle. With seat belt fastened, and in the drive mode, he gently pressed his foot on the accelerator pedal and the car moved slowly forward. Guided by the GPS, he turned right out of the hotel's entrance and concentrating on staying in the right lane, he gradually increased his speed as he began to get the feel of the car.

As his confidence grew, he further increased his speed and noticed that the drivers following him didn't tailgate him as he was obviously not a local. The Hertz sign on the rear window was there for a good reason! Before long he was tooling along the freeway leading out of the CBD and with the cruise control set at slightly below the posted speed limit of 75mph. It wasn't long before he was instructed to leave the freeway and arrived at his destination.

Feeling very pleased with the ease of driving this amazing vehicle, he signed in at reception and waited whilst Mrs. Rogers was contacted that he had arrived. A few minutes later she came down and as they rode the elevator to the top floor, she told Martin that Mr. Mason was in an important editorial meeting. He had asked that she take him to the office he has been allocated to settle himself in, and Mr. Montgomery would meet him there shortly. On the way, she showed him the small staff kitchen where he could make coffee and tea whenever he felt the need.

Setting himself up in the small office, he unpacked his brief case and then made a large mug of cappuccino from a dial-up machine that does the job as well as a barista in a café. Whilst he was in the kitchen standing by the coffee machine which gurgled and spluttered, people came in and introduced themselves in what he believed was a typically Texas friendly manner. Back in his office, he was once again working his way through the art auction catalogue when Neville Montgomery appeared bringing a chair with him. He shook hands with Martin and immediately told him to call him Neville. He placed a folder on the desk and opened to the first page. 'This section details our budget including contingencies but we'll skip these until after you have accepted and signed the confidentiality clause in the contract. Robert told me that this will take place later today.' Martin agreed with the budget details being held back. 'I am basically ready to sign the contract when I meet with Robert later but meanwhile we can work on strategy.'

'Once you have prepared a list of the paintings you have selected we should bid for,' Neville proposed, 'we'll call on Darryn Smith to mark up the list with his suggested value range. He will go independently to view the paintings in the Convention Center and then meet with us here to present his valuations. Following this, you and I will review the figures and because it is likely there will be a large variation in values, we'll decide which ones to bid for so as not to use up too much of the budget on the first couple of paintings. Our intention is to purchase quantity as well as quality. By that I mean we should try to achieve a total of at least six paintings within our budget.'

Nodding agreement, Martin asked, 'During the bidding, I am hoping you might recognise some of the people we are up against and let me know if you think they have deeper pockets than us. This may help me decide whether to continue bidding or not for a particular painting.' Neville commented, 'Working for the largest circulation newspaper in Texas brings me in contact with many high profile politicians and business people so it's possible I may know one or two of the people bidding at the auction.'

Martin then asked to see the boardroom and offices where it was intended to display the paintings. 'I'll also need a long measuring tape if someone has one in the office so I can write down the wall sizes.' Neville picked up the phone from Martin's desk and dialled reception. 'Hi Denise, this is Neville Montgomery. Please check if the boardroom will be available for the next half hour and get back to me on this extension. Thanks.' Turning to Martin, he said that there are three offices where they hope also to hang some paintings. First will be the company President's office. He is Matthew McBride, and is currently at the Hearst headquarters in New York for the annual budget meeting. I will ask his P.A. to open his office for us. After that we'll go to Emma Johnson's office and then we'll do mine. Robert is hoping we'll have an extra painting left over that we can hang in his office so we better measure his as well. After all, he is the one who came up with the whole idea.' The telephone rang and it was reception advising that the boardroom was free for the next two hours. 'This is as good a time as any so let's head there right now and I'll grab a measuring tape on the way.' Martin took out his iPad from his briefcase and followed Neville along a corridor and into what turned out to a stationery store room. Searching the shelves, he soon found a number of different types of tape measures and selected one that had a range of 30 feet. 'That should be good enough,' Neville said, 'I'm certain none of the spaces we'll be measuring are longer than that.'

Entering the boardroom, Martin cast his eyes around the smartly furnished room taking in the pictures that currently adorned the walls.

There were large photographs of an old building which Neville pointed out was the original newspaper offices in downtown Houston.

'These will be moved to the journalist's level as a reminder of the company's heritage. The paintings you can see on two of the walls are by well-known Texas artists and if space allows, we would like to retain these in the boardroom. It all depends on the size of the paintings we end up with after the auction and we'll look for your subsequent advice at that time.'

As one wall was comprised of floor to ceiling windows, they measured the length and height of the other three. Martin paused to study a portrait of a bearded elderly man and Neville told him that it was of the newspaper's president in 1920.

'The artist was Royston Nave who was well known in Texas as possibly one of the finest American portrait painters of his time.'

On the next wall was a stunning landscape which caught Martin's attention. The colours were brilliant and the brushwork was of the highest quality. At the bottom was the painter's signature, Julian Onderdonk and 1908. 'His name sounds European to me Neville.'

'His ancestors came from the Netherlands but he was actually born in and worked most of his life in San Antonio, Texas, Martin. This scene is of the countryside around that gorgeous city. His paintings are much sort after amongst serious American art collectors. If you get a chance, you should make a visit there. It's quite a unique place for Texas and is reminiscent of cities in Europe that are popular with tourists.'

Leaving the boardroom, Neville led them to the President's office which was unlocked for them by the P.A. Like the boardroom, one wall was fully glazed so they quickly measured the remaining three walls. There were some small landscape paintings hanging on two of the walls which he said were to be moved if they succeeded in meeting their goal of buying at least six new paintings at the auction, three of which would be hung in the boardroom.

They next measured the walls in Emma Johnson's office before finishing up in Neville's office. It was now after 1.30pm and Neville suggested they break for lunch in the staff canteen. Afterwards they were settled back in Martin's temporary office when Robert appeared and asked them both to accompany him to his office. Martin picked up the folder with the copy of the contract and the document with his charges and walked with them to Robert's office.

An hour later, Martin returned to his desk with a copy of the signed contract which had been amended to reflect the minor changes suggested by Isabella as well as the inclusion of the remuneration details. Neville showed him where the print room was located so he could scan documents and email them directly to his office. His email address was already in their system since Robert Mason had started corresponding that way with Martin.

Before Neville moved back to his own office, Martin told him about his fiancée's planned visit to Houston this coming weekend. 'She is arriving Friday evening,' Martin told him, 'and I will have her accompany me to the Convention Center on Saturday for my first viewing of the paintings to be auctioned. She not only has a very sharp legal mind but also a very sharp eye for fine art and good design. She'll be returning to Spain Monday so it will be a short and hopefully sweet few days.'

Knuckling down to work on the study of the auction catalogue, he was deep in thought when the phone on his desk rang. He answered and was surprised to find that it was Lonnie the chauffeur. 'Hello Mr. Taylor, hope this is a convenient time to talk. I heard that you were working here today and wanted to suggest that if you are intending to be here for the rest of the day, you could follow me to my place after we knock off around 5.30.'

Martin had momentarily forgotten that he had a dinner date with Lonnie's family tonight but didn't want to acknowledge his memory lapse. 'That's a good idea Lonnie and much appreciated. Give me a buzz on my cell phone when you are about to leave and I'll meet you in the car park out front. I am driving a white Tesla and I think it is probably the only one in the visitor's section. I don't know the license plate number but it has a big Hertz sign on the rear window.'

Up until now, he had earmarked five paintings as possibilities to be looked at *in the flesh* and as he turned to the next page, saw that it was the Robin Black painting. This reminded him to open up his emails and sure enough he found a response from Henk van den Haag. He had spoken to Sheila who told him that this particular painting had been sold to a New York gallery three decades ago. Not long after she received payment for the painting the gallery had been declared bankrupt so she wasn't a creditor when administrators were called in to sort out the mess. She couldn't be sure exactly but thinks the gallery closed about twenty years ago. There had been a suspicious fire when all records were lost and she has no idea where that painting may have finished up. It could have even been destroyed in the fire. If she was a lot younger, she might have contemplated flying to Houston to inspect it but since the Covid-19 pandemic, she had no desire to travel abroad. She suggested that Martin should take some close-up photos and send them to her via Henk so she could better study the brush strokes and style. Martin acknowledged the response and agreed to take some close-up photos when he is at the viewing on Saturday.

Later in the afternoon, Robert called to ask if Martin would like to dine with him this evening. 'Thanks Robert but your chauffeur Lonnie has invited me to partake of a Texas home cooked meal with his family tonight. Tomorrow evening I will be picking up my fiancée at the airport around 6.30 so we'll eat at the hotel and allow her to have an early night as I suspect she'll be horribly jet-lagged after flying here from Northern Spain.' Robert replied that he hoped he would have the opportunity to meet Isabella while she was here.

He had his head down and was writing lots of notes about some of the paintings that looked particularly interesting, when his cell phone rang and it was Lonnie to say he was waiting out front. Looking at his watch, Martin saw that it was now 5.45 so he quickly tidied up his desk and rode the elevator down to the lobby. He signed out in the visitor's book and walked out the front to meet Lonnie who was standing alongside the Tesla. Martin apologized and before getting into the car, asked if there was somewhere convenient they could stop on the way so he could pick up some things for his family to take with him. 'No problem Mr. Taylor, there's a 7 Eleven just up the road from my place and it has a wide range of goods.' Martin didn't want to remind Lonnie that he had asked him to call him Martin as no doubt the chauffeur's job required him to address his passengers formally.

Lonnie pointed to a large bright red Ford 250 pick-up truck and said that although the traffic will be heavy on the freeway at this time of day, Martin should be able to easily spot him ahead even if someone pulls in between them.

'I'll drive at a safe speed in the right lane and let the guys who want to get home in a hurry flash past us. In case we do get separated or you take a wrong exit from the freeway, before we leave right now punch in my address into your car's GPS and phone me to say what happened if you find yourself heading west instead of south!'

They set off out of the car park and shortly after were on the ramp to the freeway. Lonnie was correct in saying that traffic would be heavy at this time and they were soon caught up in the mass of vehicles seemingly all wanting to head to Lonnie's for dinner! Despite the volume of traffic, Martin found it easy to keep his attention focused on the road ahead and let the car glide along at a decent pace keeping the red pick-up in sight. At one stage of the journey, Martin found himself high up on a curving multi-lane road changing direction from east to south bound and saw an overhead sign that read Galveston. After some twenty minutes, he noticed the truck's rear right side light blinking and followed him onto the off ramp. They were now travelling on a two lane suburban road past some big box hardware and furniture warehouses as well as a spate of gyms before Lonnie pulled into a parking lot outside a busy 7-Eleven store. Martin went in and selected a large box of Belgian chocolates, a bunch of red roses and a bottle of Pindar sauvignon blanc. The wine was recommended by the sales clerk because this New York vineyard had been winning awards for their wines for the past few years. Back on the road again, it wasn't long before they turned into a big apartment complex and Lonnie pointed Martin towards the visitor's parking area.

He followed his host up one flight of stairs to an apartment on the second floor into a wonderfully air conditioned environment. As Lonnie unlocked the front door, his two children ran up and gave him a hug. Behind the children stood an attractive young woman who Lonnie introduced as his wife Margaret.

'Our daughter Ella is 8 and our son Alex is 7. They both attend the local public school in Clear Lake which is only five minutes away.' Alex immediately walked up to Martin and asked if he had kangaroos in his backyard at home. 'No I don't, I live in a beach suburb close to the city where the only wild animals are possums that jump on the roof at night. There are some suburbs about as far from the centre of the city as you are from the centre of Houston where kangaroos are often seen in backyards.' Ella then asked, 'What about crocodiles?' Martin laughed and explained that these creatures are only found in the north of the country some thousands of miles from where he lived. 'That is, except for those in the Melbourne Zoo which I have seen a couple of times and they are separated from the people by high walls.' Ella then told him, 'We've some alligators in our zoo which look similar to the crocodiles I have seen on the National Geographic television nature shows about Australia.'

Martin handed the roses and the box of chocolates to Margaret and the bottle of wine to Lonnie. The children excitedly asked if they could have a chocolate and were told to wait until after dinner. Lonnie passed

Martin an ice cold can of Lone Star beer and took him onto the balcony where they could sit and watch the setting sun whilst Margaret served dinner. The apartment looked out onto a well maintained tropical garden with a swimming pool located in the centre. He explained that there were different groups of apartments in the complex which was so large it had a road passing through the centre. Each group had its own pool which Martin found very impressive. He couldn't think of any apartment complex in Melbourne which had a series of pools like this.

Ella came out and told them that they should come into the living room for dinner. Like her brother, she was totally outgoing and even took Martin's hand and led him to the chair reserved for him. They started with locally caught shrimps with a cocktail sauce and then followed roast sirloin carved into thin slices. Martin was impressed by how well the children behaved as they listened intently to Martin being quizzed on life in Australia. After a delicious meal capped off with homemade ice cream and strawberries, the children were given a chocolate each and bid him goodnight and went off to bed. The three adults moved out onto the balcony and sat quietly for a while as they tried to spot any satellites moving across a starlit clear sky. Lonnie talked about the work his father was involved in at NASA. 'Dad is part of the team that is connected to Elon Musk's space program which is based in Boca Chica on the Texas Gulf Coast. Unmanned SpaceX rockets have been taking supplies to the International Space Station for some years and now take change-over crews there as well. It's a very exciting period for Texas because although we've had NASA's headquarters here for decades, manufacture of rockets and launch sites were previously located in other states. Now thanks to SpaceX, it all takes place here and employs thousands.' Martin responded that it makes sense to build and launch the rockets from one place and wondered why no-one had come up with that idea before. Lonnie explained that it was always political. 'Our leaders in Washington ensured that contracts were raised for manufacture of rocket components in states where depending on which party was in power, either Republican or Democrat votes were needed.'

Changing the subject, Margaret asked if Martin was married and he replied, 'No but I am engaged to a gorgeous Spanish woman that I met whilst travelling in Spain a few years ago. Although we currently live half a world apart most of the year, we do manage to spend time together when she can take a few days off from her work in a law partnership. In fact, she will be arriving tomorrow evening from Spain to spend the weekend with me here in Houston.'

Looking at his watch, Martin decided he shouldn't outstay his welcome and keep his hosts up late. Thanking them for their wonderful hospitality, he said goodnight and told Lonnie he would probably see him at the Chronicle tomorrow afternoon. Typing the address of the hotel into the car's GPS, he drove out of the apartment car park and onto a quiet suburban road the GPS informed him was El Camino Real. He had an uneventful run back to the hotel in light traffic and clear weather. He took the elevator from the garage straight up to his suite. As he was checking his emails on his laptop, he spotted the Texas map book he had picked up earlier and noticed that the cover had an outline drawing of the shape of the state. Something clicked and he went over to the window and looked down on the recreation area. Well, well, he muttered to himself....the course of the *lazy river* water feature reflected the shape of the state of Texas! What a terrific idea he decided as he headed off to bed, I must show Isabella when she's here.

CHAPTER 5

A HAPPY REUNION.

Up bright and early, there was a message from Isabella that had come in during the night to say she was en route and so far her flights had been on time. Checking through his other emails he found one from his accountant asking him to send through a copy of the contract so he could set up the billing system in his computer. He should have done this when he was at the newspaper office yesterday afternoon especially when Neville had shown him the scanner room. He went down to the hotel business centre, scanned the contract and sent it straight through to his accountant from the scanner. Back in his suite, he read a report from Jessica detailing progress on assignments under way which he read through and answered with his thanks and comments. He made a cup of coffee using the simple to operate pod machine on the bench above the mini-fridge. Taking the coffee to the lounge chair, he sat studying the catalogue for the next two hours before realizing it was almost time to leave for his 11 o'clock appointment at the Houston Museum of Fine Arts. He tidied up the clothes closet making sure there would be enough space for Isabella to hang her clothes.

Taking his notebook and the auction catalogue, he went down to the basement car park, unplugged the car from the overnight charger, and checked that the gauge on the dashboard indicated that the batteries were fully charged. Typing in the address of the museum, he drove out into the blazing sunshine following instructions leading him to the freeway that would take him there.

He was finding driving here easy as the freeways and roads were well signed and so far the GPS had guided him effortlessly. He rolled into the museum's car park just before 11 o'clock and asked for Michelle Robinson at reception. He didn't have to wait long before a tall, striking woman approached and introduced herself. She led him to a large meeting room which was unattended at this time and told him that they shouldn't be disturbed during their discussions. They sat down and Martin placed his notebook and the auction catalogue on the table. 'Thank you so much for giving me this time Ms. Robinson,' Martin said. 'Please call me Michelle and it's my pleasure to meet someone with your reputation. Robert Mason has given me a brief résumé of your background and it sounds like you must have some great stories to tell at dinner parties.'

Martin smiled and started to explain his role regarding the forthcoming art auction. 'The Houston Chronicle is intending to publish a series of articles about my career as a detective involved in art crime and as a conjunct to that have asked me to select and bid on their behalf for some paintings at the auction. Am I correct in assuming the Museum of Fine Arts is unlikely to bid for any of the paintings as there are no provenance certificates available?' Michelle answered, 'That's correct Martin, although I intend to take a close look at a small number of the paintings that are of particular interest after the viewing opens this weekend. I will also attend the auction. Let's look at the catalogue and you point out which ones you have chosen as possible paintings to bid for.'

For the next hour and a half, they discussed some twelve paintings that Martin had marked as possibilities. Michelle had some serious doubts that any of them were genuine… explaining, 'Extensive checks have been carried out world-wide and none of the paintings listed for auction have been claimed as stolen. This leads us to assume that the majority, if not all, are fakes. There is a very talented art forger in Mexico City who has made a fortune selling excellent copies of paintings by famous artists to people with lots of money to throw around. His customers have always included some of Mexico's drug barons as well as the Colombian narcotics king until he was recently sent to prison for life. The forger's name is Fernando de Becerra and he operates his lucrative business securely knowing the government hasn't been too fussed as long as he pays his income tax on time each year! He cleverly avoids copying paintings that are owned by museums and galleries around the world as their provenance is well documented. This guy usually copies only those paintings that are held in private collections whose ownership is not normally under public scrutiny. He obviously has accumulated a massive library of art books from which he selects the paintings to copy. Tests carried out on some of his paintings that have been confiscated reveal that the paints he uses have been manufactured in Asia based on ancient techniques to replicate those used in the original paintings. Even the canvases he uses have been especially aged using modern chemistry technology.' Martin had heard of a couple of talented art forgers during his career, particularly a famous one in New York and another in The Netherlands, but this one in Mexico was new to him.

Michelle suggested they go to the museum café for some refreshments and then she will take him on a tour of the museum. 'I want to show you some paintings in our old masters section which include some by artists listed in the auction catalogue,' she told him. Over coffee and a pastry they discussed families and interests outside of work. 'By the way Michelle, do you have any Jackson Pollock paintings?' She looked at him with an inquiring expression and replied, 'Yes we do, a number of them in fact. Why do you ask?' He answered, 'The National Gallery of Australia in Canberra acquired one called *Blue Poles* in the 1970's for a million dollars which at that time was a record price. There were outcries all over the country, with many people asking why the government had spent so much money on a painting that was a swirling mess of drips, runs and splashes. It almost brought down the government! That painting today is now worth tens of millions and the adverse publicity has resulted in it being the most looked at painting in the gallery! Jackson Pollock has a special place in my world because my first overseas art crime case involved tracking down the perpetrator of the theft of one of his paintings that was to be exhibited in the Guggenheim Museum in Bilbao, Spain.' Michelle interrupted excitedly saying, 'I remember that case and if I am correct, the mastermind tried to sell it in a number of countries before being captured in a *sting operation* somewhere in Australia, right?' Martin nodded and continued his story. 'It was fitting that the painting was actually recovered in Canberra where Australians had first heard about Jackson Pollock. That case has an even more important connection for me. It was during my involvement in assisting the Bilbao police that I met the woman who is now my fiancée. Her uncle is the chief of police in that city and introduced us at dinner one evening at his home.'

Michelle then led him to the Old Masters European section of the museum and pointed out paintings by two of the names listed in the auction catalogue. The first was a painting by Canaletto called *Entrance to the Grand Canal, Venice*. Martin opened the catalogue and compared the picture with the brilliantly coloured painting on the wall in front of him. He conceded that the two pieces of art definitely could have been produced by the same person even though he was comparing a photo with an original oil painting.

The next painting Michelle showed him was by Goya. It was a portrait of someone called Don Vicente who looked like a young nobleman with his wig and fancy suit. There is a dog jumping up wanting his master to pat him. The Goya in the catalogue was of an attractive young woman beautifully dressed and adorned with a pearl necklace and diamond pendant. The painting style and brushstrokes appeared to be very similar in the way the paint had been applied. Martin was shown a number of other *Old Masters* paintings similar to those in the catalogue with the same outcome as far as he was concerned. The similarities were uncanny but as Michelle pointed out, art forgers such as the one in Mexico City were extremely skilled.

On the way back to the meeting room, Michelle took Martin quickly through the modern section to show him their Jackson Pollock collection.

There were a number of early realist style paintings and a lot of drawings. There weren't any paintings in the style of *Blue Poles*.

Martin thanked Michelle for her assistance and promised to return to the museum some time later during his stay in Houston as it was obvious that they had an enormous collection. As he drove out of the museum parking lot he telephoned Neville to see if he was free for a quick chat in about half an hour. 'Yes Martin,' he answered, 'I'll let reception know you're on the way and ask for you to be sent straight up to my office when you arrive.' It only took twenty minutes to get there and as promised, after signing the visitor's register he was escorted immediately up to Neville's office on the fourth floor.

After the usual pleasantries, Martin asked about the budget. 'How much do I have available to spend Neville?' 'The board has allocated one hundred and seventy five thousand dollars based on a guesstimate of $25,000 each for six paintings leaving a contingency of $25,000. No-one really knows how things will pan out as an art auction of this kind has never taken place here before. Because most or possibly all the paintings are copies, many potential buyers will be afraid to push the prices too high so there might be a lot of bargains. On the other hand, because there is a very slim chance one or two may be genuine, prices could escalate especially if the bidder was willing to take a gamble.' Martin thanked him and walked over to his small office. He sat down at his desk, picked up the phone and dialled reception. 'Hi, this is Martin Taylor, can you please connect me to the person who handles staff travel arrangements as I need some information about the Houston International Airport.' A few seconds later, a woman announced that she was Jane, the company travel agent. 'Hi Jane, my name is Martin Taylor and I'll be working here with Robert Mason and Neville Montgomery for a week or so. I have to pick up someone this evening from the George Bush Intercontinental Airport. The traveller is flying here from Madrid via Dallas with Iberia and American Airlines. How and what must I do to be able to pick them up?' Jane explained that due to the enormous numbers of arrivals and departures at this airport every day, there are places called *Cell Phone Lots* where people park and wait until they are contacted by the arriving passenger. They then follow the signs to Terminal E, door number 101 or 102. You need to inform the incoming passenger that they should call you on your cell phone after they have collected their baggage and are waiting outside to tell you which door they are near. It works well if you follow these instructions.' Martin asked how he would find the *Cell Phone Lots* and she told him there are signs as you enter the airport perimeter. 'Type 17010 John F. Kennedy Boulevard into your GPS and follow the signs to the *Cell Phone Lots*. Being a Friday evening it will be very busy so allow plenty of time to get there. It is free parking in the lot so take a book to read in case the flight is running late and good luck.' He thanked her and grabbed his brief case and headed out waving goodbye to Neville as he passed his office.

Once in his car, he sent a text to Isabella with the instruction to call him after she had cleared Customs and Immigration, collected her suitcase from the Baggage Claim, and followed the signs outside to Passenger Pick-Up. He typed in the address Jane had provided and set off for the airport.

He soon discovered that Jane hadn't overstated the traffic situation….. it certainly was horrendous at this time, so he just sat back and went with the flow of bumper to bumper cars and pick-up trucks. Arriving at one of the *Cell Phone Lots* around 6.15, he parked and settled back, watching the constant stream of planes arriving and taking off. As he waited he thought about the unsatisfactory system of picking up incoming passengers at Melbourne Airport. There are dedicated kerbside places for doing this but these are for a very limited numbers of cars that can stop at any given moment. This means that if you can't find a spot within a couple of minutes, you have to drive off and circumnavigate the entire airport road network to come around again. The Houston Airport system seems to be extremely well thought out he decided. He was reading a copy of today's Houston Chronicle that he had found on his desk when he was about to leave for the airport. He was deeply engrossed in an article about the court cases that were under way with people charged over the January 2021 attack on the US Capitol when his phone beeped with an incoming text message. He looked at the time and saw it was now 6.45 and the message was from Isabella saying she was waiting by door number 101. Five minutes later he joined the queue of cars outside the Terminal E building and searched the line of people standing outside door 101. He spotted her almost immediately and hurried over to give her a big hug before taking her bags and leading her to the car. They kissed again before he drove off, and then sat in silence for a few minutes until they were out of the airport and away from the noisy hustle and bustle of such a busy place.

'Despite being tired from my long journey,' Isabella said as the car hummed quietly along the freeway, 'I am thrilled to be here with you Martin and am so looking forward to spending time with you in this city. I haven't been to Houston before but as you know, I love everything modern and I have heard that this place is as up-to-date as you can get.'

Martin was concentrating on negotiating the traffic and nodded as he watched for the signs that would lead him from the freeway to the city centre. 'We'll be at the hotel very soon now and I'll be more relaxed once we're there.' Shortly after, he turned into the hotel garage and found a spot where he could park and plug in the charger. They took the elevator straight up to the second floor and he led her along the corridor to his suite. Whilst Isabella was freshening up in the bathroom, he called room service and ordered a bottle of Champagne. He noticed an envelope on the bed and when he opened it there was a welcome message for Isabella from the people he was working with at the Houston Chronicle. When she emerged from the bathroom he handed her the note saying, 'Here's a classic example of the exceptionally courteous and friendly manner that has been my experience since I arrived here.'

The Champagne arrived and Martin poured two flutes as he proposed a toast. 'To my gorgeous Isabella, may our time together continue to flourish and these next few days bring us closer than ever. Now I'd like to hear what has been going on in your world these past months since we were last together.' As they sipped their drinks, she related stories of the high profile cases she had been involved in recently, and told of the successes as well as the ones that didn't end up as well as she had hoped. 'As I mentioned on the phone the other day,' she added, 'the most recent case was a long drawn out affair which we eventually won on behalf of our client so I was ready for a break from courtroom dramas when you suggested I visit you here.'

'Your flight from Dallas must have arrived a little early on the last leg today as I wasn't expecting you would be through Immigration and Customs until after 7 o'clock. Were your other flights on time?' Martin enquired. 'The flight from Madrid to Dallas departed half an hour late due to some heavy storms over central Spain but the pilot of the American Airlines plane was able to make up the lost time due to favourable winds over the Atlantic Ocean. I managed to sleep a few hours on that long flight so I'm not feeling too bad right now,' she answered. 'Are you hungry?' Martin asked. 'No,' she replied, 'I had a number of light meals on the different flights so if it's OK with you, I'd like to just order a snack from the room service menu.' Later, as they sat on the couch, Martin told her all about the art auction and his role on behalf of the newspaper. 'Tomorrow, I'll be going to the first viewing day of the paintings that are on show at a convention centre just opposite this hotel and if you're up to it, I'd like you to come with me and maybe make some suggestions. In the evening, we have the symphony orchestra concert to attend so we'll have an early dinner in the hotel dining room then grab a cab to the concert hall. If you think this will be too much to cope with in one day, please say so.'

Isabella leant over and kissed him passionately saying, 'If you think that I may be short on stamina then you've got another think coming!'

They watched the TV for a while as they ate and then talked about the magazine article the newspaper intended to run. Isabella was OK with her name being published and that she lived in Bilbao, but would not divulge any details of any of the cases she handled as a lawyer. The bathroom had a Jacuzzi and they both enjoyed a relaxing soak in that before Isabella suggested that Martin investigate her stamina in the bedroom.

CHAPTER 6

A CULTURE FILLED DAY.

Following an excellent buffet breakfast, Martin and Isabella returned to the suite to tidy up and prepare for the big day ahead. As the art auction display wasn't opening until 10 o'clock there wasn't a need to rush. Martin's phone rang and it was Robert. 'Hi Martin, I was just calling to check that your fiancée had arrived OK and see how you are doing.' 'Good morning Robert, Isabella is here with me and we're both well thanks. We are going to the Convention Center shortly to look at the paintings and will probably spend some hours there and we have tickets for a symphony concert at Jones Hall tonight which we are looking forward to.' Robert then asked if they were free tomorrow evening to go out for dinner. 'I'd like to bring my wife Barbara to meet you both and have in mind a nice quiet place where we can hold a conversation without having to shout.' Martin accepted the invitation saying, 'Thanks Robert, we would be delighted to spend the evening together.'

'We could pick you up at 7 o'clock from the hotel and drive to the restaurant which is outside the CBD. I'll be interested to hear your opinion about the paintings you have seen by then as none of us has had an opportunity to see them yet. Neville told me that he intended to take a look this weekend so it's possible you may bump into him while you are there. Have a great day and we'll see you tomorrow evening.'

Martin told Isabella about the invitation to dinner and she wanted to know a little more about their host. 'Robert Mason is the senior editor of the Houston Chronicle who came up with the idea of taking me on board to recommend which paintings to bid for at the auction next week. It was also his idea to have a series of articles written about me for their weekend magazine. He's a charming man and we hit it off right from our first meeting. I'm sure you will like him. As for his wife, I am completely in the dark as he hadn't mentioned her in our meetings, not even during the dinner we had together on my second night here. I was reluctant to ask about her at the time thinking maybe they were separated or divorced but obviously this isn't the case. In these matters of a personal nature I guess I'm not much of a detective!'

When they were ready, Martin took Isabella on a short tour of the hotel showing her the facilities including the gym and the outdoor pool area. She agreed that they might have a swim later if they have time when they return from the Convention Center. They then crossed the sky bridge into the centre which was bustling with people checking in. Despite the pandemic now being classed as endemic, the requirement for checking in at some public gatherings has been retained. Wearing masks is optional and Martin and Isabella chose to wear theirs. Although there appeared to be a large number of people already looking at the art on display, the area was huge and they could move about relatively easily without feeling hemmed in. One of the first paintings they came upon was one of those that Martin had marked in the catalogue as being of interest. It was listed as a Monet and was titled *The Garden at Giverny.*

It was a large highly coloured painting, showing the garden in full bloom and Isabella agreed that it was certainly attractive. They studied it for some time before Martin whispered to Isabella that it was not possible that this was a genuine Monet. The real painting would fetch tens of millions of dollars and he was certain that the majority of Monet paintings were in museums around the world such as The Hermitage in St. Petersburg and the Musée d'Orsay in Paris. In fact he had seen some in the Museum of Modern Art last year when he was working on the case in New York. 'It was a small collection….. if I remember correctly, three or four paintings. I guess that there are very few if any, in private hands. Despite it not being an authentic Monet, I still intend to include it in my list to present to the client as in my opinion it would look great on the wall of the executive editor's office.'

Ambling slowly along taking in the mix of styles and art periods represented in this amazing collection, they stopped next at the Canaletto painting that had caught Martin's eye when he opened the catalogue for the first time. He had never been to Venice but thanks to watching TV travel shows, he had seen the *Bridge of Sighs* many times and easily recognized it as the main feature in this painting. There was no signature only a small plaque on the wall stating *Attributed to Canaletto*. This could mean that it may have been painted by artists who worked as apprentices in Canaletto's studio. It was a beautiful scene and Isabella remarked that nothing appeared to have changed in the years since 1747 which was the date shown on the plaque. 'I had a vacation in Venice the year before I met you Martin, and I could show you photographs in my holiday album that depict an almost identical scene to this one.' Martin marked this one on his list as a possible choice for the Chronicle President's office. 'I haven't met the big chief yet as he is New York at the moment, but I feel a painting of this quality and timeless subject should go well in the top executive's office,' he explained to Isabella.

After consulting his list, Martin went searching for a Salvador Dali etching he thought might go well in Robert Mason's office. 'Here it is Isabella,' he quietly motioned her over to where he was standing. 'I've been a Dali fan for some time and this one has many of the characteristics he liked to use in a number of his works. It is called *The Chariot of Bacchus* and is numbered 217 of 300. As it's an etching, I am certain this would be a genuine work by Dali and as it wouldn't command an excessive price, possibly just a few thousand dollars, it wouldn't be worthwhile for someone to forge a copy.' Being Spanish, Isabella was well aware of the uniqueness of Dali's work and told Martin that as a teenager, she had travelled with a school group to a summer camp in Barcelona. 'This was a big adventure for us as it required travelling from the north of the country right down to the Mediterranean coast, a distance of more than six hundred kilometres and took most of the day on trains and a tourist bus to get there. We stayed in a youth hostel near the beach, and one day they took us to the Dali Museum which is in the town of Figueres not far from Barcelona. None of us knew anything much about Dali at that time so the visit to the museum was a revelation. They have a fantastic collection of his paintings, sculptures and jewellery. I like this etching and would be happy to have it on my office wall.'

A number of wait staff were moving around the exhibition handing out cold drinks, which were gratefully accepted by the patrons. A short time later as they were looking at an untitled painting supposedly by Jackson Pollock, Martin felt a gentle tap on his shoulder and turning around confronted Neville Montgomery. After introductions, he said, 'I was looking out for you when I spotted this lovely lady and decided she must be your fiancée!' He then told them that he was not going to view the art with them today as it would be better for Martin to decide independently at this first visit and then compare notes with him later. 'Nice to meet you Isabella, hope you enjoy your brief visit to our city and look forward to having a chance in the future to spend some more time together,' said Neville as he blended into the moving parade of people.

Martin decided to mark the Jackson Pollock painting in his list of suggestions as another possibility for Robert's office if the funds are available. He would discuss this with him and ask if he would prefer the Dali etching or the Pollock attributed painting. He was certain that this style wouldn't fit in with what he had seen so far at the newspaper's offices but had a feeling Robert would be drawn towards modern art. He believed the boardroom would be better served with realistic scenes of American landscapes and lifestyle. In this regard he remembered seeing something listed by a famous American artist named Frederic Remington. He flipped through the catalogue until he found the painting he was looking for. It was of a group of horsemen spurring their steeds into action with some of the cowboys waving rifles in the air. It was called *The Rustlers Escape* and Martin felt that it would be perfect for the boardroom and marked it down as a definite choice. Isabella commented, 'The subject of this painting doesn't appeal to me, but when I look at it I immediately get a picture in my mind of the wild-west and as such agree with you that it would fit in well here in Texas.' Looking at his watch, Martin announced, 'We have been on our feet for over two hours and your jet-lag is probably weighing heavily on you by now Isabella.' She nodded in agreement, 'Let's find somewhere to sit down while I recover that stamina I told you about yesterday. We can read through the catalogue again and mark some more paintings to look at.' They went down to street level, and a short walk away they found a café. Deciding on a table at the back where it was quiet, they ordered drinks and pastries and settled down to studying the catalogue again. Almost an hour later, they made their way back to the Convention Center and searched out the paintings they had selected during their break. These included two small artworks by the famous Mexican Frida Kahlo, one large abstract painting by Judy Wilder Dalton, a Texan, and the *Rose Bay* scene by the Australian Robin Black.

The Frida Kahlo painting, called *The Wounded Deer*, was a very interesting picture depicting a deer with a human head which Isabella really liked. Martin said that it would raise a few eyebrows if hung at the newspaper office. He wasn't sure it would be appreciated but would offer it for comment to Neville Montgomery.

The Judy Wilder Dalton abstract was an extremely attractive painting of the coastline at Corpus Christi. Martin immediately saw it as a possibility for the boardroom.

Unfortunately the catalogue does not show the dimensions of the paintings so Martin has been making his best guess and writing it down against each item he is considering.

The Robin Black painting was huge and depicted the view of Rose Bay from the small studio in the Black home overlooking Sydney Harbour. Martin explained to Isabella that Robin Black died from drug related issues in the early 1990's and his wife Sheila continues to live in the home although they had divorced three years before he died. A few years ago some fake paintings were discovered that had been sold as genuine Robin Black depictions of Rose Bay and were the subject of legal proceedings against the gallery that had sold them. 'I was still with the Victoria police force at the time and remember reading about the court case and seeing photos of the paintings. This could be one of them as they were unique being almost entirely deep blue over the entire canvas just like this one. Notwithstanding that it probably is a fake, I will still recommend it for the boardroom on the basis that a plaque be placed on the wall alongside the picture stating that it is IN THE STYLE OF ROBIN BLACK. Ultimately, the final decision will be the Houston Chronicle's whether they want me to bid or not for it.'

Noticing a large clock on the wall showing it was now after 4 o'clock, Martin called it a day and he and Isabella departed the Convention Center and returned to the hotel via the sky bridge. They changed into swimming costumes and went down to the outdoor recreation area to try out the pool. Half an hour later, after a quick drink at the poolside bar they went back to the suite to prepare for the evening's entertainment. Whilst Isabella was in the shower Martin checked his emails but being Saturday there were none of any importance. When they were both refreshed and dressed in evening clothes, they went down to the dining room and sat down to a delightful dinner. Martin found himself staring at Isabella during the meal and telling himself how fortunate he was to have such a smart and beautiful fiancée. At one stage she asked him what he was staring at and he answered smiling as he said, 'I was looking at the attractive lady sitting at the table behind you.' She turned around and discovered that there weren't any people at the table directly behind, in fact the dining room was almost empty as it was so early! Isabella decided not to comment on his joke but would bide her time till she could get her own back. There was a taxi rank outside the hotel so after they had finished their meal they wandered out to the first cab in the line.

At Jones Hall they mingled with the crowd of music lovers and Isabella found herself admiring the fashions. She was fascinated with the string neckties many of the men wore and whispered to Martin asking if he knew what they were called. 'I have no idea Isabella, but will ask Mr. Google at interval as they have just announced that the concert will commence in five minutes and we should find our seats.'

The concert began with the orchestra playing Dvorak's Slavonic Dance number one and then the soloist came out to a very welcoming applause from the audience. Sol Gabetta is a very attractive young woman who has attained world-wide recognition of her musical ability according to the program notes. The audience hushed and the conductor looked at Ms. Gabetta who nodded that she was ready. For the next 40 minutes, the Haydn Cello Concerto drifted sublimely throughout the hall with the audience totally enraptured by the music. After the last note faded away there was silence for a moment before the audience broke into a thunderous applause which continued for some time. A magnificent floral arrangement was handed to the soloist and she bowed once more to the audience before leaving the stage.

Although most people left the auditorium to head for the bar, Martin and Isabella chose to remain in their seats. He Googled string neckties and found that these are called Bolo Ties and usually have silver slides to hold the looped string together. The slides are often made by American Indian silversmiths and Bolo Ties in recent times have been declared the official neckwear in a number of states including Texas.

After a short break, the lights dimmed and the orchestra commenced the final item of the evening. It was Tchaikovsky's Symphony number 4 and was a fitting end to what had been a marvellous evening of music.

Back at the hotel, Isabella stopped to look at the tourist brochures on the display stand near the entrance and spotted one with the words San Antonio in large letters on the front. 'Martin,' she called, 'this is a brochure about a town with a Spanish name which translated is Saint Anthony and he's the patron saint of lost and stolen articles. Can you take time out tomorrow for us to go there?' Smiling as he answered, Martin nodded and said, 'It was always my intention to spend as much time as I could with you during your very short stay and I hadn't intended to work on Sunday. A day in the country sounds perfect and the saint of lost and stolen articles might help me make the right choices with the paintings of unknown origin!'

Up in their suite, they changed into more casual clothes and sat reading through the San Antonio brochure. It stated that the drive from Houston will take about three and a half hours so they decided to get up early, sustain themselves with a cup of coffee and hit the road soon after 7am. They could break the journey along the way for a snack if they were hungry, otherwise wait until they arrived in San Antonio. They had selected only three of the recommended tourist activities because some of the sights such as the art galleries and museums as well as some caves would each consume a full day to examine properly.

Martin poured a nightcap from the mini-bar for them both then set his watch alarm for 6am before they went to bed….tired but happy after such a cultural day.

CHAPTER 7

THE PATRON SAINT OF LOST AND STOLEN ARTICLES.

Up bright and early and boosted by strong black coffee they headed down to the car in the garage, Martin set the GPS to direct them to San Antonio and away they went. It was an overcast day but still humid and the air conditioning was set at a low fan speed so as not to freeze their toes off. Being early Sunday morning, traffic was light and they were soon on the highway travelling due west. Thirty minutes later they were out in open country that looked like grazing land with some rolling hills. 'There are parts of Spain that look similar to this,' Isabella said, 'but I've already noticed a major difference. Whereas in Spain almost every hill has wind turbines slowly turning in the breeze producing a large percentage of the country's electricity, so far today I've seen a lot of old oil wells with their pumps seemingly moving in slow motion as they go up and down sucking that black goo out of the ground. I imagine that many of these pumps have been working away like that for over a hundred years and from their rusty appearance, it seems that very little money has been spent on maintenance.' As they cruised silently through the ever-changing countryside, Martin remembered to tell Isabella about the job in San Sebastian that he would have managed himself if it hadn't been for the newspaper assignment. 'I had asked Jessica to see if the client could hold off until I was free but unfortunately they wanted action immediately. Juan Lopez from our Bilbao office has been assigned to this job which will have him mediating between the two protagonists, one in San Sebastian and the other in Biarritz. I would have loved the opportunity although I may have had a language problem not speaking either Spanish or French. Obviously Juan is perfect for this assignment as he speaks fluently in five languages, Spanish, French,

German, Portuguese and English.' Wanting to get her own back after the previous evening at dinner when he kidded her about the beautiful woman at the next table, she pretended to be hurt that his only reason to visit her in Bilbao was because there was an assignment on offer nearby! 'No, no,' he cried, 'you are reading something into it that is not what I meant!' She laughed and told him that he wasn't the only one that could make a joke out of nothing! She then added, 'You forgot that I was the one who suggested Juan applies for the position with your Bilbao office as I knew him well being the son of friends of my family.'

He was concentrating on his driving when he saw an overhead sign advising that there was a roadside convenience centre two miles ahead which had fuel, food and rest rooms. As they had been on the road for almost two hours by then, he decided this would be a good opportunity for a break. As he drove into the complex he thought to himself how nice it was not to have to fill up the fuel tank as he would have done if he was at home in his own car. They also had a couple of charging stations but when he checked the power meter it showed he still had more than enough to get to their destination. He would find a charging station in San Antonio where he could leave the car whilst they wandered around the sights.

Fifteen minutes later, feeling refreshed, they set off again and noticed the surrounding countryside was now somewhat more verdant. The fields were ringed with lots of tall trees and had ranches with large black cattle dotting the landscape. It didn't seem very long before they could see what appeared to be an extremely high tower on the skyline some miles ahead. Isabella had the tourist brochure open and found that this edifice was called the Tower of the Americas and read out that it had been erected for the World's Fair that was staged in San Antonio in 1968. It was called Hemisfair 1968 and was timed to commemorate San Antonio's founding 250 years earlier.

The article said it gave a fantastic view of the surrounding countryside from the lookout and restaurant at the top some 750 feet high. Martin quickly calculated that this was about 230 metres and jokingly said that having been sitting in the car for more than three hours they should walk up the stairs to the lookout for exercise. Isabella laughed and read out that in 1981 someone ran up the 952 steps in a record 5 minutes and 18 seconds. 'As I don't expect that I can better that record, there's no point in trying,' she added.

As they drove into the city they were struck by the leafy tree lined streets and how clean and tidy everything seemed. This was obviously a city that took pride in its appearance and immediately made visitors feel welcome. As they neared the looming Tower of the Americas, Martin spotted a sign pointing to a public parking garage and turned in. At the boom gate, there was a board with the list of the parking charges that also confirmed it had a number of electric charging stations. There were no attendants, parking costs plus battery charging was to be paid for with credit card at the exit. Scanners read and recorded the vehicle's license plate on entry and again at the exit. He easily found the bank of charging stations and plugged the car into one and they then followed the signs to the pedestrian exit.

The next three hours saw them being wide-eyed tourists discovering a new wonderland. They whizzed to the top of the tower in a high-speed elevator where they had a magnificent 360 degree view of the surrounding countryside. There was a souvenir shop selling the usual mix of postcards and kitsch paraphernalia from which Isabella selected a Bolo necktie for Martin. They next visited the old Cathedral of San Fernando which the brochure stated had opened in 1868 and had the distinction of being the seat of the local Archbishop. Isabella told Martin that it was reminiscent of many similar churches she had visited in Spain. 'Its external features are striking and at first I thought that the building could well have been designed by Spanish architects but the plaque on the wall out front gave what appeared to be French and Dutch names as the architects.'

They wandered the San Antonio River Walk which follows the river right through the centre of the city. It is lined with restaurants and cafés as well as shops and galleries. There is even a live theatre that has the audience on one side of the river and the stage on the other. They stopped at a shady outdoor café and had iced coffees and croissants as they watched the constant flow of people strolling past.

'This is the nicest way to spend a relaxing time in a bustling metropolis such as this and I could sit here for days if it wasn't for the fact I have to return to Bilbao tomorrow,' Isabella said with a sad look on her face. 'Yes, it really is a marvellous place,' Martin agreed, 'but we have to head back to Houston shortly as we have a dinner date this evening with Robert Mason and his wife.'

As they were walking back to where the car was parked they came across a store that sold American-Indian ceramics. Ten minutes later, they were carrying a highly decorated dish that Martin had bought for Isabella to take home.

The return to Houston was uneventful and they chatted happily about what a lovely place San Antonio was. They turned into the hotel car park around 5.30 and whilst Isabella was preparing for an evening out, Martin went for a quick workout in the gym. They were dressed and waiting in the lobby for their hosts right on 7 o'clock when Robert appeared. They followed him out to his car where they were introduced to his wife Barbara.

On the way to the restaurant, Barbara asked if they'd had a nice day. Isabella was happy to answer, 'We went to San Antonio and although we only had a few hours there, we loved the place. We'll tell you more about what we did there when we're at the restaurant.' Robert managed to get a word in just then, 'I hope you like French cuisine because we are going to one of our favourite places to dine. It's called *Toulouse* and is in River Oaks and as you will see it's an inner suburb of the city. The area was developed in the 1920's by a couple of sons of the State Governor. The restaurant is situated in a shopping centre that was one of the first of its kind in Texas, opening in 1927. Nowadays this style of shopping centre is called a mall and the largest and most popular of modern malls in Houston is called The Galleria. Apart from having most of America's high end stores, the Galleria even has an ice rink which everyone loves.'

Pulling into the parking lot nearest to the restaurant, they immediately noticed a brightly lit building with a one word sign out front proclaiming TOULOUSE. As they walked up, Isabella commented that the building exuded a French atmosphere with its Parisienne décor and large outdoor seating area. As it was lovely starlit evening, Robert had booked an outside table and they were soon seated. A waiter brought bottles of ice cold Perrier water and passed menus around. Drink orders were taken and the group sat back to get to know each other.

Barbara asked what they had managed to see in San Antonio today and Martin told them about going to the top of the Tower of the Americas. 'It was a magnificent view and it is so high it reminded me of flying in a light plane once when I was with the Victoria Police in Melbourne.' Robert commented that he and Barbara were only babies when the World's Fair was staged but they had visited San Antonio many times as adults and had been to the top of the tower. Isabella then told them about the Cathedral and how it made her feel right at home with its Spanish influence. Robert commented, 'Martin, I see that you are wearing a Texas string necktie, is that something new?' He looked down to check it was straight before replying that Isabella had bought it for him this morning in the shop at the top of the tower.

'Am I wearing it correctly,' he asked. Robert nodded saying, 'It looks very fetching on you Martin.' The waiter brought their drinks before Isabella continued to tell them about the gorgeous River Walk. 'There are lots of walks along rivers and canals throughout Europe that I have experienced, but this one in San Antonio is now one of my favourites,' she said.

The conversation halted to allow menus to be studied and orders placed. Whilst they waited for their appetisers the discussions centred on Isabella and she was asked what it was like living in a city of Bilbao's fame since the

Guggenheim Museum opened. 'I was a teenager when the museum opened and my memory of the city prior to then can be somewhat sketchy. Life was filled with school studies and parties so what the surroundings were like at that age was not considered very important. I had a middle class upbringing… my father was a junior partner in a law firm and my mother was a secondary school teacher. When I was in my early twenties my parents moved to Madrid after my father was made a magistrate in the highest court in the land. I graduated in law and joined a well-known firm in Bilbao. The city is built around a river and was a major trading port for that part of Europe until containerization created enormous ships that were too large to come up the river. Once the port closed, the city quickly degenerated, especially around the old harbour area. Warehouses and associated business buildings quickly fell into terrible disrepair. Unemployment numbers were extremely high for some years until the Guggenheim Foundation chose Bilbao for their new museum in Europe. Since it opened in 1997, many new businesses were created and tourist numbers had been growing every year until the pandemic put a halt to visitors from abroad.'

The waiter arrived with their appetizers and glasses of wine were poured. For the next hour and a half as the various courses were savoured, there was very little talk and even though the restaurant appeared to be full, there was a very quiet air of relaxation surrounding the patrons.

Delicious crêpes completed their meal and after the dishes had been removed, the *maître d'* offered coffees and liqueurs with compliments from the management. Robert had brought many business associates to this restaurant over the years and the owners were showing their appreciation in this manner.

'So Martin,' he asked, 'how did your first day at the art viewing go yesterday?' Without wishing to go into too much detail, he replied, 'Isabella and I looked at some wonderful pieces of art. Whether or not they were genuine is beside the point, most of what we looked at closely would grace any wall whether in an office or a home. So far I have marked a total of eight possibilities and will add more tomorrow after I return from taking Isabella to the airport for her return flight to Spain. As you know Robert, I met with the senior curator at the Houston Museum of Fine Arts on Friday and she was extremely helpful. Main item of interest was that she suspects some of the paintings in the art auction may have been produced by a famous Mexican art forger and I am considering a visit to Mexico City to meet with him following the auction. My reason for proposing this is to have him confirm or deny that any of the paintings we finish up with were produced in his studio.

We could then have plaques printed with a statement saying that the specific painting was a copy produced by Fernando de Becerra. This is just an idea I have right now and will require a lot more thought before proceeding with it.' Robert suggested they discuss this further when Martin is next at the newspaper office.

Returning to the hotel, Robert and Barbara farewelled Isabella and said they looked forward to seeing her should she visit Houston again. 'Have a safe journey back home, it was a pleasure meeting you.' She thanked them for the enjoyable evening and said she also looked forward to seeing them again should an opportunity arise. 'On that note, should you ever consider visiting Spain and specifically Bilbao, please let us know and we'd enjoy showing you around,' Isabella added.

Up in their suite, she turned on Martin saying he had upset her at dinner. 'You never mentioned anything to me about going to Mexico City. When did you come up with this crazy idea?' Taken aback by her reaction, he responded, 'Tonight, while I was telling Robert about my meeting with the Michelle Robinson at the Houston Museum of Fine Arts and learning about the Mexican art forger.' She replied, 'Don't you realise how dangerous this could be? You don't speak Spanish and you want to meet with an art forger who deals with drug barons…sounds like a terrible death wish to me.'

'Don't forget I was a police officer for some years and know how to take care of myself when danger lurks,' he countered.

'By the way,' she asked changing the subject, 'did you watch any of the Australian Open tennis earlier this year?' 'Why do you ask Isabella? I'm sure I've mentioned before that tennis has never been my sport of choice.' She immediately replied, 'It's because our Spanish hero, Rafael Nadal won the final match against a Russian in a five set thriller that was fantastic to watch. All of Spain was cheering him on especially as he lost the first two sets and fought back to win the next three to take the match. He was the first player in the world to win twenty one grand slam tournaments which made the win even sweeter for him. Since then he has won the French Open as well. Soon after, he was named in Time Magazine's list of the World's 100 most influential persons which stated he's going to be remembered as one of the very best athletes in all sports. He's definitely Spain's greatest hero of this age.'

Not knowing when they would next be able to spend time together, neither had a much sleep that night.

CHAPTER 8

CONCENTRATING ON THE SERIOUS STUFF....AGAIN!

Another early morning start was required to get Isabella to the airport and they were both somewhat bleary eyed as they ventured out into the heavy Monday morning traffic. Knowing his way around now, Martin arrived at the airport in plenty of time and followed the signs to the departure drop off for international flights. He gave her a big hug and a kiss as she hurried off to the American Airlines check-in counter.

He returned to the hotel, parked the car and went straight to the dining room for some breakfast. Isabella didn't want to eat anything before leaving as she knew that for the next eighteen hours or so, she would be bombarded with food on the different flights. After Martin had devoured a plate of scrambled eggs and hash browns, he went up to his suite and switched on his laptop. There was a message from his accountant with a summary of the company's financial position. It showed they were owed very little through unpaid invoices, none of which was overdue and their debt level was easily manageable. He mentioned that the New York Mayor's office was a marvellous client because they had paid the final invoice within a couple of days of receipt. He complemented Martin for achieving such an excellent rapport with the New York authorities. It's very unusual he said, for any client to pay invoices so promptly and particularly for a government entity.

There was an update from Jessica, the Brighton office manager, which showed all staff members in both offices were gainfully employed and she had received a couple of new inquiries first thing Monday morning Melbourne time. She will follow up and let Martin know more details in the next few days. Juan Lopez was on his way to meet with the client in San Sebastian and will send a report detailing what further action will be required. Phil Wilson has arranged a first meeting at the Art Gallery of Western Australia tomorrow. Martin thanked her in his reply and briefly mentioned the weekend visit of Isabella.

He spent the remainder of the morning and early afternoon at the Convention Center looking at more paintings, then drove to the Houston Chronicle office to present his initial suggestions to Robert. He had increased the number to ten paintings to discuss with him so far. It will be important for Martin to judge his response as it will help him move forward as he researches more paintings. He drove to the newspaper office for the first time without using the GPS and relied on his excellent police academy trained memory. After signing in, the receptionist told him to go straight up to the fourth floor where Mr. Mason was expecting him. Robert led him straight to his office and once seated, he started by saying, 'The management has discussed your idea about going down to Mexico City to meet with the art forger and have agreed that it would be an excellent addition to your scope. Our major concern though is security, particularly as this person you want to meet no doubt deals with people in the drug trade. Have you seen today's paper?'

Wondering what could be so important in today's news, he answered, 'No Robert. I had to leave the hotel very early to take Isabella to the airport and on my return to the hotel, rushed through a light breakfast before coming straight here.'

Walking over to his desk, Robert picked up a copy of today's paper and handed it to Martin. 'There at the bottom of page one is a story about Mexican investigative journalists being murdered for writing articles about corruption being rife throughout the country. There is nothing new about these revelations except that the latest stories provide names showing that corruption reaches the highest levels of government and police. Even army officers have been reported as receiving payments for not following through on tip-offs when they are ordered to raid drug warehouses. The number of journalists shot is growing every week and not all are Mexican nationals. We have a small news office in Mexico City staffed with locals who work under the direction of one of our senior writers at this office. So far our team has not carried out any direct investigation of Mexican officials and their reporting only mentions the seriousness of the allegations without providing any names. Our team recently praised the current Mexican President and the Chief of Police saying they are working hard to stamp out corruption but unfortunately it won't happen overnight. Our senior management has decided that should you indeed feel it helpful to visit that art forger in Mexico City, we will provide you with an escort. The person we have in mind not only knows how to handle himself in dangerous situations, he speaks Spanish fluently which is definitely advantageous.' Martin agreed that this would certainly help to make his job a lot safer and easier. 'You have met him,' Robert said, 'That person is our chauffeur Lonnie. Not only is he a Karate black belt, he also spent two years with the Special Forces in Afghanistan where he earned the *Medal of Honor*. This is our highest military award for bravery.'

Martin considered what Robert had just told him and answered, 'I've faced some tough situations during my policing years and later as a private investigator, but having someone of the calibre of Lonnie alongside for the ride would definitely be an asset. Isabella might feel a little more comfortable as well. Come to think of it, he would have been very useful to have along when I was attacked in New York a year and a half ago although I must congratulate the NYPD who appeared within minutes of my being set upon.'

'OK,' said Robert, 'that's settled so now let's hear what you have for me regarding painting suggestions.' Martin handed him the list of ten paintings he had prepared which had the artist's name each was attributed to as well as the title and in which office Martin thought they might best suit.

1.0	MONET - GARDEN AT GIVERNY	EXECUTIVE EDITOR
2.0	CANALETTO - BRIDGE OF SIGHS	PRESIDENT
3.0	SALVADOR DALI ETCHING-THE CHARIOT OF BACCHUS	SENIOR EDITOR
4.0	JACKSON POLLOCK – UNTITLED	SENIOR EDITOR
5.0	FREDERIC REMINGTON – THE RUSTLERS' ESCAPE	BOARDROOM
6.0	JUDY WILDER DALTON – CORPUS CHRISTI	BOARDROOM
7.0	FRIDA KAHLO – THE WOUNDED DEER	FINANCE DIRECTOR
8.0	ROBIN BLACK – ROSE BAY	BOARDROOM
9.0	EL GRECO – ADORATION OF THE MAGI	BOARDROOM
10.0	JAMES McNEILL WHISTLER – NOCTURNE, CHILE	EXECUTIVE EDITOR

They spent the next hour and a half looking at the photos of the listed paintings in the catalogue with Robert commenting here and there about which office to hang them. He agreed with Martin's assumption that the other executives probably wouldn't have chosen the two modern abstract paintings that Martin had earmarked for his office should funds be available. 'I also love the painting by the Australian Robin Black which you have marked down as a possibility for the boardroom,' was Robert's final comment. 'It's too large for the walls in your office Robert and that is why I suggested it for the boardroom,' Martin explained. 'Understood Martin, I have to rush now to my afternoon editorial meeting. Will you come by tomorrow?' Martin grabbed his papers and brief case and answered that he would be back tomorrow after another session at the Conference Center. 'I'm going to my office now to type up my notes on the ten paintings selected so far.'

As he passed Neville's office, he was waved in. 'Good afternoon Martin, how are you going with your assessment of the artworks?' Martin remained standing as this was only going to be a short and sweet chat. 'Robert and I have just reviewed my first ten suggestions and so far I seem to pressing the right buttons. What did you think of the collection after I saw you on Saturday?' Neville smiled at Martin's response, 'No doubt about it …that is one helluva collection of art even if they are fakes. I saw a lot of paintings that really caught my eye although I have to say I am not a fan of abstract art. Speaking of pressing buttons, the company has had a couple of charging station installed in the employee car park and I have a key card for you to use whenever you are here. Assuming one of the charging stations is not in use when you are here, please plug your car in and recharge. Very few of our people have electric vehicles so you shouldn't have any problem finding one free when you are here. Many Texans love their gas guzzling pick-up trucks and as far as I know none of these types of vehicle are battery powered at this time. We have a special contract with Hertz which enables our reporters to hire cars from them whenever they are sent away on assignment. As well as making it simple for our people when they require a car, this entitles us to special rates. In light of this, I have spoken with Hertz and they will bill us directly for the car you are using so you won't receive an account from them.' Martin thanked him and picked up the key card to the staff parking lot as he went along to his temporary office.

Settling down with a strong mug of coffee, he switched on his laptop and started preparing his report on the paintings selected so far. It is important to note the reasons for his selections and why each would suit a different office due to size and/or the likes and dislikes of the office occupant. He was so engrossed in his report that he hadn't realised that it was now late afternoon and he looked up to see Neville standing at the door of his office.

'Would you like to join me for a beer at a nearby pub before you go back to your hotel Martin?' Shaking his head as he answered, Martin explained, 'Neville, we have an ad campaign in Australia that says, *IF YOU DRINK AND DRIVE, YOU'RE A BLOODY IDIOT!* I was raised with that slogan imbedded in my brain.

Alternatively, you could come with me back to my hotel have a drink and a meal there, then take a taxi home.' Neville replied, 'That sounds like a better plan Martin. My wife is in Florida with the children visiting her parents so I'm on my own at the moment and don't have to rush home. I'll come with you and later take a taxi home. I'll send Lonnie a message to pick me up in the morning so I can have a glass or two tonight without any problem. I do like that road safety slogan but not sure the average Texan would care for it. They don't like being told what to do!'

Later on, the two men were comfortably ensconced in the Marriott Marquis Hotel upper level sports bar which had the longest bar and largest TV screens Martin had ever seen. Neville told Martin that this was a favourite place for baseball fans to watch in comfort as the Houston Astros battled it out against their rivals. 'Further to what we were talking earlier about Texans not liking to be told what to do, in the 1970's a law was passed that made it mandatory for everyone to wear seat belts in cars. Many Texans believed this was an infringement against their *God given rights* to choose whether or not they wanted to wear a seat belt… so they refused to put them on. The carmakers first installed a system that used weight sensors in the seats to set off an annoying alarm when the engine was started and seat belts weren't clicked into their restraints. This so upset some Texans that a number of car workshops around the state began specializing in disabling the alarm. The authorities then had the carmakers go a step further by connecting the seat sensors to the ignition so that the engine wouldn't start unless the seat belts were employed. Texans then had those smart car mechanics rewire the car's entire electrical system so the ignition activated despite bottoms being on the seats!'

Martin was amazed that people would go to such extremes in order to flout the law. Neville continued his story, 'Texans have always enjoyed thumbing their noses at authority. Some years ago our freeways were widened and extra fast lanes were designated for cars carrying the driver and at least one passenger to promote ride-sharing. Cars with only a driver were not permitted to use these lanes and hefty fines were imposed on those caught by the highway patrol police. Suddenly a new business began to counter this regulation. Drivers were buying store mannequins and strapping them in the passenger seats so from the distance it looked like there were at least two people in the car. Police soon cottoned on and a lot of heavy fines stopped that game.'

Martin laughed and then changed the subject. 'Australia was one of the first countries to mandate seat belts in cars after Sweden had set an example for the whole world. Until recent times, our citizens have usually accepted government decrees without a lot of fuss but there is now a different mind-set growing in numbers, with protests in front of state and federal parliaments.' He then asked if Neville had ever been to Australia. 'I was conscripted during the Vietnam War,' he answered, 'and we had the choice to spend our R & R either in Hawaii or Australia. In 1974 I chose to relax on the golden beaches of Surfers Paradise in Queensland and really enjoyed the place. I took my wife Estelle there for a vacation a few years ago and couldn't believe the way the place had grown with a skyline that surpasses Miami which is where she is right now. If it wasn't for her close-knit family here, Estelle would have cheerfully moved to Queensland after our visit.'

Martin ordered two bottles of Stella Artois which he explained is a beer he was introduced to when he was in Belgium a couple of years ago winding up a case after rescuing a kidnapped gallery owner. 'This will be one of the stories you will hear about when your newspaper writes its articles about me.' They decided they were enjoying the atmosphere in the sports bar so instead of going down to the more formal dining room, they ordered meals at the bar and continued their conversation staying right where they were.

'I heard from Robert that you are considering going down to Mexico City after the auction to meet with the art forger who is suspected to have produced some of the paintings we are considering buying. As the auction will be held later this week and continue over the weekend, I assume you are talking about going down to Mexico after the auction and this depends on which paintings we finish up with, is that correct?' Martin nodded, 'I believe it will be important for the Houston Chronicle to acknowledge publicly if any of the paintings they purchase are copies and this can only be satisfactorily proven if admitted by the forger. He's got nothing to lose because I understand from Michelle Robinson at the Houston Museum of Fine Arts that he is proud of his handiwork and doesn't mind publicity.'

'I'm sure you appreciate the risks involved Martin,' Neville replied, 'and we as your client can only assist up to a point in providing you with some security. Robert told me earlier that our news office in Mexico City will make the initial contact with…. I believe his name is Fernando someone or other, and try to arrange a meeting for you. Now, that's enough on the subject for one evening, please tell me all about your gorgeous Spanish fiancée. I only saw her for those few minutes when we met at the Convention Center on Saturday.'

'Isabella is a partner in a law firm in Bilbao and not only is she beautiful but is extremely smart and has an enviable record in winning court cases involving business law. We met when I was in Bilbao on vacation three years ago. I happened to witness the murder of a man on the city's funicular and assisted the local police whose chief happened to be her uncle. He had invited me to his home to meet his family and she was there that evening. So began a long distance relationship that somehow manages to endure and recently we became engaged. We get together as often as our careers allow and sometime in the future we will have to face up to marriage and where we'll make our home. The most likely scenario is that we'll have a home in both Bilbao and Melbourne so we can spend time together in both cities.'

Neville noticed the time on the large clock on the wall and said, 'It's time for me to head home as I have a full day scheduled at work tomorrow with the company auditors. It's been a most enjoyable evening thanks Martin, and if you are still in Houston when my wife returns from Miami,

I'll have you over to have dinner with us.' Martin went down with him to the lobby and saw him into a cab. 'I'll wave to you when I'm at the Houston Chronicle office tomorrow afternoon if I see you unless you're still tied up with the auditors.'

Up in his suite, he checked his emails whilst getting ready for bed and saw one had come in from Isabella. She had arrived in Madrid and was awaiting the onward flight to Bilbao. She was tired but feeling OK and would send him a message once she was home.

Feeling relieved that the longest part of her journey was now over and she was well, he turned off the lights and fell into a deep sleep.

He was dead to the world when his telephone rang the next morning and it was Neville to say that his meeting with the auditors had been postponed for a week so he had decided to come to the viewing at the Convention Center. 'What time will you be there Martin?' Rubbing the sleep from his eyes Martin looked at the clock and replied, 'It's only 6 o'clock Neville and the viewing doesn't open until 10.00am so there's plenty of time to get ready. I'll go to the gym and work out for a while then have a swim, shower and go to breakfast. Look for me soon after 10 o'clock near the entrance to the art viewing area.'

Neville apologized for waking him up and mentioned that he had to be up early as Lonnie would be picking him up at 7.30 to take him to the office. He agreed to meet around 10 o'clock at the Convention Center. Sitting at the desk after he switched off the phone, he noticed that the laptop was still powered up from last night and there was a new message from Isabella. She had arrived home and the flights had all been on time…..something she wrote must be a record! She had decided to spend the day at home resting and shaking off the jetlag.

Martin trained hard at the gym sweating out some of the food and alcohol from the night before. He then took a shower before swimming laps for half an hour. As arranged he was waiting for Neville at the Convention Center precisely at 10 o'clock. Martin walked Neville around the twelve paintings which he had earmarked for them to bid for and hopefully purchase at least six. The current list has expanded by three more items than when Martin had run through them with Robert the day before.

1.0	MONET - GARDEN AT GIVERNY	EXECUTIVE EDITOR
2.0	CANALETTO - BRIDGE OF SIGHS	PRESIDENT
3.0	SALVADOR DALI ETCHING-THE CHARIOT OF BACCHUS	SENIOR EDITOR
4.0	ACKSON POLLOCK – UNTITLED	SENIOR EDITOR
5.0	FREDERIC REMINGTON – THE RUSTLERS' ESCAPE	BOARDROOM
6.0	JUDY WILDER DALTON – CORPUS CHRISTI	BOARDROOM
7.0	FRIDA KAHLO – THE WOUNDED DEER	FINANCE DIRECTOR
8.0	ROBIN BLACK – ROSE BAY	BOARDROOM
9.0	EL GRECO – ADORATION OF THE MAGI	BOARDROOM
10.0	JAMES McNEILL WHISTLER – NOCTURNE, CHILE	EXECUTIVE EDITOR
11.0	FREDERIK MARINOS KRUSEMAN –AT THE CREEK	PRESIDENT
12.0	PETER PAUL RUBENS – ANTWERP STUDIO	FINANCE DIRECTOR
13.0	PAUL GAUGIN – TAHITIAN LANDSCAPE	EXECUTIVE EDITOR

Neville particularly liked the Rubens painting but said he would be happy with the Frida Kahlo work as well if they were unsuccessful with their bid for the Rubens. Overall, he told Martin that he had marked some of the same items when he had made his first viewing on Saturday. 'It's hard to know what competition we'll face when the bidding starts on Friday,' he said. 'At least there is such a large collection we should have some success bidding for six or seven of the paintings.'

They stopped briefly in front of the Robin Black painting whilst Martin took some close up photos to send to his art gallery friend who would pass them on to Sheila Black. 'Right at the end of the catalogue,' Martin pointed out, 'is a photo of a Picasso etching depicting a face of one of the artist's friends named Robbie. According to the write up in the catalogue, some years after Picasso passed away, his daughter Paloma sold some of his works that had been in storage. There were also some ceramic works and etching plates. One of the latter was called *Pour Robbie* and was bought by an American art dealer. After it had been verified by The Collector's Guild in New York that the etching plate was genuine, copies were produced from the plate and sold to collectors. There is no record of how many copies were made but it's likely to be in the hundreds which means its value is probably somewhere between five hundred and a thousand dollars. Although Picasso did not actually produce these prints they are none-the-less a result of his design and etching the plate. I suggest we search for it now and if it looks as good in reality as it does in the photo, I would add it to the list and we can find a suitable spot somewhere in the office for it.'

Fifteen minutes later Martin and Neville were admiring it and trying to guess its dimensions. Neville thought it was around eleven inches by fourteen inches. Martin calculated that this would be 28cm by 36cm and agreed they were in the same ballpark. 'Put it down as a possibility for my office Martin as I really fancy having a Picasso on the wall opposite my desk,' he added.

The two men spent the next three hours looking at the remainder of the works on display before declaring that they have now seen enough. They marked a few extra paintings in the catalogue as spares if they don't achieve the required number out of the thirteen first-choice suggestions. The small Picasso etching is excluded from the list and considered only as a bonus if they secure it.

'I assume you are coming to the office this afternoon Martin,' Neville asked. 'Yes,' Martin replied, 'do you have something special for me to do?' Neville told him that Janita Sullivan had returned from her trip *down under* and would like to spend some time with Martin to run through the schedule for the magazine article interviews. 'Excellent timing,' said Martin, 'I look forward to meeting her.' They parted ways to retrieve their cars and would see each other shortly at the Houston Chronicle headquarters. Martin stopped by his hotel suite and collected his briefcase and laptop before driving off. Once settled in his office he found a note on his desk from Janita asking him to call her extension and make a time for them to meet. After he had introduced himself on the telephone, they agreed to get together in his office at 2 o'clock as she said it would be quieter there than in her busy space in the journalist area on the third floor.

Martin worked on preparing the format for the acquired paintings report and was deep in thought when Neville poked his head in and said, 'I'm going to the canteen for a bite, would you like to join me?' It was one o'clock and Martin nodded, saying, 'I have to be back here at two to meet with Janita so let's go.' Over lunch Neville told him that the auditors were now here and he would be tied up all day tomorrow with them.

They had been going through the accounts this morning whilst he was at the Convention Center and he expected they would raise any concerns they had with him tomorrow. 'I'm not really worried that they'll find anything seriously wrong with our financial management Martin, but to justify their existence they'll always uncover one or two minor issues that they can blow up in their report.'

Back in his office, Martin had just emailed a copy of the final list of thirteen paintings to Robert Mason when there was a knock on his door and in walked Janita Sullivan. He had brought in a spare chair when he returned from the canteen earlier and invited her to sit facing him at the desk. She was carrying an iPad and a cup of coffee which Martin considered must be the modern journalist's most important *tools of trade!*

He guessed her age as mid-forties and noticed she was wearing a wedding ring. She was tall and of striking appearance. 'My visit to your Brighton office,' she said breaking the silence, 'was my first time in Australia and I was disappointed that my time there was so short.' Martin apologized saying it was his fault because he had changed plans and stayed a few days longer in New York.

'I've put together a questionnaire document on a USB which I'll leave with you to fill in and hand back to me tomorrow. This will provide me with the basic personal information I'll need for the lead-in to your story. It includes some questions about your parents and their backgrounds. This document is headed Personal Data. There's another virtually blank document headed Important Cases and here I'll want you to make a list of the cases of your choosing that we could write about in the articles. Please list them in chronological order giving them a descriptive name and the location of the crime. If possible, please list at least five cases and depending on the length of each story, we'll decide how many cases to write into the article. There will be a series of photo shoots during your stay here. We may use local independent photographers to take some pictures of you in the Brighton office and of your fiancée in Spain. Over the next week or so whenever you are available, we'll interview you for the details of the cases. These interviews will be recorded and then typed up for review before inserting into the overall article. If you have any questions as we move forward, please don't hesitate to call me on my office extension number. It's really nice to have finally met you and I look forward to working with you on the magazine article.' Martin stood up and shook hands with Janita as she left his office.

Later, his telephone rang and it was Robert asking how he was settling in. 'Fine,' replied Martin, 'Neville and I are virtually in agreement on the paintings we will bid for and as well as that, I have had my first meeting with Janita Sullivan. She has provided me with a couple of questionnaires which I will complete this afternoon and return to her before I leave today.' Robert then told Martin that he had forwarded his list of thirteen paintings to Darryn Smith, the art valuer to add suggested price ranges for each item. He would attend the viewing tomorrow to look closely at the paintings and send his price guide to Robert tomorrow evening. He then inquired if there was anything else he could help with at this time. 'Well Robert, I would like to visit some private art galleries around Houston to get a feel for pricing so if you have someone here that can provide me with some gallery names and addresses, it sure would help.'

'I'll send up our art critic who is familiar with almost every gallery in Houston. His name is Ben Scott and I will ask him to bring you a printout of the best gallery names and addresses,' Robert replied. Ten minutes later, a young man appeared and introduced himself to Martin then handed him a sheet with about a dozen gallery names on. 'I would suggest you start with the gallery at the top of the list and work your way down until you have seen enough. I have also provided the name of the contact at each gallery and I'm sure they will make you welcome and assist in any way they can. Mr. Mason explained to me what your role is at the Houston Chronicle so if at any time you have any questions please telephone me on the extension number shown at the top of the list.' Martin thanked him and said, 'I'll let you know how things went Ben after I've visited some of the galleries.'

He spent the remainder of the afternoon filling in Janita's questionnaires and called her to say it was ready. She replied that she would send a junior trainee up to collect it. He had not long put the phone back on its base when there was a knock at the door and a young lad appeared. Martin handed him the USB and the boy retreated *post-haste* probably thinking there was some news item on it that had to go to print tonight!

He had printed out a copy of the cases he had proposed for inclusion in the magazine article and was now reviewing them and adding some notes for the forthcoming interviews.

2016   Major Australian Art Fraud.

An international crime syndicate with operatives in Sydney and Melbourne were importing paintings from Europe that were being sold to large businesses with false provenance documents. The certificates showed that their previous owners had been museums scattered around the world and although the artists were relatively unknown, the paintings were of a high standard and generally attractive to look at. The fraudsters were able to sell these paintings at considerably higher prices because of the false certification….sometimes at ten times their real value. Corporate art buyers were swayed by the false belief that the paintings may have once hung in the New York Metropolitan Museum or the Tate in London. Martin became the lead investigator after one of the largest mining companies in Australia which had its headquarters in Melbourne, became suspicious and called on the Victoria Police to follow up. Spent some months gathering sufficient evidence to enable the state prosecutor to bring charges against the fraudsters and subsequently ended with substantial custodial sentences being handed down.

2017   The Jackson Pollock Case.

Promoted to Detective Senior Sergeant in the Victorian State Police to head up the Art Crime Division. Sent to Madrid to participate in an international symposium on art fraud. Afterwards, took some vacation time to go to Bilbao to visit the Guggenheim Museum. Witnessed a murder on the funicular railway and then became part of the investigation team tracking down the perpetrator behind the murder and the theft of a Jackson Pollock painting.

The hunt passed through a number of countries before reaching its conclusion in Canberra. It was in Bilbao that Martin met Isabella who is the niece of that city's police chief.

2018   Gallery Owner Kidnapping.

This case involved stolen diamonds being hidden in the frame of a painting that was sold at an auction in a Melbourne art gallery. The gallery owner was subsequently kidnapped and spirited out of Australia to The Netherlands and used as a hostage in exchange for the diamonds. Martin was the go-between in a sting operation to release the kidnapped gallery owner and capture the criminals in a Dutch town near the Belgian border.

As the diamonds had been stolen from a company in Antwerp, the successful solving of the case resulted in a celebration at the Belgian royal palace hosted by the king and his family.

2019   The Mislaid Painting.

This is more of a humorous anecdote than a case of fraud or theft. Martin had recently resigned from the Victoria Police and started his own private investigation firm.

The art gallery in the regional Victorian city of Ballarat had been preparing for a retrospective of a famous 19th century artist who specialized in paintings of local landscapes and was unable to find one by this artist that had been in their collection for more than a hundred years. They had wanted to include this painting in the exhibition and searched their basement storeroom as well as the warehouse where large items were stored until needed for an exhibition. Assuming that it might have somehow been stolen, they called in Martin's company to investigate. Turned out that it had been sent away for some restoration work two years earlier but before it could be returned to the gallery, the restorer passed away and the painting sat in his studio awaiting collection for more than a year.

2020   Theft of Maltese Cathedral Treasures.

As a result of a friendship that commenced in 2017 with a Los Angeles police officer he had met in Madrid that year, he was invited to assist the NYPD in tracking down the perpetrators of the theft of an extremely valuable collection of gold treasures belonging to a Cathedral in Malta. They were stolen after being on show in a New York private gallery. The investigation uncovered an organized international crimesyndicate and an outlaw motorcycle gang that had carried out the theft which culminated   in a military style confrontation at the organization's European headquarters.

Obviously, Martin would need to elaborate on each story in detail when interviewed and figured that the notes he had written should provide enough for Janita to formulate her questions. He printed out another copy and telephoned Janita to tell her he would bring these notes down to her except he wasn't sure where she was located on the third floor. 'Take the elevator down one floor and I'll wait there to meet you,' she told him.

He packed up his things and went down to the third floor to meet Janita. She showed him the partitioned cubicles where the journalists were hard at work preparing for tomorrow's newspaper and led him to her desk. After handing her his notes, she asked Martin if he would be free tomorrow afternoon for the first interview. 'I'll be visiting a private gallery or two in the CBD tomorrow morning and will aim to be here around 2 o'clock. If that's convenient, I'll call you when I arrive.' She nodded and thanked him for being so co-operative.

He retrieved his car from the staff parking lot and joined the throng of vehicles on the freeway back into town. Once in his hotel suite, he sat writing emails to Isabella, his office and his accountant bringing them up to date on what he had been doing in Houston the past few days. He then remembered that he hadn't corresponded lately with his friend Charlie Watson, the Los Angeles police officer who had introduced him to the New York Police Commissioner. The fact that Charlie was the Commissioner's cousin certainly opened the door to a whole new world for Martin. He composed a long email to Charlie filling him in on what had subsequently transpired following the recent court case in New York. He finished by mentioning the possibility of visiting Mexico City to meet with an art forger.

Thursday morning after a solid work-out in the gym, Martin checked the address of the private art gallery at the top of the list and found it was within easy walking distance from the hotel. It was called Sophie Fine Art Gallery & Sales and opened at 10 o'clock. It was a cloudy day and not as humid as it had been every day since he arrived in Houston, making it far more comfortable for strolling around town. He arrived at the gallery after a fifteen minute walk and introduced himself to the manager, Ms. Sophie

Fine. 'How can I help you Mr. Taylor?' she asked. 'I am representing the Houston Chronicle at the upcoming art auction which starts tomorrow at the Convention Center and am hoping to get a feel for current values of quality paintings in the US. As you will no doubt hear from my accent, I'm not a local so any assistance you can give me will be appreciated.' She smiled as she answered, 'I am guessing you are either an Australian or New Zealander…both accents sound the same to me. The Houston Chronicle has bought a couple of paintings from me in the past and they have written positive reviews of exhibitions I have had so I am more than happy to show you around and discuss prices.' Martin thanked her and added, 'We know that the majority of the items being offered for sale are copies of well-known artists so pricing will be reduced accordingly. My intention today is more to get a feel for what buyers might be prepared to pay for attractive well-presented artworks.'

For the next hour, Ms. Fine showed Martin some excellent paintings, the majority being from American artists of the 20th century. He made some notes on his phone of the size and value of a few of the landscapes. Thanking her again, he departed to walk to the second place on the list. This gallery was called Studio Westheimer and was located on the street of the same name. The owner of the gallery was Marcel Dupont and following introductions explained, 'I moved here from Paris twenty years ago and started this studio where I initially gave art lessons to students. This progressed over the years to include more mature people who had been painting for some years but lacked the skills to produce what we call fine art.

I select the best of the works to hang in the gallery and sales have been excellent, particularly during the pandemic when most people were stuck at home staring at blank walls.' Martin told him about his role in the forthcoming art auction and was then given a tour of the studio and look at the paintings currently on display.

Prices were discussed and it was Martin's conclusion that these prices would be more in line with those he would be bidding for. As he said goodbye, Marcel told him that he would be attending the auction as a spectator not as a potential buyer and would look out for Martin when he was there.

It was now after mid-day and he decided to grab a snack on his way back to the hotel. As he walked along he found himself passing the Aussie Café and decided to stop and have a smashed avocado on toast. Today he was waited on by a young backpacker from Sydney who was hoping to work her way up to New York after a couple of weeks here in Houston. She had already spent three weeks in Los Angeles before taking a train to Houston. They chatted about home for a few minutes whilst she brought his food and coffee. Later he grabbed his things from the hotel and drove out to the Houston Chronicle

Martin found a note on his desk clipped to a copy of the suggested paintings list which now had some indicative prices added by Darryn Smith. The note was from Neville saying that he would like for him to come to his office to run through the pricing later this afternoon after he had finished his interview with Janita. He then made a cursory look at the pricing noting that the largest paintings attributed to famous artists had been marked at $25,000 to $75,000. Smaller paintings by lesser known artists were marked at $15,000 to $25,000. It will be interesting he thought to see how keen his opponents will be to acquire these works and how far they will push the prices.

He heard a soft knock on his door and looked up to see Janita coming in carrying some sort of recording device. He jumped up and moved the chair out for her to sit at the desk. They talked briefly about his visits this morning to the two private galleries and then settled down for the interview.

'I'd like to start with the first case on your list if that's agreeable with you?' Janita said switching on the recorder. She explained that it is a battery powered device that records onto a hard drive which makes it very portable.

'What rank did you have with the Victoria Police at this point in your career?'

'I was a detective sergeant in the art crime division. This was a small group of dedicated police officers selected because they had had some experience in working on cases connected to museums and art galleries. I landed the job of checking whether or not the museums that were listed on the provenance documents as having been the previous owners had in fact ever owned the painting. I visited the headquarters of the companies that had bought these paintings from the fraudsters, examined the items and took photographs. I then sent these photos to the nominated museum requesting their comments. The more I delved, the more I was amazed at the extent of the crooked art dealers' out and out brazenness.

They had managed to convince purchasing officers employed by some of our largest corporations to pay outrageous sums for these paintings. It was an interesting case in that it was not illegal to sell these paintings to prospective customers but providing false documents to clinch the sale was illegal. The total sales netted many millions of dollars for the criminals. It was an extremely embarrassing situation for the companies that had been tricked so not to further embarrass them I won't divulge the names of those unfortunate businesses. Incidentally none of the funds was ever recovered and it's no doubt stashed away in offshore banks for use when the crooks are released from prison.'

'I'd like to backtrack a little now,' Janita advised, 'and hear something about your childhood and subsequent education up till the time you started at the Police Training College. The reason I am interviewing you this way is because I intend to start the article with your first major art case then revert to your childhood before going onto your next big case.'

Martin then talked for the next hour or so about his family and what it was like growing up in a happy household with a police officer for a father, a wonderful caring mother and a smart sister who achieved top honours at university. Janita picked up her recorder and told Martin as she headed back to her cubicle that she now had plenty of information to start writing his story.

Martin picked up the painting list with the prices and walked along to Neville's office grabbing two mugs of coffee on the way. 'Come on in Martin and make yourself comfortable while I finish off this financial report for the boss. There's a copy of today's paper on the table if you haven't already seen it.'

Robert walked by and saw Martin sitting in Neville's office so turned around and came in to say hello. 'As the auction starts tomorrow, I guess you guys are finalizing your strategy for the bidding. By the way Martin, how did you go at the private art galleries this morning?' Martin told him that the second gallery he went to was the most worthwhile as it was also an art school and sold paintings produced by their most experienced students. 'I was shown paintings that were currently for sale and these were of excellent quality but because the artists are not well known, the prices were very reasonable. In my opinion, this visit gave me a good feel for the type of bids we can expect at the auction. Of course the fact that the majority of the items being auctioned are copies of famous works means they are more recognizable and will attract higher prices accordingly.' As Robert turned to leave he said, 'Good luck tomorrow guys, we're looking forward to hanging some new pictures on our walls.' A short time after Robert had departed he closed the folder on his desk and moved over to the table where Martin was sitting. The two men sat reviewing and discussing the pricing recommendations from Darryn Smith.

Later, Neville excused himself saying that he had to get to the airport to pick up his wife and kids who were returning from Miami. 'I'll see you at the Convention Center tomorrow morning at 9.30 because we have to register for the auction before it commences at 10.00.

We'll get a numbered card which you'll hold up each time you wish to make a bid.' Martin agreed on the time to meet and followed up with,

'Hope your family enjoyed their visit to your in-laws and look forward to meeting them sometime soon.'

Before leaving the office, he walked by Robert Mason's office and seeing him alone, knocked on the door and entered. 'Hope I'm not interrupting you Robert, but something has been bothering me and you may have the answer.' Robert looked puzzled and asked how he could help. 'When the Houston Police or the FBI searched the home after Miguel de Cristobal was murdered did they find a cache of drugs?'

'I'll have to check our stories that were front page news for a while after the murder but off the top of my head, I can't recall anything like that. Now that you've raised the question I am thinking that a person like that never really turns into an honest citizen so I'll also make some inquiries with my contacts at the law agencies. I intend to pop in at the auction some time tomorrow when I can get away from here for a couple of hours, so will look for you there. You obviously have some underlying thoughts that have arisen since you started working on the art auction and I'm looking forward to hearing about them soon.' Martin didn't elaborate as he made his exit, 'Goodnight Robert, I'll look for you at the auction tomorrow.'

Later in his hotel suite he looked on-line to see if there were any fish and chips cafés in Houston and was surprised to find one called *Platypus Brewing* which as the name implies, turned out to be another Australian venture. It was a pleasant walk from his hotel and once settled at the bar sampling a craft beer called *The Freckled Dingo Pale Ale,* he smiled when he read the label which advised the drinker that a Dingo would walk 500 miles through the blazing sun to get to this tasty brew! The red haired barman grinned when he topped up Martin's glass and introduced himself as Bluey. 'I can hear from your accent that you're an Aussie, and I welcome you to our establishment.' Martin told him that he came from Melbourne and was in Houston on business. Looking around the neatly furnished and decorated dining area, he quickly came to the conclusion that it was considerably smarter than any fish and chip café he had been to in Melbourne. A short time later, he thoroughly enjoyed the fish and chips that he had chosen from the extensive menu before returning to his hotel.

He telephoned Isabella and they talked about what she had been doing since she returned to Bilbao. She was now working on a case for a client that was one of the city's best known business families and involved a fraudulent charity organization that had swindled them out of hundreds of thousands of Euros in donations. It is expected that the trial will last two to three weeks. Promising to call every couple of days, they said goodbye and hung up.

There were routine emails from his office and the accountant to which he responded before settling down to watch a late night talk show on TV.

CHAPTER 9

LET THE GAMES BEGIN!
THE BIDDING WAR GETS UNDER WAY.

A bright and sunny day greeted Martin the next morning as he ventured outside to walk a couple of blocks for exercise before going to the hotel buffet because he knew he would be sitting for hours at the auction today. After a light breakfast, he took his iPad and the marked up list of paintings and strolled across the sky bridge at precisely 9.30 to meet Neville just as he approached from the other direction.

They joined one of the queues of people waiting to register their names for the auction and they were through in minutes. Moving into the auditorium, they found two seats somewhere in the middle which they decided should give them a good view of the proceedings. Martin looked around the entire seating area and estimated that there could be somewhere between two hundred and two hundred and fifty seats. By the time the auction team appeared at the front just before 10 o'clock, there were very few vacant seats left.

A tall man with a somewhat large moustache stood up and introduced himself as Sydney Bartholomew and told the crowd that he was the authorised auctioneer. He had a pronounced British accent and Martin assumed he had been sent from the auction company's London head office to conduct this very important event. He welcomed the audience and then ran through the way the auction would be managed explaining firstly that a photo of each item would be projected onto a huge screen behind the auctioneer and the title would be announced. The auctioneer would then call for an opening bid. If no opening bid was offered from the crowd, the auctioneer would start things off and then ask for further bids. He explained that they had established reserve prices for every item and if this figure was not reached then that item would be passed in and open to negotiation after the end of the three days of auctions. Bids could only be made by persons who had registered their details prior to the auction.

The first painting displayed on the screen was attributed to Manet and was a beautiful French landscape of brilliant colours. Immediately the auctioneer called for an opening bid, a card was raised and the bidder offered twenty five thousand dollars. Seconds later another card was raised and the bid increased by five thousand dollars. The two bidders fought it out with bids of one and two thousand increments until the hammer fell at thirty five thousand dollars. Neville whispered to Martin that the successful bidder was a well know Houston businessman connected to the oil and gas industry.

The next three paintings finished with prices from fifteen thousand to twenty five thousand dollars. Finally, one of the paintings on Martin's list appeared on the screen. It was *The Adoration of the Magi* attributed to El Greco. Martin raised his card and started the bidding at fifteen thousand dollars hoping to frighten some prospective buyers off. There was a short lull before someone raised the offer to seventeen thousand five hundred dollars.

Martin waited quietly and when no other bid was offered he held up his card and increased the figure by five hundred dollars. His opponent raised it by a further one thousand dollars and Martin immediately made it twenty thousand dollars.

The room was silent and it was knocked down to Martin at that price. Neville nodded and whispered to Martin, 'Well done, that's one down and only five more to go!'

Another hour passed with paintings sold that were not on Martin's list before the Jackson Pollock untitled painting came up. No opening bid was offered and the auctioneer started things off with a bid of ten thousand dollars. A number of bidders joined in and pushed the price up in small increments to twelve thousand two hundred dollars and Martin stepped in with a bid twelve thousand five hundred dollars. An aggressive bid was then made of thirteen thousand and Martin immediately raised it to thirteen thousand five hundred dollars. No further bids were received and it was knocked down to Martin.

Soon after, the auctioneer announced that there would be a one hour break for lunch and the auction would resume at 2 o'clock sharp. Martin and Neville went to the café in the hotel for a sandwich and coffee where they discussed their success so far….two paintings at less than the budget figure in the first session. They considered this as a successful morning's effort. As they re-entered the auditorium, Martin caught sight of Marcel Dupont from Studio Westheimer. He walked over and shook his hand thanking him for his helpful advice when Martin had visited Marcel's gallery the day before.

The afternoon session only included one more of the items on Martin's list and that was the Frida Kahlo painting titled The Wounded Deer. Martin suspected that being Mexican, it was possibly a genuine Frida Kahlo, and despite making a couple of early bids for it, three other potential buyers fought it out taking the final price to seventy five thousand dollars. Neville agreed with Martin dropping out when the bids reached fever pitch and the price skyrocketed. He believed that it was now more certain that this was a genuine Frida Kahlo and the three bidders had the same view, hence the spirited bidding for it. Around mid-afternoon, Robert arrived and found a spare seat near them. Martin spotted him and signalled that they had achieved two successes. As soon as the last painting was put up for the day, the three men headed out of the auction room to the foyer where they could talk. Martin explained that the two paintings they had bought included the Jackson Pollock that was earmarked for his office. 'Well done guys, I can already see that picture hanging on the wall of my office. I'll try and call in again tomorrow to see how you are doing. Oh, before I forget Martin, I checked my sources and your suspicion was correct…no drugs were found in the murdered man's mansion despite thorough searching by the authorities.' Martin responded with, 'I'll fill you in with my thoughts on the subject when I'm next in the office Robert, probably tomorrow afternoon.'

Before leaving the Convention Center, Neville had to collect the invoices for the two paintings they had successfully bid for today. He had to take them to the office early tomorrow morning to arrange for the payment by electronic transfer. He would then meet Martin at 10 o'clock for the second day of the auction.

Martin walked back to the hotel and changed into his swimming costume so he could work by the pool. Collecting his iPad and notes he went down to the recreation area and found a vacant table and chair. There were few people around so he shouldn't be disturbed as he worked. He researched the history of the genuine paintings that he had bought for the Houston Chronicle today and wrote up his notes accordingly.

An hour later, he switched off the iPad, covered it with his towel and dived into the pool where he swam 20 laps. Suitably refreshed, he lay on a sunlounge and let the late afternoon sun dry him off. A waitress approached and told him that the gentleman in the light fawn jacket sitting at the bar would like to buy Martin a drink. He ordered a pint of Lone Star draft beer and told her that he would take it at the bar so he could personally thank the gentleman. Slipping on his shirt, he walked over to where the man was sitting and asked if it was OK to join him.

'Please take a seat,' the man replied, 'my name is Ray Barrett and I was sitting near you at the art auction today. I will be attending the auction every day on behalf of the IRS and seeing you out by the pool just now I decided I'd like to get your opinion on the way the auction is panning out so far.' Martin shook hands and asked, 'I've heard that acronym used once before so what is the IRS?' Ray smiled and replied, 'From your accent it seems you are not an American and obviously unfamiliar with the acronyms related to our government departments. The IRS is the Internal Revenue Service which is our taxation department and the art being auctioned will compensate our department for some of the unpaid taxes owed by the late owner of the collection. By the way, if it is not too rude of me to ask, where do you hail from?'

'I'm an Australian and my name is Martin Taylor. The Houston Chronicle has contracted my services to assist them in selecting and buying some of the art on offer.'

'Wow, did they bring you all this way to do their bidding for them?'

'Not exactly Ray, I was in New York when they contacted me.'

'That's interesting as my branch of the IRS is based in New York. What were you doing there?'

'It's a long story but in short, I was a witness in a murder trial. The woman I was investigating was a possible member of a gang which stole in New York some items belonging to a Maltese cathedral. I was assisting the NYPD in that case and I'm an ex-police officer running my own private investigation business specializing in art crime.'

'I followed that trial every day and can't believe that suddenly out of the blue I am now sitting having a beer with the star of the show!'

Martin then thanked Ray for the beer and excused himself saying he had work to do. 'I'll be spending the day at the auction again tomorrow so will no doubt see you there.' Returning to his suite, he showered and changed into casual clothes and went walking for the next two hours.

Not wanting to sit alone in the main dining room, he took the elevator to the top floor sports bar where at least there was a bunch of cheering baseball fans eating and drinking as they watched the Astros hit the winning home run on the big screens. Martin decided baseball was almost as boring to watch as cricket but didn't dare make any such comment to the raucous crowd surrounding him. Nonetheless, he was pleased to be amongst a happy-go-lucky mob after the seriousness of the bidders at the art auction earlier today.

Later when he was sitting at the desk in his suite, he was turning over in his mind the chances that there might be drugs hidden somewhere in some of the paintings. The idea had come to him when he was writing some notes for the magazine article.

The case of the kidnapped art gallery owner that he was involved with two years ago concerned stolen diamonds that were hidden in brilliantly designed and executed compartments in a picture frame. It's possible that the drug baron had something like this made to hide drugs particularly when the collection was moved from Mexico to Texas. He would certainly suggest searching the pictures they finished up with after the auction. Obviously the chances are small that out of the whole collection one or more of the six paintings they obtain might have drugs hidden somewhere, but who knows?

Next morning Martin and Neville were in their chosen seats at 10 o'clock waiting for the first painting to be offered up. Unfortunately they had to wait more than an hour before one of their choices appeared. This was the Rubens attributed painting called *Scene in the Antwerp Studio*. It depicted a large studio filled with lots of paintings on easels being worked on by Rubens' assistants and students. It is a magnificent scene and there is so much to study closely, one might take years to really appreciate every aspect of the detail. A first bid was made of ten thousand dollars and was immediately raised by two thousand dollars. There was a slight lull before Martin bid another two thousand dollars. Bidding halted whilst someone at the back was talking to an out-of-town client on the phone, and after a couple of minutes, raised the price to sixteen thousand five hundred dollars. Martin jumped in with a further bid making it eighteen thousand dollars and the person on the phone shook his head and it was knocked down to Martin. Turning to Neville, he whispered, 'We're halfway there!'

No further selected paintings came up prior to the lunch break but mid-afternoon the Dali etching called *The Chariot of Bacchus* showed up on the screen. The auctioneer, Sydney Bartholomew, emphasized that it was number 217 of 300 prints made and independent art experts had considered it to be genuine. The room was silent with no-one opening the bidding. Martin waited patiently while the auctioneer called twice for a bid to start the process and again there was silence. He was about to bring the gavel down to pass it in when Martin held up his card calling out, 'I'll open the bidding sir with fifteen hundred dollars.' There was a gasp from the crowd followed by silence. A minute passed and the gavel was raised again when suddenly a new bidder entered the fray! He added five hundred dollars. Martin immediately raised it to two and a half thousand dollars. The other bidder added two hundred and fifty dollars and Martin immediately made it three thousand dollars. The bidding war continued this way until it reached five thousand dollars.

The speed of Martin's raising the price must have scared off the other bidder as she dropped out and it was knocked down to him. Neville leant over and smiled giving Martin the thumbs up. The afternoon dragged on with most paintings fetching between ten and twenty five thousand dollars. There was one exception which was the one attributed to Monet called *The Garden at Giverny*. Two bidders fought for this as seriously as the combatants in Russia's recent invasion of the Ukraine, pushing the price well above fifty thousand dollars. The winning bid came from someone on the telephone. Martin was pleased he hadn't participated in that *bidding war!*

The last picture offered for the day was the small Picasso etching called *Pour Robbie* that had been printed some time after the artist's death. The auctioneer pointed out that this print was one of many produced from an engraved plate made by Picasso but unlike the earlier Dali etching, the prints were made by an American company. There was a label on the rear stating that an independent company had verified that the plate was genuinely etched by Picasso. Bidding was slow for this item starting from three hundred dollars and eventually realising a price of three thousand dollars bid once again by Martin. After Neville had collected the three invoices for today's successful purchases he and Martin chatted outside on the sky bridge. 'That was great today Martin, I am particularly satisfied with the two items that we bought today for my office. Your bidding was outstanding and achieved our aims splendidly.'

'I'm also pleased with today's results Neville,' Martin said, 'Hopefully we'll be able to complete our purchases early tomorrow as I want to spend the afternoon at the Houston Chronicle office. Robert must have been in meetings all day as he didn't make it to the auction as he had hoped. I need to discuss some matters with him tomorrow and you might want to listen in. I have some thoughts that are bothering me about the paintings in the collection that I want to expand on. Despite the fact that we sat for all those hours in the Convention Center, it's somewhat exhausting and I'm going to turn in early tonight. By the way, how did you get on with the auditors?' With a grin from ear to ear, Neville replied, 'Absolute clean slate. They were pleased with my management of the paper's finances and my records were squeaky clean. See you tomorrow bright and early.'

Martin worked out in the hotel gym where he met up with Ray Barrett. 'I didn't notice you today during the auction Ray.' 'Someone else had taken the seat near you when I arrived there this morning,' he answered, 'so I finished up sitting near the back of the hall. I noticed that you managed to win the bidding war on some more paintings before the auction ended today. Are you free to join me at dinner in the hotel dining room, say in half an hour?' Martin agreed and ended up having a pleasant evening chatting with someone over a meal instead of sitting on his own. Ray wanted to know more about the case he worked on in New York that led to the death of a young woman. 'I found myself in a somewhat dangerous situation during the investigation of the Cathedral's items that had been on display in a Manhattan gallery. It is a very long and involved story and I'd prefer not to go into all the details right now as the Houston Chronicle will be writing a series of articles about me that will be published in their weekend magazine some time in the not-too-distant future.

Suffice it to say I was investigating the victim at the time of the murder and was called as a prosecution witness at the trial of the killer.' Ray was disappointed not to learn more about the case and said that he will look out for the articles about Martin when they have been published.

They parted ways around 9 o'clock saying they expected to see each other tomorrow morning which would be the third day of the auction. 'I expect the remaining paintings will go under the hammer in the morning and the afternoon will be dedicated to selling the sculptures and ceramics,' Ray advised as he walked away. Back in his suite, Martin gathered together the growing stack of receipts of charges incurred this past week to scan and send to his accountant. He then sent through the close-up photos he had taken of the Robin Black painting to Aart van den Haag.

Next morning, Martin and Neville were seated five minutes before the first item was presented so had a few minutes to chat. 'I didn't get a chance yesterday to tell you about the guy I met who is staying at my hotel. He is the IRS representative monitoring the sales at the auction. He is sitting to our left in the row behind.... we had dinner together last night. As far as I can tell, he seems to be quite pleased with the way the auction is being managed so I assume the sale prices are meeting their expectations.'

The room became hushed as Sydney Bartholomew arrived and banged his gavel to signal commencement of the day's auction. The screen lit up and the first picture of the day turned out to be the Canaletto painting of *The Bridge of Sighs*. The auctioneer reminded the patrons that although this item was signed Canaletto, it could not be verified. He then asked for an opening bid for this very beautiful painting. A woman right at the back of the room held up her card and said that her client was on the telephone and bid fifteen thousand five hundred dollars. It was obvious to Martin that this was not going to be a bargain. He whispered to Neville that he really wanted this painting for the company president's office. 'Go ahead Martin, I'll let you know when you are to stop bidding.' Deciding to play it cool, Martin made a series of small incremental bids which slowly pushed the price up to eighteen thousand seven hundred dollars. There was a pause whilst discussions followed with two telephone bidders at the rear of the hall and the price stalled at twenty one thousand eight hundred dollars. The auctioneer banged the gavel twice and had raised it for the third time when Martin called out twenty two thousand dollars. One of the telephone bidders added one hundred and fifty dollars and Martin immediately made it twenty two thousand three hundred dollars. The two people on telephones shook their heads and another painting was knocked down to Martin.

A series of smaller paintings attributed to lesser known artists followed during the next hour and then the instantly recognisable exotic *Tahitian Landscape* attributed to Gaugin was on offer. There was spirited bidding for this painting but once again Martin played it cool and won the fight at nineteen thousand four hundred dollars. Neville was keeping a running tally of their purchases passed a note to Martin showing so far they had spent $101,200 so still had $48,800 available from the original budget.

'Don't forget we also have a contingency amount of twenty five thousand dollars should we need it,' he said. Just then, Martin spotted Robert passing their row along the aisle and nodded to acknowledge that he had seen him.

Fifteen minutes later the cowboy painting that Martin was sure would be great in the boardroom appeared on the screen. It was called *The Rustlers Escape* and was attributed to Frederic Remington. Knowing that this would be a popular choice for many Texans, Martin held off bidding to observe the reaction of the patrons.

Once bidding was down to two people Martin made his first offer of twenty two thousand dollars. One of the two bidders dropped out and it was then between Martin and one other person. Bidding slowed after it reached twenty four thousand two hundred dollars against Martin and Neville nudged him to make one more bid. He won this bidding war at twenty four thousand six hundred dollars so clocked up another one for the boardroom.

During the next batch of paintings that were not on the suggested list, Martin inquired of Neville, 'Not including the little Picasso etching, we have seven paintings to hang on walls, two of which are definitely for the boardroom. We have finished up with two abstract pieces of art and as far as I know, the only person who likes this style is Robert but originally he wasn't to get any paintings for his office. We did agree early on that if there was some money left over we could buy one for his office and we more or less settled on the Dali etching. Because we didn't succeed in bidding for the Monet we then won the bid for the Jackson Pollock. Two paintings on our list which haven't come up yet are the James McNeill Whistler and the Aussie Robin Black. We could stop right now and shuffle the ones we have bought around until we get an agreement, or bid for one of the two still available and this would need approval to dip into the contingency.' Neville thought for a minute then replied, 'There is still twenty four thousand two hundred dollars remaining in the budget and if you can get the Robin Black for around that amount let's try.'

'The Whistler painting would certainly be more popular in the US and could reach a high price whilst Black is probably less known,' Martin stated authoritatively. 'OK, let's do battle and hope to win!' declared Neville.

As it turned out the Robin Black painting came up soon after the discussion and there were only three bids with Martin winning with a bid of twenty five thousand dollars. The Whistler painting followed soon after and sold for seventy thousand dollars so they decided they had made the right choice. They had succeeded in buying a total of nine pictures which was three more than originally expected and spent only eight hundred dollars of the contingency to achieve this result.

Neville took off to collect the invoices for the days' purchases and Martin found Robert and told him he was going to the Houston Chronicle this afternoon. 'I'll be working in my office on the Art Chronicles report Robert, so please call me when you are free for me to come and see you.'

Around 3 o'clock, Martin's phone rang and it was Robert inviting him to come to his office and to bring Neville along as well. Although it was Sunday, the saying that a newspaper never sleeps was well demonstrated by the number of people Martin saw dashing back and forth past his office. He wandered down to Neville's office and asked him to join him for a meeting with Robert Mason.

When all three were settled in the Senior Editor's office, Robert congratulated the guys for what they had achieved at the art auction. 'I have just spoken with the company President, Matthew McBride, and he told me he was looking forward to meeting Martin on Monday morning.' Addressing Neville, he asked, 'When will we be able to collect the paintings we have bought?'

After consulting the calendar on his phone, he answered, 'I am making the final payments this afternoon for today's purchases so they should show up in the auctioneer's account tomorrow morning. I'll call them around midday to confirm that they have received all of our electronic funds transfers and if so, we'll arrange with the specialist art transport company we have used before, to collect the paintings Tuesday.'

Robert then turned to Martin and suggested he expand on his thoughts about the possibility of drugs being stored in some of the paintings. 'The more I thought about it, the more viable it seemed,' he replied. 'When Miguel de Cristobal moved from Mexico to Houston, hiding small packs of heroin inside paintings being transported with his furniture and other home-wares would have made it easy for smuggling across the border. This of course is only speculation on my part, but in my experience once someone has spent their adult life dealing in drugs, no matter how much money they have made, they never stop. In my years with the Victoria Police in Melbourne, I witnessed the same drug dealers time and time again released from prison and go straight back to spreading their evil products to the unfortunate addicts who can't escape the habit. Some are ultimately assassinated in gang wars such as your *infamous art collector* but that never appears to convince the drug barons to think twice about staying in the business.'

At this point, Robert interrupted Martin to say that earlier this year the biggest drug baron in the world had been extradited to the USA. 'His name is Dario Antonio Usuga and he led a cartel based in Colombia called the *Gulf Clan*. He was the most wanted person in Colombia for seven years during which the clan shipped hundreds of tons of cocaine abroad every year worth billions of dollars.'

Martin said that he hadn't heard of that particular person but had read a lot about the other notorious Colombian drug baron, Pablo Escobar. He continued his theory about the possibility of drugs having been hidden in the paintings that have just been auctioned. 'It is probable that if my assertions are correct, only a small number of paintings would have been used to hide the drugs. He would have worked out a system together with his most trusted sidekicks that would enable them to find the drugs at a later date. Up till now I haven't come up with what their system might be and the chance that any of the paintings we bought could be carrying drugs is extremely low.

I'm interested to hear your comments on my theory, and if you have any ideas how their choice of pictures to hide the drugs might have worked, please let's hear them.'

The other two men had sat in silence whilst Martin had explained how he arrived at this notion but now Neville wanted to throw his hat into the ring. 'My immediate reaction was that hiding drugs in some of the paintings is a definite possibility and if this is the case, then those paintings will now be in the hands of innocent buyers and somehow will have to be warned by the authorities. As for which paintings they might be hidden in is quite a conundrum but I have one suggestion. Consider the effect these drugs have on people's minds….. they addle the mind so everything looks out of focus and screwed up therefore my guess would be they would use abstract paintings to tuck their little packs of hallucinating powders somewhere in the back between the canvas and the rear cover board.'

Robert jokingly remarked, 'I always knew you were more than just a pretty face Neville with a good handle on numbers.' Martin followed with, 'That's an excellent idea Neville, two of our paintings fall into that category, the Dali and the Jackson Pollock. My suggestion is that before we remove the back from any of our acquisitions, the Houston Chronicle request representatives from either or both the Houston Police drug squad and the FBI be present to witness just in any case drugs are found.'

Robert concurred, 'I totally agree Martin, and we'll have someone from our legal department also on hand. Thanks for devoting your Sunday to the auction and let's call it a day and I'll see you both here tomorrow morning.'

As Martin and Neville were walking back to their respective offices to get their bags, Neville again congratulated Martin for his efforts. 'I suggest an early night as I have a feeling the rest of this week is going to be full on for all of us.'

CHAPTER 10

WHEN ART IS MORE THAN JUST A PRETTY PICTURE.

A Tuesday morning like no other greeted Martin as he sat reading the newspaper whilst eating breakfast. There were dire hurricane warnings on the front page describing a massive build-up of dangerous weather over the Gulf of Mexico. As he had never experienced weather conditions as described in the newspaper he wasn't sure what he was expected to do. He decided his best plan of action would be to get himself to the Houston Chronicle and follow their directions on safety protocols.

Also of concern was an article about two further deaths of journalists in Mexico City both of whom worked for international news organizations. He was checking his phone for messages when he noticed one had come in overnight from his L.A. police officer friend, Charlie Watson. He expressed concern over Martin's intention to visit Mexico City and offered his assistance as he explained that he had a lot of experience in dealing with criminals in that city. Because it was still early morning in L.A., Martin decided to call him from his office at the Chronicle later.

When he arrived at the office, he found a note from Janita asking him to phone her to make an appointment for another interview. He called her extension and they agreed to meet at 11 o'clock. He was working on his report of the auction when Robert called to say that the company President would like to meet him at 10.30. He was to first go to Robert's office and he would take him to meet Matthew McBride. As he passed the executive editor's office Emma Johnson waved him in. 'Good morning Martin, I have been briefed by Robert that you succeeded in buying us a lovely new art collection for our offices and I'm looking forward to seeing them.' He responded that it was an amazing auction, 'I hope you are pleased with our final selection and we are hopeful that the paintings will be delivered here later today. I have to keep moving right now as Robert is about to introduce me to Matthew McBride and we don't want to keep him waiting.'

Right on 10.30, Robert introduced Martin to the company President who formally thanked him for his reported success at the art auction. 'If things go to plan,' Martin told him, 'we'll be able to start hanging paintings in their new home later this week. I don't know if Robert has filled you in with a possible hitch to the program regarding my concern that there might be some drugs hidden in the paintings. We'll check them once they are here.'

'Yes,' Matthew McBride answered, 'and I'm in agreement that we need to be certain that we are not in possession of any drugs, albeit that we didn't put them there. Please keep me up to date on your investigation. I am also looking forward to the series of articles about you that will be published in our weekend magazine.'

Martin and Robert took their leave and returned to their offices. Neville phoned five minutes after Martin was seated at his desk. 'I have just confirmed with the auctioneer that our payments have been cleared and we can pick up the paintings this afternoon. Our logistics department is making the arrangements as we speak.'

'That's great Neville, will you have someone from your legal department contact the police to be here tomorrow when we open up the backs of the pictures?'

'I've already set the wheels in motion Martin…. the Houston police commissioner, Madison Reynolds will have someone from their drug squad here at 10 o'clock and she will also speak with the local FBI office to see if they wish to attend. I've alerted our maintenance department to have a carpenter available for what I am calling *the grand opening!*'

'I should have known that you would be right on top of things Neville.'

A few minutes after putting down the phone, Janita appeared with her recording machine and her usual mug of coffee. 'I heard on the grapevine that you did well at the art auction Martin and congratulations are in order. I also heard some rumour about possible drugs being involved, is that correct?' He smiled saying, 'Well Janita, it doesn't surprise me that you might have heard about it. After all, this is a newspaper and gathering news is the reason you're all here. I have an idea that there could be drugs hidden in some of the paintings so we'll be investigating my theory tomorrow morning. No doubt one of your reporters with a photographer will be on hand to record whatever we find…if anything.'

She straightaway declared, 'I'll make sure it's me as it will be an important adjunct to my story about your adventures.' For the remainder of the afternoon, Janita questioned Martin about his training at the Police Academy and expanded on the details of his first overseas case that started when he witnessed the murder of a man on the Bilbao funicular railway.

Around 4.30, Neville popped in to invite Martin to his place to meet his wife Estelle. 'I'll be leaving here around five so if you can drag yourself away from your work, you can follow me home. I hope you like barbecue food as I'll be cooking tonight.' Martin laughed as he thanked him for the invitation, 'BBQ's are a favourite of Australians and we never get tired of them.'

When he was following Neville later to the upmarket suburb of River Oaks, he noticed a florist shop and signalled Neville to stop so he could buy flowers for his hostess. Upon arrival at the Montgomery home, Martin was introduced to Estelle. Handing her the floral arrangement, he thanked her for the invitation to dine with them. 'It's our pleasure Martin and having heard so much about you from Neville since I returned from Miami, I look forward to hearing more from you first hand tonight.'

He was taken through to the deck at the rear of the house where Neville was busy setting up the barbecue. Martin raised his concern about the weather, 'This morning's newspaper warned of a threatening hurricane building up over the Gulf of Mexico and I forgot to ask what one does in such circumstances when I was at the office. So far, everything seems normal to me….have I missed something?'

'No,' Neville answered, 'this happens often in the southern states when these storm systems develop over the Gulf of Mexico and then fizzle out without making landfall. We can never be certain what they will do, and therefore the authorities often err on the conservative side. When one of these hurricanes does move onto land the damage can look like there has been a war and sadly there's always a loss of life as well. The one that developed yesterday offshore New Orleans appeared to be threatening Texas but has actually now moved away towards Cuba. According to the weather bureau it is no longer intense enough to be a serious problem. These storm events are always given names and this one was called Minnie. Thankfully it lived up to its name!'

Just then as Neville put the steaks on the BBQ, two young women came outside with Estelle and were introduced as Rosalie and Sandra. Martin guessed their ages as fifteen and sixteen. 'They both attend the local high school,' Estelle mentioned as she asked them to set the table in the family room. 'I heard from Neville that you have a beautiful Spanish fiancée and that she visited Houston last weekend while I was in Miami. I'm sure he has told you that I have holidayed on the gorgeous Queensland Gold Coast and if it wasn't for my parents in Miami, I would have happily moved there.'

Martin replied, 'Queensland advertises itself as the state that has beautiful weather one day and perfect the next! Unfortunately this is not always the case as was demonstrated earlier this year when Brisbane and the Gold Coast were devastated by unprecedented rainfalls. This resulted in extensive flooding with thousands of homes completely submerged up to their rooflines. Sadly, a number of people drowned trying to escape the floodwaters.'

They sat down to a delicious meal of perfectly grilled steaks with Idaho potatoes done in their jackets and a variety of condiments. The talk centred on the success of the art auction and the mystery surrounding whether or not drugs may have been secreted behind the canvases of some paintings. 'Tomorrow, all will be revealed,' said Neville with some conviction. The meal concluded with a fresh fruit platter and a pot of strong coffee.

The two girls had returned to their rooms to finish their homework straight after dessert and did not come down again before Martin headed back to town. He had thanked his hosts sincerely for a pleasant evening and promised to see Neville early at the office in the morning. Although he felt that he was getting to know his way around Houston by now, he still used the car's GPS to lead him back to the hotel the most direct way as this was the first time he had to find his way back from River Oaks.

He wrote long informative emails to Isabella and his office manager detailing the events of the past two days and the results of his bidding at the art auction. He also briefly mentioned the forthcoming examination of the paintings looking for hidden drugs. Once again, he highlighted the wonderful hospitality of the people he had met so far in Houston and hoped he would have some way of returning their generosity before the assignments were over and he returned to Australia. Switching on the FOX late news, he watched various reports of dramas in Europe and Asia before deciding it was all too depressing so decided to try his hand at the Houston Chronicle crossword instead before turning off the light.

He skipped breakfast the next morning and went straight to the newspaper's offices as wanted to take a look at the paintings before the witnessed examination took place at 10 o'clock. When he pulled into the staff car park and plugged the car into the charging station, he saw Lonnie arriving and went over to speak with him. 'Hi Lonnie, I don't know if anyone has brought you up to date about the paintings we bought at the auction, but today is a very important occasion.' Obviously he hadn't been given any specific details but apparently Robert had asked him to remain at the office all morning. 'What's it all about Martin?' he inquired. 'Lonnie, I had a feeling that the murdered drug baron who owned these art works may have hidden illicit narcotics in some of the paintings. We are going to examine them this morning under the watchful eyes of the Houston police department and the FBI. Do you have any idea where the paintings would have been offloaded when they arrived yesterday?' Lonnie led Martin to the reception to sign in and replied that they are in a warehouse behind the main office building where huge reels of newsprint and inks were stored. 'I saw them being unloaded from a large truck late yesterday afternoon but you'll need management permission to enter the warehouse before I can take you there.'

'OK Lonnie, thanks for the info, I'll go up and see Robert and get his permission then call you.' As he made his way to his office on the fourth floor, he noticed Neville was not in yet but after dropping his brief case and laptop on his desk, he continued on to Robert's office. He was hard at work and at first didn't hear the quiet tap at his door. He looked up when Martin knocked a little louder and waved him in. 'Hi Robert, I understand the paintings were delivered yesterday as expected and are sitting in the company warehouse right now. I met Lonnie in the parking lot earlier and he told me that I need permission to enter the warehouse. Can you please arrange for me to go in and examine the paintings as I believe it's important for me to be completely familiar with them before the authorities arrive at 10 o'clock?' Robert picked up his telephone and asked the receptionist to connect him with Lonnie. 'Good morning Lonnie, I'm sending Martin Taylor down to the front right now and I'd like you to accompany him to the warehouse and provide him with whatever assistance he might need to look over the paintings currently stored there.' Martin nodded and asked, 'Will you be with us when we formally examine the paintings Robert?' Shaking his head, he apologized, saying, 'I would like to be there but I have a major editorial meeting scheduled that will start at 10 o'clock and last for some hours but I have asked Neville to be there with you.'

Martin had brought his high-end Nikon digital camera with him today and slung the strap over his shoulder before going down to meet Lonnie. He was led out and around the main office complex to the warehouse at the rear and introduced to the security guard on duty at the front door. Once inside, he immediately caught sight of the paintings which had been transported on special stands belonging to the art transport company. Each had been completely covered in bubble wrap and Martin took photos showing them in that condition before asking Lonnie to have one of the store personnel bring cutting tools and start removing the bubble wrap.

He was pleased to see that this person was a young woman and thought that she would probably be more careful not to damage the paintings than a gung-ho warehouseman.

The auctioneers had labelled each painting which enabled Martin to easily select the ones he wanted unwrapped first.

Lonnie whispered that her name was Zoe. 'Hi Zoe, my name is Martin, please unwrap the one with the label JACKSON POLLOCK-UNTITLED.' She very slowly and carefully peeled back the bubble wrap until the painting was exposed in all its glory. He immediately took photographs of the front and back then moved closer to examine the frame as well as the Masonite backing board. There were no obvious signs of anything out of the ordinary. 'Please unwrap the one with the label SALVADOR DALI-THE CHARIOT OF BACCHUS.' Once again the picture was carefully exposed and photographed. His examination of the backing board revealed some small scratches at the corners which he photographed close-up. Being a print of an etching, it was protected by a glass front. Martin was deep in thought when Lonnie's phone rang and he announced that the authorities had arrived. 'That was Mr. Montgomery and he said to tell you that he is on his way to greet the visitors at reception and escort them to the warehouse.'

While they waited for the detectives, Martin pointed out to Lonnie, 'There's something very unusual about the way these paintings have been packaged. Paintings on canvas such as the Jackson Pollock are normally open at the back. This one has a Masonite sheet covering the rear of the frame so that could provide an excellent hiding place. As for the Dali print, this would normally have a thick sheet of ply or plastic to press the print paper flat against the glass front. In our case, the frame seems to have been made much wider than normal leading me to suspect that there is a second sheet of ply at the rear leaving a gap between it and the front sheet.' He was interrupted by Neville arriving with the visitors. Introductions were made of everyone now gathered around the paintings. The newspaper's legal representative was Deidre Bush, the Houston detective was Daniel Gunn, and the FBI inspector was Ron Stephens. Martin was asked to explain how he had arrived at his suspicions that drugs may have been hidden in some of the criminal's paintings. Choosing his words carefully, he told of the case he was involved with a few years ago when he was a police officer in Australia. 'Stolen diamonds had been cleverly concealed in the frame of a valuable painting so it could be transported out of Europe undetected and imported into Australia where the Customs inspectors considered the painting to be quite innocuous. This method of hiding goods to pass through Customs at borders has remained with me since that time. This past week, I represented the Houston Chronicle in bidding for some of the art that was auctioned on behalf of the US government that had been removed from the home of a murdered Mexican drug baron. The more I thought about the background of the owner of these art works, the more I came to the conclusion that he could have hidden illicit drugs in some of the paintings. Just prior to your arrival I had the store person here unwrap two of the pictures I thought could be examples of my suspicions. I photographed the unwrapping so you can see we haven't tampered with them in any way. I would now like to have everyone witness the removal of the boards covering the rear of each picture and I will record these events on video.'

Martin then asked Zoe if she could bring the appropriate tools to remove the boards from the backs of these two pictures. A table was brought from the warehouse lunch room and the cast-off bubble wrap laid over it to prevent damage to the pictures.

Lonnie and Zoe carefully lifted the Jackson Pollock painting from its transport stand and laid it face down on the table with some blocks under the picture frame. Zoe then selected a small Phillips-head screwdriver from her tool kit and slowly removed the six countersunk screws that were holding the rear cover in place. She then lifted the cover board out of the frame to reveal what was behind. The group of onlookers moved forward to get a better look and there was a pronounced gasp at what was now revealed in full view. The cover board had a number of compartments attached and squeezed into each was a small plastic bag filled with a white powder. The Houston Police Officer picked up one of the bags and examined the powder carefully before declaring that he was certain it was heroin. Martin had continued filming the entire operation whilst the FBI detective took lots of photographs on his cell phone. The drug-loaded board was set aside and the painting returned to its transport stand.

Zoe was then asked to carry out the same actions on the Dali framed print. Sure enough, the extra rear cover board was fitted with similar compartments each with its little bags of white powder.

Ron Stephens from the FBI instructed Martin to have each of the remaining pictures unwrapped to enable examination. This took the rest of the morning and proved Neville's theory was correct. Only the abstract pictures had the false rear cover boards so no further drugs were found. The two compartmented boards were wrapped and sealed with duct tape. Both the lawmen signed their names with a permanent marker on the bubble wrap and the package carried out to the FBI's black SUV and locked inside. A security guard was instructed to wait by the vehicle until Ron Stephens came back.

Everyone involved was then taken to the boardroom to discuss what actions were required following today's discovery. The newspaper's legal representative, Deidre Bush, took charge of the meeting and started by addressing the two lawmen, Daniel Gunn and Ron Stephens. 'Obviously we have uncovered what is possibly only the tip of the iceberg and no doubt there are more drugs hidden in some of the other paintings sold at the art auction. As we are not involved with any of those other sales, it is clear to me that our responsibilities end with what you observed here this morning. We can provide you with copies of the videos that were made in your presence and copies of our sales receipts for the pictures. Is there anything else you require from us at this time?'

Detective Daniel Gunn spoke first. 'Thank you Ms. Bush, we appreciate everything the Houston Chronicle has done to uncover these drugs and we'll be working with the FBI to follow up examination of all the items sold at the auction. Today's discovery will provide new clues to our team investigating the murder of Miguel de Cristobal.'

Ron Stephens then added, 'No doubt some of the paintings could by now have been delivered to their new owners in Houston and other American states, or could even be on their way abroad. Your theory about only abstract style pictures being used for the concealment of the drugs appears to be correct and we'll tackle all such items first. We have resources available throughout the continental USA and I'll start the ball rolling as soon as I return to my office today.

Thanks to all of you for your well managed operation today and if any of you are considering joining the FBI, you can contact me at our Houston office.'

Lonnie was asked to escort the two lawmen to their cars and then come back to the boardroom. Deidre Bush left to inform the company President about the events that had taken place this morning. Martin and Neville went straight to Robert's office to give him the news. He had just returned from the editorial meeting and was amazed when told about what he had missed. 'We'll be running an exclusive first hand story of the discovery of the drugs….do we have any photos?' Martin told him we have lots of photos and videos. 'I used my digital camera instead of my cell phone today so they should be of excellent quality.' Robert told him that he would send one of their reporters up to borrow the camera and download the photos and videos. 'Are there any of your personal shots in the camera.' Martin shook his head, 'No Robert, I had already cleared everything out last night onto my laptop so what is there now is only the record of today's events.' They were walking back to their offices when Lonnie appeared. 'I was instructed to return to the boardroom but there was no-one there when I looked in.' Martin asked him if he could assist him for about half an hour if he is not tied up right now. 'I need help to measure the pictures so I can be certain they will fit in the spaces on the walls they have been allocated.' Lonnie said that would be OK and it would also give him a chance to discuss accompanying Martin to Mexico City should that still be on the cards. 'Good, let's go Lonnie. I'll pick up a tape measure as we pass the stationery room.' Grabbing his iPad to write down the dimensions, they took the elevator down to the ground level and walked around to the warehouse.

The largest painting they measured was the Rubens *Scene in the Antwerp Studio*. It was five foot four inches wide by two foot six inches high. The second largest was the untitled Jackson Pollock which measured three foot eight inches wide by two foot ten inches high. The Dali etching *The Chariot of Bacchus* was two foot six inches wide by two foot three inches high. The Canaletto painting of *The Bridge of Sighs* was two foot six inches wide by one foot six and a half inches high. All the other pictures were smaller so would not present any spatial issues.

Martin and Lonnie went to the canteen and over lunch they discussed their possible excursion to Mexico City. 'I have travelled there a couple of times and found it a very interesting place to visit. There is a fantastic museum there filled with artefacts from the Mayan, Incan and Aztec civilizations, a lot of which was discovered when they were tunnelling for their Metro rail system some years ago. Unfortunately, for quite some time Mexico's economy has suffered due to corruption amongst the highest levels of government and law enforcement agencies. This has left the country with an extremely large number of very poor people, many of whom are continually trying to enter the USA illegally. The result of this poverty has created a crime rate that makes it dangerous for visitors, especially American tourists who are seen as easy pickings.'

Martin mentioned that the management of the Houston Chronicle had chosen Lonnie to accompany him because of his excellent army record and his knowledge of the language.

'I will be pleased to have you watching my back although I am sure your wife won't be happy about it.' Lonnie grinned as he answered Martin. 'As a matter of fact, Margaret took quite a shine to you when you came for dinner and more or less insisted that I accept the bodyguard job looking after you for a couple of days! Make sure you take good care of this lovely man she said, or you'll have me to answer to.'

'Now we have the paintings in our possession,' Martin explained, 'I will be taking a series of close-up photographs to show the forger in Mexico City and ask him to confirm or reject our suspicions that he was the painter of all or some of these.' Lonnie's cell phone rang and he said he had to go to the airport to pick someone up and would see Martin during the day tomorrow.

Martin returned to his office and was checking the list of the paintings he had successfully bid for and realised in all the excitement they now had an extra painting that they needed to find a home for. He prepared a list showing which painting was currently allocated to whom and emailed it to Robert and Neville for comment.

EL GRECO – ADORATION OF THE MAGI	BOARDROOM	$20,000
FREDERIC REMINGTON – THE RUSTLERS' ESCAPE	BOARDROOM	$24,600
ROBIN BLACK – ROSE BAY	BOARDROOM	$25,000
CANALETTO – BRIDGE OF SIGHS	PRESIDENT	$22,300
PAUL GAUGIN – TAHITIAN LANDSCAPE	EXECUTIVE EDITOR	$19,400
PETER PAUL RUBENS – ANTWERP STUDIO	FINANCE DIRECTOR	$18,000
PICASSO – POUR ROBBIE	FINANCE DIRECTOR	$ 3,000
SALVADOR DALI -THE CHARIOT OF BACCHUS	SENIOR EDITOR	$ 5,000
Not yet allocated JACKSON POLLOCK – UNTITLED		$13,500

Janita called and asked to meet Martin in half an hour in the warehouse for a photo shoot. She would bring a photographer and wanted to get photos of him in front of the line-up of paintings. He spruced himself up and wandered down to meet her. She escorted him into the warehouse and introduced him to the photographer, Sammy. As they approached the row of paintings, Martin was surprised to see both Robert and Neville were there studying the lined up pictures. Robert greeted the newcomers and told them that he and Neville were reviewing the allocation list they had just received from Martin. 'We are basically in agreement with the way you have allocated the pictures Martin, and as I was originally only to receive one if there were surplus funds, the inexpensive Dali print was ultimately a welcome solution. I also like the Jackson Pollock painting but Neville and I believe it should be hung in the boardroom if there is space on the walls after the other three are in position. We'll run it past Matthew McBride and Emma Johnson and let you know what they decide.' Neville added, 'I will have Zoe, who did such a good job when the Houston police officer and FBI inspector were here, call you to fix a time to start bringing the pictures into the office building so you can manage the positioning of each.'

Janita explained that she and the photographer were about to take some photos of Martin with the paintings, and Neville replied that they were leaving them to it and going back to their respective offices. The photo shoot was carried out and afterwards Martin took the opportunity to take close-up shots of the paintings he believed may have been produced by the

Mexican forger. Janita arranged for the next interview session to take place at 2 o'clock this afternoon in his office.

He grabbed a sandwich from the canteen and was checking through the photos he had just taken of the paintings when Neville phoned to say that the management had agreed to have the Jackson Pollock painting hung in the boardroom if space allowed. 'We'll continue to use the name of the artist when talking about the paintings even though we know they are actually only attributed to them. It's much simpler that way, especially amongst us.' Martin agreed, and raised the issue of his visit to Mexico City. 'I have talked this over with Lonnie and would like to proceed with making arrangements to call on the art forger, Fernando de Becerra. Please have your manager at the Mexico City office contact him to see if he will meet with me say the day after tomorrow. I'm assuming there are plenty of flights between here and Mexico City and we shouldn't have problems getting reservations at short notice.' Neville responded, 'I'll get onto it straight away. Are you remaining here for the rest of today?' Martin told him that he would be here continuing his interview with Janita. 'If time permits, I'd like to start hanging pictures later this afternoon.'

He downloaded the photos of the paintings onto his laptop and then saved them onto a USB which he took to the operations room and printed them off. Collecting a couple of folders from the stationery department, he returned to his office and sat printing the name of each painting onto the relevant photograph. While he was busy doing this, there was a knock on his door and it was the art critic, Ben Scott. 'Hi Martin, I have just been in a meeting with Mr. Mason and was on my way to the elevator when I decided to stop by and see how you went the other day with the art galleries I had given you introductions to?'

'Hi Ben, thanks for dropping by. The most relevant information came from my visit to Studio Westheimer....Marcel Dupont was extremely helpful, and because his gallery is really an extension of his art classes selling works by his best students, the prices helped me to better understand what might be expected at the auction.' Ben departed pleased that he had sent Martin to the right place.

Janita appeared shortly after Ben had left, and she and Martin settled down for the next phase of the magazine article interviews. Today's session concentrated on the *2018 Gallery Owner Kidnapping* case. This was a very complicated story and explaining the intricacies of the crime took a long time. The further Martin detailed the events, the more intrigued Janita became and the interview dragged on as she asked more questions. Finally she switched off her recorder and thanked him for being so open about the case. She was just walking away when his phone rang and it was Zoe from the warehouse asking which pictures he wanted brought up first. 'Please bring up the Jackson Pollock, the El Greco, the Frederic Remington and the Robin Black. Each picture has a label attached with the artist's name and title so you can easily identify them. These are all to go to the boardroom on the fourth floor.

By the time you get here, I will have the room unlocked and meet you there.' As soon as he hung up from Zoe, he called Neville to have the boardroom made available for the next hour or so. 'There are no meetings booked for today Martin so there won't be any issue. I'll wander down later to assist in any way if that's OK with you.' Martin went to the stationery room and borrowed the long measuring tape and a marking pencil. Looking along the extensively stocked shelves in the room, he was pleased to see a selection of picture hooks. Taking two boxes of large hooks, he walked along to the boardroom.

Entering the boardroom, he took down the old pictures and carefully stacked them near the door. A few minutes later Zoe arrived wheeling the first picture on some sort of a trolley. It was the Jackson Pollock brightly coloured abstract painting. 'Please take that one and stand it against the end wall.' Noticing that she was wearing a tool belt, he asked Zoe to go around the room and remove the old hooks from the walls. A young man arrived wheeling another picture, the El Greco *Adoration of the Magi*. Martin directed him to stand it against the wall to the right of the door. Zoe introduced the apprentice as Bill and asked him to bring up the next picture. As soon as she had finished removing the old hooks, she took off to get another picture also. Whilst they were gone Martin started measuring and marking the walls where he wanted the picture hooks located for the two pictures on hand at the moment. Bill returned with the Frederic Remington painting of *The Rustlers Escape* and was directed to stand it against the wall to the left of door. Just then Neville arrived and asked what he could do to help. 'Please take a look at where I have placed the pictures and tell me if you think they look OK in those positions before we start with hammering picture hooks into the wall. The fourth and last picture will be here in a moment so we'll have the complete set to finalize then.' Neville was standing back and studying the layout when Zoe arrived with the Robin Black *Rose Bay* painting. Martin asked her to stand this one against the other end wall.

Neville commented, 'I agree with positioning the two abstract pictures on the end walls and the two more traditional pictures either side of the door. As to whether the two modern pictures should be swapped around end to end or the others changed left to right is not important. My feeling is that the entire atmosphere in the boardroom has been improved by the introduction of these works of art and the proof will be when the board next meets.'

Martin then completed marking the walls with the picture hook locations and asked Zoe to nail each hook accordingly. Half an hour later, all four pictures were hanging in their new home. Thanking Zoe and Bill for their assistance he told them they would start on the individual office paintings tomorrow morning. As it was now late afternoon, Neville suggested that he invite Matthew McBride, Emma Johnson and Robert Mason to see the result of today's efforts in the boardroom.

Around 5 o'clock they all gathered in the boardroom for the viewing and congratulations were offered for the new look. Emma voiced a comment on the modern pictures. 'As I have mentioned previously, I was never a lover of abstract paintings but I really like the one signed Robin Black called *Rose Bay*. Who is he and where is that bay?'

Martin gave her a brief run-down on the artist and she responded with, 'I have been to Sydney a couple of times and their harbour is truly a magnificent sight. Next time I visit, I'll make sure I go to Rose Bay as it looks so serene, a place to get away from the hustle and bustle of the city.' Martin then told her that the late artist's wife lived there and she had created a beautiful park out of some unused land between her house and the harbour which is now a favourite picnic spot. 'You are absolutely correct in your assumption that it is a relaxing quiet place to enjoy the views of the harbour. If you are lucky you may even spot Sheila Black pottering around in the park which is right outside her front door.' As expected, Matthew McBride told the gathering that he particularly liked the Frederic Remington painting called *The Rustlers Escape*. 'This scene could well have been taking place in Texas,' he added.

Martin then asked the assembled group, 'How do you feel about the abstract painting by the American Jackson Pollock we have hung on the end wall?' They moved closer to examine it and there was a soft murmuring before Emma Johnson turned to Martin and replied, 'We'll accept it for the moment and raise it with the other board members when we have our next full board meeting at the end of the month.'

Matthew McBride then asked where they were with Martin's planned visit to Mexico City. Neville told the group that their Mexican office was at this moment trying to arrange a meeting with the art forger for Martin the day after tomorrow. 'We had hoped to have an answer late today but it now seems we should hear from them tomorrow. Meanwhile we have made tentative reservations for flights for Martin and our chauffeur Lonnie Macpherson.'

The group moved out of the boardroom and Martin picked up his briefcase and laptop and made his way out to the parking lot. Driving back to the hotel he was deep in thought about his upcoming venture to Mexico City assuming that the forger would agree to meet with him. Once back in his suite, he decided to call his friend Charlie Watson in Los Angeles and ask him for advice as to how best to handle the dangers he might face. Due to the time difference between Texas and California, it was still afternoon there and Charlie was at his desk when his phone rang. 'We are waiting for a response from the art forger to agree to my visit,' Martin told him, 'but we should know tomorrow morning if the meeting will take place. I need to be properly prepared ahead of time and although the newspaper is sending one of their personnel to accompany me as my bodyguard, you had offered me some guidance when I mentioned it to you recently.'

'There's no question Martin that the situation in Mexico is extremely dangerous for journalists who have been blowing the whistle on officials involved in wholesale corruption. Although you are not a journalist, you will be there as a representative of a newspaper and most likely would be considered to be in the same category. Tell me more about the guy who will be acting as your bodyguard.' Martin described Lonnie's physical attributes and his Special Forces background in the conflict in Afghanistan resulting in him receiving America's highest medal of honour.

'I would like to have a talk with him tomorrow if you can set it up as a three way telephone discussion so you can hear what I am going to recommend.' Martin agreed to arrange this when he is at the Houston Chronicle in the morning. 'What time would be best for you Charlie?' He answered that as Los Angeles was two hours behind Houston, 'Call me soon after eleven o'clock your time and I'll be at my desk waiting to hear from you.' They said goodbye and Martin then decided he would like to speak with Isabella but when he checked the time it was 3.00am in Bilbao so decided he would call when it was around 7.00 o'clock there and she'd probably be eating breakfast. Switching on his laptop he spent the next couple of hours researching news reports about crime in Mexico City and noted that it had very high murder numbers. According to these reports, the majority of killings could be attributed to drug gang warfare. Obviously, since their discovery of drugs hidden in paintings that were possibly produced by Miguel de Cristobal, Martin could be jumping right into the deep end of a very dangerous situation.

He decided to play things down a little when he talked with Isabella later. Making himself a cup of very strong coffee to keep him alert until midnight, he switched on the TV and found a quiz show to occupy his mind until it was time to telephone Isabella. He must have dozed off and was awakened by the sound of his mobile phone ringing. He glanced at the clock and saw that it was only just after 10pm as he grabbed his phone. 'Martin, it's Neville here, sorry to disturb you at this time of night but I wanted to let you know that Miguel de Cristobal has agreed to meet with you the day after tomorrow. For security reasons, your meeting will take place in a popular restaurant in the centre of the city. Whether or not you will then be invited to see his studio will be up to him. He has been told that you will be accompanied by an assistant and that you'll be driven around by one of our staff from the Mexican office. I'll have more details when I see you tomorrow, goodnight.'

After disconnecting from Neville, Martin made another cup of black coffee stronger than the earlier one which obviously didn't do what it was supposed to do. He then sat at the desk and worked on *The Houston Art Chronicles* for the next hour and a half writing more detailed descriptions of the pictures that were now the property of the newspaper. At five minutes after midnight, he dialled Isabella's number. It rang for quite a while and just before going to her message-bank she answered, 'Hello my darling.' Taken aback, Martin asked how she knew it was him calling. 'It's very unusual for anyone to call me so early in the morning and I was hoping it might be you' she replied. 'What if it hadn't been me at the other end of the line and you greeted them that way?' he asked, feigning shock. 'In that case, I would have apologized for making a mistake, that's all. If you prefer, I could address you as Mister Taylor whenever you telephoned, how would that be?' He quickly answered, 'I'd rather you continued to guess it was me calling at weird times and to keep up the endearing dialogue.'

Changing to a more serious tone he then said, 'Isabella, I wanted to let you know that the Mexico City visit is going ahead and the forger has agreed to meet with me in a restaurant the day after tomorrow. I will have Lonnie the chauffeur looking after me the whole time and we'll also have the resources from the newspaper's Mexican office driving us around while we are there.

On top of all that, do you remember my friend Charlie Watson, the Los Angeles police officer that I met in Madrid three years ago? We have stayed in touch and tonight he has offered his assistance and advice regarding the Mexican trip. In fact we will be having a conference call tomorrow morning with Lonnie when Charlie is going to give us specific advice what to watch for and what to do in case things turn nasty.'

'Martin, you know I am not happy about you taking this action but I do understand that you want to clear up any doubts as to authenticity of the paintings. I would never try to stop you following your path to completing an assignment with no stones left unturned as long as you take every reasonable precaution. From what you have just told me I accept your decision.'

'Thanks for that my love, I promise you I am not intending to do anything stupid down there. I'll call you tomorrow after the final arrangements are in place so I can give you details of flights and the name of the hotel we'll be staying in. Have a good day in court.'

CHAPTER 11

A "CHILLI" RECEPTION IN MEXICO!

Martin arrived at the Houston Chronicle office early as he knew there was a lot to get through today. As it happened, as he was plugging his car in to a charging station in the staff parking lot when he met up with Lonnie. 'Good morning, I'm glad to catch up with you early today. Our trip to Mexico tomorrow has been confirmed so please inform your family ASAP so they can be prepared. I have a Los Angeles police officer friend who wishes to give us some advice later this morning which I'm certain will be very helpful for us both. I have to telephone him around 11 o'clock so please be in my office before then.' Lonnie replied that he would make sure he didn't take on any chauffeuring jobs at that time.

Up on the fourth floor, Martin greeted Neville telling him that he expected to hang his pictures during the morning as well as Emma Johnson's. 'Martin, I'll have all your Mexican travel arrangements ready by lunchtime so leave mine until then.' Martin told him that should work out well as he'll have Lonnie with him then.

He called Zoe in the warehouse and asked her to bring up the Gaugin painting called *Tahitian Landscape* to the executive editor's office. 'Where's that,' she asked. 'Next to the boardroom Zoe, where we hung four pictures yesterday. I'll meet you there in fifteen minutes.' He then called Emma Johnson to check that this arrangement was convenient to which she replied, 'Absolutely Martin, I am looking forward to being transformed spiritually to Tahiti every time I look at the painting.' They had satisfactorily located and hung the Gaugin *Tahitian Landscape* by mid-morning and Martin then asked Zoe to bring up the Dali etching. 'That's the only one with a glass

127

front so it's easily recognisable. This one is to go in Mr. Mason's office. He's the senior editor and his office is opposite the one we've just been in.' By the time they had hung *The Chariot of Bacchus*, it was almost 11 o'clock and Martin told Zoe he would be tied up on a conference call for the next hour but she could bring up the Rubens *Scene in the Antwerp Studio* and the little Picasso picture of a face. 'These are to be taken to Mr. Montgomery's office which is two along from where we have just been. Thanks Zoe, I'll expect to see you there around midday.'

As she headed to the elevators she passed Lonnie who appeared making his way towards Martin's office. They nodded to each other and kept walking. He borrowed a chair from the staff amenities room and placed it facing Martin at his desk. 'Please close the door Lonnie as I am putting the phone on speaker.' He dialled the number and Charlie Watson answered on the second ring and was introduced to Lonnie. He started the conversation with, 'I've had quite a lot to do with cases involving Mexican drug barons. These people are vicious and brutal and cannot abide anyone looking into their illegal operations. Martin, open your note pad and start writing as I speak. First thing you are to arrange is for the people in the newspaper's Mexico City office to buy two disposable cell phones and these are the only phones you use the entire time you are in that country. Do not give them the numbers of your usual cell phones or any other contact numbers. Next, do not tell them your surnames or where you are staying.

Now this is very important…. as soon as you get your Mexican cell phones I want you to call me on my personal cell phone using a public phone and give me the numbers of these phones. You are then to enter the following cell phone number I'm about to give you into both phones and name it with the letter "A". It will be at the top of the contact list which means it is quick to dial and in the type of situation where you would need to contact me, speed is of the greatest essence. The number is 1-299-878 9900. This is a special number we have for emergency situations. Martin, should you or Lonnie realise that you're suddenly in a situation that you are unable to get out of, hit the "A" and I'll know you need help. We'll be able to track precisely where you are through those phones and I'll immediately alert my colleagues stationed in Mexico City. Let's assume some thugs have grabbed you and removed your phones….all they'll find is one number which is untraceable and if they dial it no-one answers so it tells them nothing of any importance. Whatever you do, should you have to speak with the people you meet down there, only use those phones. Do not call me or the local newspaper staff that are assisting you from those phones. If you have to make non-emergency contact with us, find a public phone.' 'Do they still have public phones in the streets in Mexico?' asked Lonnie.' Charlie laughed, 'Believe it or not, there are still a small number of people around the world who do not have cell phones.' Martin added, 'I know of only one person back home who refuses to have a cell phone and it's my mother.'

Charlie continued, 'You will certainly be searched for weapons or hidden recording devices so make sure you are clean in that respect. Leave your iPads, personal cell phones and laptops in your hotel rooms. If you carry wallets, leave them behind as well in your room safe. Just carry some cash, say not more than a hundred to a hundred and fifty dollars each. When you know your flight details and the name of the hotel where you'll be staying, please send them to me by email. My department is heavily involved in monitoring the movement of drugs between Mexico and the US so your visit is of extreme interest to us. You won't see any of my officers keeping an eye on you but we will be doing our best to keep you safe while you're in Mexico City.'

Martin and Lonnie thanked him for his advice as well as the news that the LAPD would have someone watching over them whilst they are in Mexico. They had just disconnected when Zoe appeared at the door. 'I've brought up the pictures for Mr. Montgomery's office, if you are free now,' she asked. 'Good timing Zoe, we'll go with you right now. Lonnie come along too because Neville should have the details of our travel arrangements by now.'

Neville looked up when he saw people at the door of his office and waved them in. Martin marked the only wall where the somewhat large Rubens painting would fit and Zoe set about attaching two hooks for it. He then held the small Picasso print up on the wall facing the desk and asked Neville to say when he was happy with the position. Once this was done and both pictures were satisfactorily on display, they thanked Zoe and she departed.

'Here are your airline tickets and the vouchers for the hotel. I suggest that you two go to the airport together from here. The flight departs at 10.30am so you should drive here and leave your vehicles secure in the staff parking lot around 7.30.

That should give you plenty of time to get to the departure terminal and pass through the various time consuming security checks to the departure lounge. I will have one of our reporters drive you to the airport in the company car. Take face masks with you as there are still quite a lot of Covid-19 cases being detected daily in Mexico. Our travel department checked if Australians need a visa and none is required for short visits. Should you wish to obtain some Mexican pesos to buy things there, do not use the ATM's in the street.... change money inside your hotel where it is considerably safer. Do you have any questions?'

Lonnie shook his head and Martin briefly explained the role of his L.A. police officer friend Charlie Watson. 'May I please have the name and email address of the person in charge of your Mexico City office so I can make contact this afternoon. We need to set up some way they will be able to recognise us when we exit from the terminal. We also need them to buy two disposable cell phones to use whilst there instead of using our personal phones.' Neville promised to get that information and email it to Martin in the next half an hour. 'Thanks again for your choice of pictures for my office Martin.... it sure has brightened up my workspace.'

Lonnie had to leave to take two of the senior journalists to the Hobby Airport which was Houston's original airport and is much closer to the CBD than the newer George Bush international airport. The Hobby Airport has flights to many US cities and some Mexican, Central American and South American cities, but generally not to the major cities in those countries. Travellers like using it because it is not as busy and therefore less time is needed moving through the security checks. Unfortunately, their flight will depart from the international airport which is why they have to leave so early. They agreed to meet in the staff parking lot around 7.30 tomorrow morning.

Back in his office Martin picked up the USB with the painting photos he wanted to show the forger and took it down to the print room. He made two sets so he could give one to Lonnie in case his briefcase was snatched. He also discovered that there was a setting on the photo printer that enabled enlarging the picture so he managed to print off some excellent close-ups as well to show the forger.

Searching the stationery room for a suitable folder to use for carrying the photographs, he found one that had built-in plastic envelopes into which he could slide the pictures. Taking two of the folders back to his desk, he prepared two complete sets and then printed labels for identifying each picture. He was admiring his handiwork when he received a telephone call from Robert requesting his presence in his office. He went straight away and was greeted with a smile. 'Good to see you Martin, I wanted to have a chat before you set off on your mission tomorrow. Neville told me a little about the assistance you've been offered by your LAPD friend and I have to say that sounds like a great boost to your security. Naturally we all hope there won't be a need to call on their help but realistically there's always a chance of some nasty incident occurring in the sort of company you are likely to find yourselves in tomorrow. I wish you and Lonnie a safe and successful trip and look forward to hearing all about it on your return.

Meanwhile, I want to say that I really love the Dali print I can admire every day on my office wall. The more I look at it, the more I can see and appreciate the hallucinations that brilliant artist was passing on to the world.'

Checking his emails before turning off his laptop, Martin found the one from Neville providing him with the contact details of the person in charge at the Houston Chronicle office in Mexico City. It is a woman named Leticia Chavez and her email address is leticia.chavez@thc.com.mx. She had been advised of the arrival time of Martin and Lonnie's flight from Houston tomorrow morning and would have someone collecting them from the Mexico City airport. The driver would be holding up a placard with their names on. He immediately composed an email to Leticia introducing himself and asking her to obtain two disposable cell phones for them to use during their brief visit in her city. *'We will be staying at the Hyatt Regency in downtown Mexico City and we wish to go there directly from the airport. After we have checked in, we'd like to meet with you to run through the plans for our visit with Fernando de Becerra. Please email by return the full address of the restaurant where we are to meet with him. Looking forward to meeting you tomorrow.'*

He next sent an email to Isabella telling her that he would be flying with United Airlines to Mexico City and staying at the Hyatt Regency Hotel for two nights. A few minutes after he had pressed the SEND key, an email came in from Leticia. *The restaurant where the meeting is to take place is called PUJOL and the address is Tennyson 133, Polanco IV Section. It is reputed to be one of the city's finest restaurants and Fernando de Becerra has reserved a table on the side of the main dining room. We will pick up two disposable cell phones from the supermarket for you to use. I'll be with my assistant when we pick you up at the airport so we can get to know each other as we head to your hotel.*

Martin forwarded the details of their flights, hotel accommodation and restaurant name and address to Charlie Watson. He sent the restaurant details also to Robert and Neville to ensure their movements were known to all. He packed up his brief case and said goodnight to his colleagues as he made his way to the elevator. Driving to the CBD he decided to have an early dinner at the Aussie fish & chip place then work out at the hotel gym before turning in for an early night.

After garaging his car in the hotel car park, he walked to the Aussie café called Platypus Brewing. Sitting at the bar, he ordered a pint of *Dazzler Blonde Ale* which he enjoyed as he watched the comings and goings of young people. It appeared to be a very popular venue for office workers calling in for a drink and a snack on their way home. The guy behind the bar came over to where Martin was sitting and asked, 'Do I detect a genuine Aussie accent?' Smiling, he replied, 'My name is Martin and I'm from Melbourne, how about you?' The barman had moved along the bar to serve a customer then came back saying, 'I'm Morgan and my partner over there talking to someone at a table is Sean. We are both from Brisbane and Sean's wife Rachna is the third member of our brewing team. She's a genuine Texan from Houston. We hope you enjoy your time in our city, it's a great place to live. Would you like to order some food?'

Martin asked what the fish was tonight and was told flounder. 'OK Morgan, I'll have the traditional Aussie fish and chips please and another pint of your delicious beer.'

Later he was seated at a table and Sean came over and shook his hand. 'Welcome to our city Martin, are you working here?' 'I'm on a special assignment for the Houston Chronicle,' Martin answered, 'which should be completed in a week and then I'm heading back to Melbourne. Congratulations on your business, it's a very welcoming establishment and I wish you every success with it.'

Back in his suite, he packed his suitcase ready for the morning and set his alarm for 6 o'clock. He sent a message to Isabella saying he would try to call her from his hotel in Mexico City.

Despite the prospect of the potential danger surrounding his visit, Martin managed to sleep well and sprang out of bed when the alarm woke him up. He made a strong cup of coffee as he dressed and finalized his packing. He stopped at reception on his way to the car and advised them that he would be out of town for a couple of days but would retain his room until he returned. The clerk would check with management to reduce the room rate while he was away and Martin felt that this was a very generous offer.

Arriving at the Houston Chronicle fifteen minutes early, he parked the car and went into the lobby to wait for Lonnie. He arrived shortly after and they chatted for a few minutes until a young man approached them and said he was their driver. 'Call me Joe, I am a junior reporter and start work every morning at 7 o'clock. They walked outside and saw that Joe had brought the car around so they could load their luggage at the front door. The traffic was bumper to bumper all the way to the airport but Joe demonstrated his skill at the wheel and managed to get them to the United Airlines terminal in forty five minutes. They thanked him and checked their bags in at a self-serve station and took an elevator to the departure level. Passing through security and then immigration was very slow due to the number of passengers flying to a variety of destinations at that time of the day. Although the flight time was only two and a half hours to Mexico City, the company had provided them with business class tickets which meant that they could wait in the Club Lounge. Martin looked at his watch and saw that they had over an hour before their flight was due to depart. He suggested they take advantage of waiting in comfort in the Club Lounge. 'We can grab a breakfast there although we won't have a lot of time to eat it. Probably best to just get a coffee and wait to see what is served on the flight.' Once they were in the lounge, the decision was made for them as there were long lines at the self-serve food buffets. They picked up copies of the morning newspapers and sat quietly reading them with their coffees. In what seemed to be no time at all they heard the announcement for their flight so headed off to find the departure lounge for the flight.

They enjoyed a comfortable flight and a tasty snack served soon after they took off. On arrival into the Mexico City airport they passed through customs and immigration relatively smoothly and speedily. They wheeled their bags out of the terminal into brilliant sunshine.

Lonnie pointed to a woman holding up a placard with their names on and he waved and proceeded to walk towards her with Martin following. 'Hi, I'm Leticia and I welcome you to Mexico City.' They shook hands and followed her to a car that was parked in the pick-up zone. After they stowed their bags behind the rear seats of the Renault SUV, the driver introduced himself as Jaime. 'Pleased to meet you,' he told them in excellent English as they buckled up.

As they drove away from the airport, Martin noticed a huge slum area filled with sad looking houses made from scraps of rusty corrugated iron and broken packing case timbers. Some of the buildings seemed perilously close to a runway and as he watched he saw a plane taking off over the top of some of the houses. He decided not to ask Leticia about it as no doubt it's a sad reflection on the city's approach to taking care of the nation's poor. They were soon driving past modern buildings in the CBD giving the appearance of a thriving rich metropolis in stark contrast to what he had seen near the airport. In between some of the modern office towers, Martin could see ruins of what appeared to be very old buildings. When he mentioned these to Leticia she explained that Mexico City had been built on top of an ancient Aztec city and whenever they dug foundations for new buildings or were extending the Metro underground rail system, they unearthed more of these ruins. 'Our national museum is filled with a magnificent collection of pottery and artefacts much of which was found undamaged, she added.

Jaime pulled the car into the driveway at the entrance to the Hyatt Regency and Martin and Lonnie retrieved their bags. Leticia accompanied them into the hotel lobby and Jaime went off to find somewhere to park the car. She waited in the lounge while the men checked in and took their bags up to their respective suites then came back to join her. They moved to a corner where they could talk privately and not be disturbed. Leticia opened her brief case and took out two cell phones. She gave one to each of them and they had tags showing their respective phone numbers. As they were iPhones, they could plug them into the chargers that are supplied in modern hotel rooms nowadays. 'The arrangement for tomorrow morning is Jaime will pick you up at 9 o'clock and bring you directly to our office where we'll finalize our security details. We'll then take you to the restaurant at 11 o'clock.' Just then they spotted Jaime walking around the lounge looking for them and Lonnie jumped up and brought him over to the group. 'I had to drive around the block twice before someone moved out of a parking spot and I managed to beat someone else for it. The other driver was so angry he threatened to ram our car but luckily a police patrol car came past just at the right moment and he changed his mind and took off.' Leticia handed Martin a business card and told them to call if they have any questions before she and Jaime departed for their office. After they had gone, Martin reminded Lonnie that the cell phones they had been given are not to be used to call anyone but the forger or his cronies.

There was an ATM on the wall of a gift shop alongside the entrance and they each changed a hundred dollars for two thousand one hundred pesos. Their rooms were next to each other and after they had unpacked, Lonnie joined Martin in his room. Martin sent an email to Robert informing him of their arrival at the hotel and confirming that they had been welcomed by their representatives in Mexico City.

He next sent a message to Charlie Watson in Los Angeles giving him the two disposable cell phone numbers. Lonnie returned to his room to call his wife and change into shorts and T-shirt to work out in the hotel gym. Martin said that he would meet him there shortly. For almost two hours the two men lifted weights, ran miles on the treadmills and strained every muscle in their bodies on the exercise bikes before showering and relaxing in the pool. 'We're now ready to face whatever is thrown at us for the next two days,' Lonnie declared and then added, 'Unfortunately as we are unarmed, our fitness is our only defence should someone attempt to harm us.' Martin agreed and said, 'We'll have a light meal and turn in early. No alcohol tonight as we need to keep our heads clear so we can focus on watching our backs.' As they walked to their rooms after dinner, Lonnie pointed out that there was a connecting door for families with small children, 'Could be useful in an emergency.'

Next morning after a healthy breakfast, the two men were waiting in the lobby for Jaime to pick them up. They had followed Charlie Watson's instructions and left all their personal items locked in their rooms. They had also taken their electronic room keys to the front desk and asked that they hold them until they returned later in the day. All they had with them were the pesos, the cell phones which now had the special emergency number installed and the folder of photographs of the paintings. They then waited in the lobby until precisely 9 o'clock when they recognized the Renault SUV pull up and went out to greet Jaime. They drove off and immediately noticed the cloudless sky had turned a pinkish shade. 'Is that smog?' asked Martin. 'Absolutely sir, unfortunately the combination of the low altitude of our city and the surrounding mountains together with too many cars, some of which are in very poor condition, creates this terrible smog. It occurs far too often and many people suffer dreadful respiratory problems from inhaling these toxic fumes.' Lonnie proudly told them that despite the overcrowded roads around Houston, he had no recollection of smog conditions such as they were witnessing here.

Arriving at the office, they were led to a small meeting room and Leticia brought in a pot of strong Mexican style coffee. She started off by asking if they had heard about the recent murders of journalists in this city. Martin's reply was that he had been told about it when he first raised the idea of meeting Fernando de Becerra and since then had seen some reports in the newspaper. She elaborated, 'We are being very cautious not to provide names of anyone accused of corruption when we file our stories.

You may not have noticed when you arrived here but we have a security guard stationed near the entrance to our office. He does not wear a uniform and the security firm changes the person every day so it's not obvious we have this protection. Of course, we can't be watched over 24/7 and so we need to be alert at all times. It's not the happiest situation to live in but this is Mexico and we have learnt to be strong. We are thankful that we have not been invaded by another country and are governed by elected Mexicans even if some may not be entirely honest.'

Martin then asked about the arrangements at the restaurant and how would they find Jaime following the end of the meeting with the forger. 'Jaime will drop you at the front of the restaurant and go and park the car. He will then return and we have reserved a table for him near the front door. He will look around to see where you are sitting and keep watch on your movements the whole time you are there.

This is such a popular eating place it is always crowded so it's very unlikely the forger and his cronies would try anything in front of so many witnesses but desperate and ruthless people don't necessarily follow the rules. If Jaime notices something out of the ordinary, he will call me straight away.' Martin then told her about Charlie Watson and his LAPD team working in Mexico City who would also be watching out for them. Jaime looked at his watch and announced that it was time to leave for their appointment. Twenty minutes later he dropped Martin and Lonnie at the entrance to the restaurant and took off to park the car.

There was a waiter standing just inside the door and asked in Spanish if they had a reservation. Lonnie replied in Spanish that they were to meet a Señor Fernando de Becerra. The waiter looked at his iPad and gestured for them to follow him to a table at the far end of a very large dining room. As they approached the table they saw that there were two men already seated and drinking glasses of wine. One of them had a neatly trimmed white beard and was dressed in a light blue suit with a pink shirt and a bow tie. He also wore an artist's blue beret. The other man was burly and clean shaven except for a pencil thin black moustache. He wore a black suit with a black shirt and Martin decided he looked similar to the Mafia types he had seen in Italy two years ago. They didn't stand up to greet them but just gestured them to sit down. Martin introduced himself to the bearded man saying, 'Good morning, I assume you are Mr. de Becerra? I am Martin and my assistant is Lonnie.' The forger replied in Spanish saying he didn't speak English. Lonnie spoke up and said he spoke fluent Spanish so he would interpret for Martin. The minder was not introduced.

Martin then placed the folder of photographs on the table and opened it to the first set of pictures. Before he could continue, a waiter deposited dishes of Mexican delicacies in front of them which featured bright red chillies and asked if the two visitors would like any drinks. They ordered glasses of fruit juice then Martin started to discuss the first photograph. This painting is attributed to the American artist Jackson Pollock but we are certain that it was not painted by him. Can you please look at it and tell us if you painted it?' Fernando de Becerra studied the photographs for some time then pulled out a magnifying glass and concentrated on one corner of the main photo. 'Si, si,' he proclaimed and continued in Spanish which Lonnie translated for Martin. 'He said that there is a small f in the bottom right hand corner that he hides in every forgery he produces and is not obvious to anyone casually looking at the painting. It was especially hard to spot on a Jackson Pollock picture filled with squirts and splashes. You have to look very closely to find it.' Martin then showed the photographs of the Canaletto *Bridge of sighs* and received the same answer. The only paintings Martin bought at the auction for the Houston Chronicle that were not produced by the forger were Remington's *The Rustlers Escape* and Black's *Rose Bay*. Martin showed him the photos of the Dali print and Fernando immediately claimed that it was most likely an original etching so of course he hadn't produced it. Martin agreed this made sense but was astounded by what the forger told them next. Translated quickly by Lonnie, Fernando told them that his paintings are sold via a small gallery he owns next to his studio and they provide a framing service as well. 'Martin, it seems that they were given the Dali print to fit into a special frame designed by the customer.' Lonnie was then requested to ask Fernando why the Dali etching had a double cover behind the print. The answer came back that Miguel de Cristobel often requested that feature when ordering picture frames. Martin turned to Lonnie and remarked that he believed they had sufficient information now on which paintings were probably genuine and which were produced by the man sitting opposite. 'Please thank him and tell him we won't stay for lunch but would pay for the snack and drinks as we leave the restaurant.' They stood up and walked around the table to shake hands with Fernando and suddenly Martin felt something cold and hard pressed into his back. Lonnie whispered, 'The thug has a gun in his coat pocket and is gesturing for us to walk in front of him and out the rear door.' Fernando quietly spoke to Lonnie that he was *inviting* them to visit his studio where they could talk some more in private. The four person procession walked slowly past a group of happy diners enjoying themselves at the outdoor section of the restaurant. Martin and Lonnie both had their hands in their pockets and pressed the emergency button on their cell phones. They had no sooner reached the street when a black Mercedes screeched to a halt and they were pushed into the back seat with the thug and the car took off at breakneck speed.

Meanwhile back at the restaurant, Jaime Rodrigues had seen Martin and Lonnie hustled out the rear door and immediately called Leticia Chavez with the bad news. At the same time, Charlie Watson acted immediately on receiving the alarm signal. His colleagues in Mexico City were alerted and a team was now tracking the signal from the cell phones.

On arrival at Fernando's studio, Martin and Lonnie were taken into a store room and sat down on chairs with their hands tied together behind. They were searched by the thug who they now knew was Luis, and their cell phones taken from them and placed on a table out of their reach. Fortunately, they were not switched off because Fernando had said he wanted to see what information he could get out of them. Luis also took the cash they had in their pockets and told them that this would cover them for the snacks and drinks they had at the restaurant. Fernando was elsewhere in the studio calling someone for instructions on what to do with his captives. Luis was standing guard by the door and Lonnie was quietly rubbing the rope back and forth across his metal watch band which had a sharp edge from damage that had occurred when he was in Afghanistan with the special forces. Fortunately he had enormous strength and stamina to keep this up as he knew it would be a slow drawn-out process. Fifteen minutes later, Fernando appeared and told them that a colleague would be here shortly to ask them some questions. In the meantime he scrolled through their phones and all he could find was one number programmed in both phones. When he dialled it no-one answered which he thought was somewhat strange. He asked Lonnie what that number in their phones was for, 'I have no idea,' he answered in Spanish, 'they were already programmed in when we bought the phones at a supermarket.' Before he could be questioned further, there was a knock at the door and man entered nodding to Fernando and Luis. He was of heavy build with olive skin and a thick black moustache. He was not introduced and walked straight over to stand in front of Martin and Lonnie. In heavily accented English, he started his questioning. 'Did you find anything hidden in any of the pictures you bought at the auction in Houston and if so, what did you do with them?'

Lonnie replied cautiously, 'Before I answer your question, we'd like to know where you fit into this scenario.'

'I was a business partner with Miguel de Cristobel who owned the art collection that was auctioned. We had some serious personality issues which resulted in the dissolving of our partnership prior to his unfortunate demise. He had never paid me for the goods we had supplied to him and I am now keen to be compensated for my loss.'

Martin now joined in saying, 'As you understand English, listen carefully to what I have to say. Anything we may have found in the paintings is no longer in our possession so we really can't help you with regards to any compensation. In any case, we only purchased nine items at the auction and found strange packages in two of them. I assume you had hidden packages in more than only our two pictures.'

'There were a total of ten pictures with the frames modified by Fernando here in this workshop that we used to hide our *goods* so I now have the following proposal for you to consider. One of you will return to Houston with a list of the ten pictures that were used to transport our hidden *treasures* out of Mexico and track down the new owners of the other eight. We will *take care* of the other man here until you have sent us details of who now owns those remaining eight pictures. Once we have that information, we'll release our *guest*. We'll leave you alone for five minutes to consider our proposal.' They left the room and locked the door after them.

Lonnie whispered that he was almost through cutting the rope around his wrists. 'I probably need another five to ten minutes to free my hands.' Martin told him that if they accepted the crook's demands, he would insist that Lonnie be the one to go back to Houston and once we have the list we can implement an escape plan. 'In any case, I am anticipating that the local team of the LAPD drug squad should appear any moment…. assuming Charlie Watson acted immediately on receiving our cell phone signal.'

They heard the key turn in the lock and the door opened to admit the drug baron and his buddies. 'Have you agreed to our proposal?' Martin told him they would accept his plan and added, 'My assistant will return to Houston and track down the information you require. I will stay here as your guest until you are satisfied with the information he gathers on the new owners. How do you want that information transmitted?'

'My personal email address is at the top of the page I will hand to you now. This is the complete list of the artworks that our goods were hidden in.

You understand that if either of you try to contact authorities here or in the USA, we have ways of making you disappear permanently.'

As he finished making his threat, the cell phones on the table both started to ring. Fernando, who was standing nearby, grabbed one of them and punched the answer icon. 'Ola,' he yelled into the phone and suddenly the door burst open. Two men in navy blue uniforms called out in Spanish for everyone to lie down on the floor with their hands behind their heads.

Fernando and the drug baron did as they were told but Luis the thug, swung around and crouched behind Lonnie using him as a shield. He held a pistol at Lonnie's neck and threatened to shoot unless they let him leave. The officers turned their guns to the side and all of a sudden Lonnie gave a huge grunt as he strained to break the last few strands of the rope. 'Gotcha,' he cried as he swung around and elbowed Luis in the face knocking him off balance then followed up with a massive kick to his groin.

He doubled up in pain and Lonnie quickly removed the pistol from his grip. One of the officers came over and clamped handcuffs on Luis then turned to Lonnie and asked him if he would like to join the LAPD drug squad team. 'You have the strength and determination that would be a great asset for our group,' he said admiringly. 'Thanks, but my family and home are in Houston and that's where I am looking forward to going as soon as we can leave.' Lonnie then removed the rope from Martin's wrists saying, 'The others seem to have forgotten you sitting there all trussed up… now you can massage the circulation in your hands back to normal.'

As the two LAPD officers were putting handcuffs on Fernando and the drug baron, a group of four Mexican police officers rushed into the room. They were led by a man who introduced himself as Felipe de Ortega. 'I am the chief of police in Mexico City,' he told the assembled group in only slightly accented English. He had a row of badges pinned to his jacket signifying that he had been awarded a number of honours during his tour of duty. 'We were contacted by Leticia Chavez at the Houston Chronicle that two men had been kidnapped by Fernando de Becerra, a person we know very well.' He walked over and shook hands with the LAPD drug squad officers addressing them by name. 'Good to see you Andre and Joe, I half expected you guys might have been involved but am curious to know how you were able to get here before us.' Andre answered saying he would explain all when they came to the police headquarters later to make their statements. As the three handcuffed men were led out to the police van in front of the studio, the police chief congratulated Andre and Joe for their assistance in capturing the drug baron Alejandro Alvarez. 'We have been trying to get hold of him for a long time but until now he has eluded our efforts.' Turning to Martin and Lonnie he said, 'We would be pleased if you also came to headquarters to provide us with detailed statements as we are anxious to know what your roles were in this event.' Andre stated that they would bring Martin and Lonnie along with them this afternoon.

They all departed and two police officers were left to search the property and ensure it wasn't looted whilst the owner was in the lockup. 'News spreads quickly whenever there's been a police raid and the *vultures* would appear from nowhere as soon as a property is known to be unattended,' one of the uniformed officers told Lonnie in Spanish as he was walking out.

Martin and Lonnie were led to a large black Ford Explorer SUV and driven to the LAPD drug squad local office. Once inside, they were shown the bathroom so they could freshen up. Later seated in a meeting room, Martin handed Andre the list of the ten pictures which had drugs hidden in the back and asked if he could please make copies.

'I would like one to take back to Houston, no doubt the police here will ask for one and your department will naturally be interested as well.' Joe went off to make the copies, and Andre called Charlie Watson to report on what had taken place. When he had finished speaking, he handed the phone to Martin. 'Hi Charlie, just wanted to thank you for arranging what turned out to be a very timely intervention. Your team performed outstandingly for which my assistant and I are truly grateful. We have to attend the police headquarters this afternoon to make statements and will return to Houston tomorrow morning as planned.'

Andre then told them that Charlie had suggested they all go out for dinner after they have finished making their statements at police headquarters to celebrate a successful mission. Joe came back into the meeting room with the copies of the list and coffees for everyone. 'We'll head to the police headquarters shortly but before we do, would you like to make any phone calls to Houston?' Martin said he should call the Houston Chronicle to let them know what had happened today, and Lonnie wished to call his wife. During their subsequent phone calls they both gave low key descriptions of being held captive for a short time promising to elaborate further when they returned to Houston tomorrow.

All four men piled into the SUV and drove across town to the Mexico City police headquarters. On arrival they were taken directly to the office of Felipe de Ortega who told them that the arrested men had been charged with numerous offences. 'Depending on the statements you will now make with my officers, we may be able to add to those charges.' Each was taken to interview rooms and questioned separately. It was late afternoon when they gathered out the front of the police headquarters. Andre suggested they go to an English style pub where they thought Martin might feel at home. 'Well actually I'm Australian not British,' he told them, 'but an English pub is OK with me as long as they sell other than British beers. If it's not out of the way, could we stop by our hotel and pick up our cell phones as I'm certain I will have some urgent messages to attend to. We also left our wallets and passports back at the hotel and we should have those with us as well.' Andre apologized saying he thought Martin's accent sounded British. 'The pub is not far from the Hyatt Regency so we'll take you first to the hotel and sit and wait for you in the hotel's forecourt.'

When Martin got to his room there was a note under the door. It was a message from Leticia asking him to call her on her cell phone no matter what time it was. He suddenly realized that he should have called her when they were at the LAPD drug squad office. Grabbing his cell phone from the charger where it had been all day, he dialled her number. She answered straight away very concerned. 'Mr. Taylor, are you and Mr. Macpherson alright?' He immediately apologized for not contacting her earlier. 'Leticia, sorry for not calling you but we have been flat out all afternoon since being rescued by the officers from the LAPD drug squad. We also spent a long time at police headquarters giving statements and have only just now returned to our hotel. Other than some minor rope burns on our wrists from being tied up, we didn't suffer any injuries. Will Jaime be available to take us to the airport in the morning? Our flight is scheduled to depart at 11 o'clock?' She answered, 'Jaime will be driving but I'll be coming with you as I would like to hear a little more about your Mexico City *adventures.*'

She paused for a moment while she gave an instruction to Jaime who was nearby then continued, 'Robert Mason called me half an hour ago with instructions to write a first-hand account for the newspaper. I'm assuming you haven't been interviewed by anyone other than the police which means we'll have an exclusive story for our paper. I'll pick you up at 9.00am so please be out front by then.' Martin told her that they would be waiting by the hotel's revolving doors at that time. 'I have to go now as we are having dinner tonight with the two LAPD officers at an English style pub apparently somewhere near the hotel we are staying in.'

He then ran down the stairs instead of using the elevator for some exercise and when he opened the rear door of the SUV, Lonnie was already there and wearing his seat belt. 'What took you so long?' Martin replied that he had received a note from a worried Leticia from the Houston Chronicle local office concerned about their disappearance earlier. 'I stopped to call her immediately and briefly explain what had happened.'

Five minutes later they arrived at the pub which was called *The Hunters Arms* and Andre found a parking spot just along the street. When they entered the pub they were immediately impressed by the décor which the owners had tried carefully to make look as near as possible to a British pub. It was obviously a popular venue for ex-pats as they could hear more English being spoken than Spanish in the bar as they walked through to the dining room. They found a table and settled down for a pleasant chat. Joe went to the bar and returned with four pints of Heineken which was one of only two beers they had on tap apart from a huge British selection. Andre told them that he and Joe had been in Mexico City for close to twelve months and reported to Charlie Watson in Los Angeles. 'What's the connection between you guys and Charlie?' Martin spoke up, 'I met Charlie a few years ago at an international police convention in Madrid, and we have been corresponding ever since. He was instrumental in recommending me to the New York Police Department to assist on a robbery case that developed into one of the most complicated assignments I have ever worked on. I had only recently started my own private investigation business when Charlie contacted me about the job in New York. This was a huge feather in my cap and the publicity from it led to this special contract with the Houston Chronicle. Lonnie is an employee of the newspaper and only knows about Charlie because of my relationship with him.'

Keeping with the theme of the pub, they all ordered the roast of the day which this evening was roast beef and Yorkshire pudding. Martin was the only one of the four who actually knew what the pudding was! 'My dear mother used to often prepare this meal for Sunday lunch during the winter. We all liked it and I hope it's as good here as she used to make.' Considering that this was Mexico and the chef was probably a local, the resulting meal was in fact excellent, and everyone enjoyed a dish that was very different to what they were accustomed to.

Martin found himself glancing around the dining room studying the patrons as he was taught to do at the Police Academy and suddenly spotted a face that somehow seemed familiar.

He was searching through his memory of all the people he had met since arriving in Mexico City when Joe interrupted his chain of thoughts. 'Have you guys been to Mexico City before?' Lonnie answered on behalf of both of them, 'I have made a couple of trips here with my family as I live not far away in Houston, but this is Martin's first time. I learnt to speak Spanish at school which has been helpful as I found that English was only spoken in tourist hotels and venues.' Martin's mind drifted away from the conversation again trying to find a link to the face he had seen across the room. Digging deep into their movements since arriving in Mexico he looked up and got another glimpse of the face.

Bingo! He remembered who it was. Yesterday when they had been taken to the Chronicle's Mexico City office, Leticia had pointed out that they had a security guard out front. This was the person he now saw in the pub. Was this a coincidence or could it be that he was in the same place as them to keep them under surveillance for the newspaper. He raised this with their LAPD hosts and Andre responded that he should call Leticia right away and check. Martin excused himself and walked outside to make the call. She answered right away and told him that the guard was definitely not there on her instructions. 'Please be very vigilant,' she told him, 'and I'll see you in the morning.' He thanked her saying they were with the LAPD team and would be escorted back to their hotel after they left the pub.

Martin returned to the dining room and passed on Leticia's conversation to his colleagues. Andre suggested that they follow them to the airport in the morning just in case it wasn't a coincidence that the security guard just happened to be in the same place tonight. 'Do you really think that's necessary?' Martin asked. 'I do,' Andre told them, 'besides, we have to report back to Charlie Watson that we completed our mission satisfactorily and that will only be after you are on the aeroplane heading for Houston.'

Later, back at the Hyatt Regency, Lonnie assured Martin that the concerns for their safety raised by both Leticia and Andre are genuine and necessary. 'Mexico is a lovely country and in general the inhabitants are friendly and helpful, but unfortunately the drug industry here is so large it dominates every aspect of their lives. Take my word for it Martin, now that we have been involved in the arrest of those crooks, I have no doubt that there are people out there who have instructions to settle the score.'

'I'm sure you're right Lonnie, so we'll stay in our rooms tonight and not go anywhere else until we leave tomorrow morning. Checking out will be quick and easy as the company has prepaid our stay here. See you in the lobby just before 9 o'clock.'

Martin turned his key in at reception just after 8.30 in the morning and was looking in the hotel gift shop when it opened. He looked around for something to buy for Isabella and settled on an exquisite modern design silver choker necklace. The woman in the shop explained to Martin that it was made from the highest quality sterling silver from Taxco, a town a short distance east of Mexico City. 'The silver mined from that region of Mexico is amongst the finest in the world and you have selected a necklace handmade by one of our best jewellery designers. I'm sure the person you will give this to will be thrilled with your choice.'

She gift-wrapped it in a beautiful box and he walked out of the shop wondering when he would next see Isabella to present her with the gift. Lonnie appeared and the two men waited in the lobby until they saw the Renault SUV turn into the driveway out front then wheeled their cases out to greet Jaime and Leticia. As they drove out of the city Leticia turned on a portable recorder and started the interview. Martin and Lonnie took it in turns to answer her questions and by the time they were on the freeway to the airport, she had most of the facts to enable her to enlarge into a full story of the kidnapping and subsequent rescue.

They had been driving for about twenty minutes when Jaime exclaimed that he had noticed the same car following them for the last few kilometres. 'Whenever I pull out to pass another vehicle, the car behind makes the same move and then returns to the same lane behind us.' Martin decided to tell them that the LAPD team had offered to monitor our movements to the airport. 'What kind of car is it Jaime?' He replied that it was a dark grey Mercedes van. 'That can't be our guys,' Martin said, 'they drive a black Ford SUV.' Leticia told them they were only about ten kilometres now from the airport and she instructed Jaime to leave the freeway at the next exit onto a side road which was the original road to the airport before the freeway was built. 'If it follows us at that turn off I will telephone the police chief, Felipe de Ortega and let him know we seem to be in danger.'

Sure enough, the Mercedes followed them onto the old airport road and drew closer. There wasn't a lot of traffic on this road at that moment and Jaime called out that the car behind had pulled out as if to pass them. Leticia immediately called the police chief and gave him their location. As the Mercedes drew level with them, Martin saw a passenger window opening and a gun barrel appear. 'Everybody bend down, they are going to shoot!' Jaime hit the brakes and as the other car zoomed past, gunshots were heard and bullets hit the front of the car. As they came to a complete halt and before the Mercedes could stop and turn around, a big black SUV shot past and skidded to a 90 degree turn across the road blocking the path of the shooters. Whilst the others watched, the LAPD officers shot the tyres of the Mercedes and two men jumped out with their hands in the air. Lonnie remarked on the driving skill of the officer behind the wheel and the fantastic timing of their arrival on the scene. As the officers handcuffed the two men, a police helicopter appeared from the direction of the airport and landed in the open field alongside the road. Jaime tooted the horn and they waved thanks to the officers before he turned the car around and they returned to the freeway to continue their unforgettable journey to the airport. Leticia had taken a number of photos on her phone of the incident which will no doubt embellish the story she was writing for the Chronicle. Martin had Andre's business card and told Lonnie they would call him from the airport to thank him formally for once again being in the right place at the right time.

What they didn't realise at the time was that as soon as the Mexico City police had arrived on the scene and taken charge of the two men who had shot at their car, the LAPD team had followed them to the terminal. They had parked their vehicle in a special area reserved for authorities and watched over Martin and Lonnie whilst they checked in and walked through to the departure lounge. Andre and Joe did not leave until they had seen the flight called and all passengers had boarded the aircraft.

They watched as the plane took off for Houston and then sent a message to Charlie in Los Angeles that their mission was complete and Martin and his assistant were safely aboard the plane taking them to Houston.

Once the plane reached its cruising altitude, refreshments were served and Martin turned to Lonnie expressing relief. 'We've certainly had a harrowing couple of days and believe we have earned some R & R.'

Lonnie smiled as he reclined his seat, 'Well Martin, to tell you the truth, what we have just experienced reminded me of the dangers we faced when I was in Afghanistan. It saddens me to compare those two countries because I do like Mexico and its people, but on reflection it is similar in that they face enormous problems with corruption and hard drugs are the prime industries in both places.'

By the time the plane landed at Houston International Airport, the two men were relaxed and passed through immigration and customs cheerfully greeting the authorities. After collecting their bags, they walked out into the sunshine where they spotted Janita Sullivan who had come along with a photographer. Photos were taken and she explained that Ben Scott had driven them to the airport and was waiting in one of the cell phone lots for her to call and tell him which pick-up door they were waiting at. Five minutes later the company SUV arrived and they all piled in for the drive to the Houston Chronicle headquarters.

CHAPTER 12

FRONT PAGE HEADLINES.

On arrival at the office, there was a message at reception asking them all to go straight to the boardroom for a welcome back celebration. Depositing their luggage in Martin's office, they walked into the boardroom where they were greeted by a cheering crowd. Flashlights were popping and there was a lot of hand-shaking before the company president, Matthew McBride stood and made a speech. 'As most of you know by now, Martin Taylor was contracted by us to purchase a number of paintings at the recent auction of art that had previously been owned by the murdered drug baron Miguel de Cristobel. As you look around this room you will see four of the pictures now hanging on these walls. Hidden in two of them were bags of heroin that were discovered once the pictures were in our possession. Martin had suggested that drugs could have been concealed in some of the items and we arranged for representatives of the FBI and the Houston Drug Squad to be here when the backs were removed from the pictures. The auctioneers had advised potential buyers that although the paintings were attributed to mostly well-known artists, it was likely they were forgeries.

After some research, it appeared possible that some of these artworks may have been produced by a famous Mexican forger called Fernando de Becerra. Martin discussed with us that he wanted to meet with him to confirm if he had painted any of the pictures we had bought. Because of the anticipated dangers involved, our war hero Lonnie Macpherson agreed to tag along to help if any crisis arose. As you will be able to read in our next edition, an extremely dangerous situation did arise and Lonnie was able to show his mettle at the right time. Janita Sullivan who is working on a series of articles about Martin that will be published in our weekend magazine over three weeks, will also be one of the reporters putting together the exclusive story of what happened in Mexico City these past two days.' At this pause in Matthew McBride's talk, staff from the canteen appeared bearing dishes of finger food and fresh fruit.

Robert Mason walked over to Martin and Lonnie and told them they could take the rest of the day off to recover from the trauma they just had been through. 'We have received a comprehensive report from Leticia Chavez that will be part of the front page story. It details the work of the LAPD team who were instrumental in protecting you and apparently making arrests on behalf of the Mexico City police. Your story will be headlined on the front page of tomorrow morning's Chronicle. I'll see you guys back here tomorrow at the usual time and you'll find copies of the paper with you in the headlines on your desks.'

Martin walked out with Lonnie to their cars and thanked him for his company on the trip to Mexico City. 'I really appreciate your help on what turned out to be a much more dangerous adventure than I had anticipated. I'm glad that you are returning to your family in one piece Lonnie, see you tomorrow.' As he walked to the Tesla, he decided that tired as he was, he would work on the Houston Art Chronicles report and draw up the plaques that will be affixed to the wall alongside each picture.

But prior to devoting the evening to working in his hotel suite, he would write an email to Isabella with a brief description of what took place in Mexico City. He also needed to catch up with his manager, Jessica at his Brighton office.

After advising the front desk that he was back from his Mexico trip, he unpacked in his suite, sent some clothes to the hotel laundry then changed into his tracksuit to work out in the gym for an hour. He ran into Ray Barrett also working out who asked him where he had been these past few days. 'I went down to Mexico City to follow up the authenticity of the paintings we bought and ran into a spot of bother there. You will be able to read all about it in tomorrow's Chronicle. Suffice to say that it involved being confronted by some ruthless people in the drug trade.'

'My New York office told me that some drugs had been found in a couple of your pictures and that the FBI and Houston police are working together on this to track down all the pictures sold at the auction and check them for any further hidden drugs. There were nine paintings not sold as well as a small number of the sculptures and all have been searched for drugs and none found. More than two million dollars has been raised from the auction so far. Next phase of our tax recuperation program will be to auction off the furniture and accessories from the home and finally the mansion itself. These other auctions will be carried out over the next couple of weeks so I'll be staying in Houston until they are concluded. How much longer do you expect to be here Martin?'

'I'm not sure Ray, but hope to be heading back to Melbourne within a week.' Martin's cell phone rang and when he answered, it was Robert. 'Sorry to interrupt your free time Martin, but we've had a call from the Houston police requesting an urgent meeting with you and Lonnie to fill them in on the recent events that took place in Mexico City. Lonnie will pick you up in half an hour and take you to police headquarters. If you are confronted with any difficulties, telephone our legal officer, Deidre Bush. I'll text you her cell phone number. I don't expect you'll have any issues but this has become such a high profile case, one never knows what will turn up next. Please keep me informed.' Martin disconnected and apologized to Ray that he had to go out shortly and would see him around later. He returned to his suite and hurriedly washed and dressed to wait for Lonnie. He walked out front just as the car pulled into the drive-through. 'Long time no see,' Lonnie greeted him as he climbed into the front passenger seat, 'I have a feeling we are going to be questioned on every minute of our time in Mexico City as this could lead to who was involved in the importation of the drugs into the USA and who ordered the slaying of Miguel de Cristobal.

It will no doubt be a gruelling experience.' Martin responded that he didn't believe they had broken any American laws in meeting with the art forger. 'The fact that this led to our grilling from Alejandro Alvarez was not of our doing and was totally unexpected. Although I was never a member of the drug squad when I was with Victoria Police in Melbourne, I am accustomed to how police interviews are carried out and am not concerned about it. This will be my chance to reverse our roles and watch out for you.'

Lonnie drove past the police headquarters in Travis Street until he spotted a public parking lot and turned in. They walked back and followed the signs to the main entrance.

At reception they asked for the drug squad detective, Daniel Gunn and were asked to please wait a moment whilst the officer checked that they were expected. A few minutes later, Daniel appeared and after they had signed in, he led them through a metal detector and to the elevators.

Arriving at the second floor they were taken to an interview room where they recognized the FBI detective Ron Stephens who was already patiently awaiting their arrival. He stood up and shook hands then invited them to take a seat. 'I'm sure you guys understand the importance of the events that occurred whilst you were in Mexico City and the information you provide to us today will be of particular interest to our investigation team. Daniel has a number of officers chasing down the locations of pictures that were purchased by buyers here in Texas and my team is carrying out a similar exercise throughout the entire USA. To date it doesn't appear that any of the items have been sent abroad which makes out task a little simpler. Obviously, you stepped on some toes down there and the reaction of your kidnappers confirms our suspicions that there are a lot more hidden drugs out there yet to be found. The LAPD team that assisted you just when you needed help was apparently a fortunate result of a friendship between you Martin and one of the top officers in the Los Angeles police force. The officer in charge, Charlie Watson has sent us a very comprehensive report for which we are extremely grateful. What we require now is your first-hand details of the events.' At this point, Daniel spoke up. 'We will record our conversation today and before you leave, we'll have it typed up and you can sign it to confirm that it is a true record of our interview. It is our understanding that your reason to visit Mexico City was only to talk with the art forger so you could establish whether or not he had produced any of the paintings you had successfully bid for at the auction. Is that correct?'

Martin answered, 'Yes sir that is correct. We met with him at a restaurant called Pujol.'

'What did you learn from Fernando de Becerra?'

'He told us which of our pictures had been produced in his studio.'

'How did you then come to meet the drug baron, Alejandro Alvarez?'

Lonnie answered this question. 'We thought that our meeting had been successful when all of a sudden the thug Señor de Becerra had brought along as a bodyguard, pushed a concealed gun into my side and we were hustled out the rear of the restaurant into a waiting car. We were taken to the forger's studio somewhere in the suburbs and tied up on chairs. The forger looked at the photos of the paintings and told us which of our pictures had actually been produced in his studio. Shortly after he received a phone call which we later learnt was from his colleague Alejandro Alvarez. We were kept locked up until Señor Alvarez arrived. Meanwhile, I was rubbing the rope that bound my wrists together across my metal watch band. It was a slow and painful way to cut a rope but I persisted and the delay in our questioning was actually a bonus.' Martin took over the story at this point. 'Some time later a gruff looking Alejandro Alvarez arrived and started questioning us on what we knew about the paintings sold at the auction.

I told him we didn't know who bought any of the pictures apart from the ones we successfully bid for on behalf of the Houston Chronicle newspaper. He became very aggressive and proposed that one of us would return to

Houston and track down the buyers of the eight other pictures that were listed on a sheet he handed to us. To ensure we didn't go to the authorities, the other one of us would be kept locked up in the studio until they had received the information they wanted. We were threatened with serious consequences should we attempt to countermand his instructions.' At this juncture, Martin handed them a copy of the list of the paintings carrying drugs.

The FBI detective added, 'As we understand the sequence of events, your eventual release from those criminals was thanks to the Mexican branch of the LAPD drug squad who had been looking out for you. The Mexico City police have the crooks under lock and key right now and we have been told that they have applied for bail today. We are waiting to hear if the judge will let them out. It would not surprise us if they were released even if the bail amount is set high. You will probably be interested to know what sort of value we are talking about if those small bags of heroin were released on the streets of our cities. Based on the twenty bags we took from your two pictures and assuming there are similar quantities in each of the other eight pictures, we'd be looking at fifteen to twenty million dollars. Those crooks are going to do everything they can to retrieve the drugs. The list you have just given us will make our search a lot easier and we thank you for that.'

Daniel said that he would keep them advised of the result of the bail application. 'This mob is a ruthless bunch and there's no telling what reprisals against you they could come up with. Please contact me should you see anything suspicious or out of the ordinary and we'll look into it immediately. Your statements will be ready for signing in a few minutes so you can relax with a coffee now and we can chat off the record.'

Ron told them about a case he was involved with a few years ago. 'An ocean going yacht departed San Diego with a cargo of two tons of drugs destined for Australia. The FBI heard about it the day after the yacht had stopped in Hawaii to pick up fresh food and water. One of the crew had consumed too much booze in a Honolulu bar and bragged about the cargo they were delivering to Brisbane. I was given the task of flying to Canberra where I set up a working party with the Australian Federal Police. The yacht was kept under surveillance as it sailed into a marina on the Queensland Gold Coast. The gang had thought things out fairly smartly by registering the yacht as Australian owned and flying the Australian flag from its mast. They hadn't allowed for a drunken sailor shooting his mouth off at the only stop they made across the Pacific! The AFP had a team of officers ready to board the yacht as soon as it tied up in the marina. The two Americans who were part of a well-known Californian drug ring and the four Australian crew members were immediately arrested and are still in prison serving long sentences. I believe it was one of the largest drug busts in the past decade. I spent some days in Canberra and found it to be beautiful well laid out city with some marvellous institutions such as the National Gallery and the incredible War Memorial.'

By the time Ron had finished his story, an officer brought the typed statements which were read through and signed by Martin and Lonnie.

They were given copies to take with them back to the Houston Chronicle. It was quite late in the day by then and they went straight back to the newspaper office to retrieve their vehicles and call it quits for the day. Feeling exhausted from the events of the past days, he wanted to have an early night but had to wait up until it was a convenient time to call Isabella in Bilbao. They had a thirty minute discussion whilst he ran through all that had taken place during his visit to Mexico City. He simplified some of the details of the kidnapping and subsequent interrogation. She was shocked but happy he was back in Houston safe and sound.

The following morning, Martin found a copy of the newspaper on his desk at the Houston Chronicle with the front page headlines proclaiming:

TROUBLES ERUPT IN MEXICO CITY – OUR PEOPLE KIDNAPPED

The exclusive story that followed was spread over about a quarter of the front page then continued on page three. There were photos of Martin and Lonnie in the article and as he read it, he realized just how it shone the spotlight on them which may not have been in their best interests. The article was well written and shown to be a joint effort between their senior reporter Janita Sullivan and their chief photographer Sammy Gollings. For security reasons, there was no mention of the Mexico City team led by Leticia Chavez. The more he considered the enormity of being headline news, the more he realised that this kind of publicity could bring unwanted consequences. He flipped through the pages of the news section and saw an article about more floods in southern Queensland and northern New South Wales. The federal and state governments were once again blamed for not doing enough since similar floods took place only two years before.

He saw an advertisement on page two for a rodeo to take place in the NRG Stadium this coming weekend. In large script it stated NO GUNS ALLOWED. He smiled as he thought to himself how this might upset the local cowboys and reduce the numbers in the audience. From what he had been told by friends who had spent time living and working in Texas, many locals, particularly men, would never leave home without taking a gun with them.

Robert called in to see Martin and asked about yesterday's interview with the Houston Police and the FBI. 'I have copies of our statements,' Martin told him, 'and will give them to Deidre Bush but I don't know where her office is.' Just then Neville walked by and when he saw them together decided to join in the conversation. 'Hi Martin, are you OK after your ordeal down south?' Martin nodded and told him he was glad to be back. 'I was just saying to Robert that I have the statements that we made to the authorities yesterday and thought that I should hand them to your legal officer.' Neville suggested that he and Robert would like to look them over before they are given to Deidre.

'Further to the subject of our police interview,' Martin told them, 'they raised the possibility of reprisals from associates of the criminals who are now in custody with the Mexico City police. Daniel Gunn insinuated that the drug cartel won't take the loss of drugs worth millions of dollars without some sort of action. They can't be seen to be weak. Now with our names splashed over the front page it won't be difficult for anyone to track us down.'

'I can fully understand your concern,' Robert stated, 'would you like us to arrange for surveillance professionals to keep an eye out for you until you return to Melbourne?'

'No thanks Robert, I don't think that will be necessary and in any case it's only conjecture that Lonnie and I might be targets now we are back in the USA. We'll keep our eyes and ears open and at the first sign of anything untoward, I have a direct line of contact to Inspector Daniel Gunn at police headquarters. Meanwhile, I am almost finished drawing up the wording to go on the plaques for each of the pictures which I'll give you later today so you can have them printed. Regarding my report on the artworks I estimate that it will require two more days to complete. At the same time, I still have at least two more sessions with Janita for the magazine article.'

Neville decided to put in his ten cents worth proposing that Martin not wander around at night alone and remain indoors at the hotel whenever he's there. 'I don't think anyone would attempt to harm you or Lonnie whilst you are here in our offices. Our buildings are extremely secure 24/7 and can even withstand devastating hurricanes from the Gulf. I'm not sure we could survive a Putin style rocket attack though! Meanwhile I'll talk with Lonnie for his take on the potential risk to himself and his family.'

Robert walked out of Martin's office with Neville saying he would see Martin later when he delivered the picture plaque details.

He was busy at his desk shortly after when his phone rang and it was Janita to make an appointment for his next session. They agreed on 2 o'clock and he returned to the plaque layouts on his laptop. A typical plaque for a copied painting was worded like this:

Adoration of the Magi

Attributed to El Greco 1541 – 1614

Copied by Mexican artist 2014

Oil on canvas

A typical plaque for an original print was worded like this:

The Chariot of Bacchus

Original etching by Salvador Dali 1904 – 1989

Number 217 of 300

Print on paper

He had just returned to his office from taking the layouts to Robert Mason when Janita Sullivan arrived for his next session. She set up her recorder and before commencing her questions regarding the *Mislaid painting* case, she wanted assurance that he was up to her prying into his life.

'I know that you had been grilled by the Houston police yesterday and you may have had enough of nosy parkers like me.' He told her that he was cool with her questioning and to switch on the recorder and get the show on the road. 'This somewhat humorous tale didn't involve any criminals and was purely an example of a gallery not controlling their records of where a particular piece of art was at any given time. In this case it was a combination of the retirement of a gallery employee and the passing of an art restorer that led to the belief a painting was lost or stolen.'

As this story was covered in less than half an hour, Martin agreed that they could continue for another hour with more details of his family including his father's untimely death. They then discussed his relationship with his widowed mother and lawyer sister. When Janita advised that she had enough to work on, she switched off the recorder and went back to her desk. Martin opened up the *Houston Art Chronicles* report and spent the rest of the afternoon deep in thought as he read through what he had written so far. Eventually, he looked up and noticed that it was getting dark outside and it was very quiet on the fourth floor. Deciding that he had better turn off his laptop and head for the hotel, he went down to the parking lot and set off for downtown Houston.

As he drove along the Southwest Freeway towards the city, Martin was surprised to find that the traffic was much lighter than he had been accustomed to. Looking at the dashboard clock he realised that this was because he had missed the peak hour rush of commuters. He tuned the radio to station KUHF to listen to classical music and was humming along to Mozart's Clarinet Concerto when all of a sudden there was the unmistakable roar of a Harley Davidson motor bike in the next lane. He glanced at the driver and couldn't see his face as he was wearing a helmet with tinted glass. The motorcyclist accelerated and pulled over in front of Martin's car. He immediately recognised the logo on the back of the rider's jacket….. a Mexican toreador with his sword drawn facing a bull. Emblazoned in large red capital letters on a yellow background was the name *THE VILLAINS* Martin had had previous dealings with the Australian chapter of this outlaw motor cycle gang and they were certainly not a friendly organization. He was about to move into the next lane and drive past the motorcycle when another member of *The Villains* came up alongside him. He looked in his rear-view mirror and saw that there was a third biker almost touching the back of his car. They were moving as if in a convoy at just on the posted speed limit. Martin calmly searched his phone log which he had earlier transferred to the car's control screen and clicked on Daniel Gunn, the Houston drug squad detective. He answered almost at once and Martin told him he was surrounded by a motorcycle gang on the Southwest Freeway about two miles from downtown heading east. Daniel told him he'd have the highway patrol attend as soon as he hung up. Two minutes later he saw flashing lights approaching from the rear at breakneck speed and the motor cyclists escorting him gunned their engines and took off like greased lightning.

There was no sign of them again before Martin safely entered the hotel car park and docked his car at a charging station. Once in his suite, he called Daniel to thank him for his prompt action and tell him that he was now in the hotel. As he hung up the phone, he thought that the police officer's surname was so appropriate for a Texan.

He telephoned Lonnie to tell him about what had just taken place. 'Quite frankly Lonnie, I doubt if the motorcycle escort I had just now on the freeway would have taken any more serious action, it probably was just some sort of warning. Did you see any *The Villains* on your drive home?' Lonnie replied that his drive home was completely hassle-free. 'There weren't a lot of cars on the freeway and I got home quicker than usual. I will keep my eyes open tomorrow now that you have told me about *The Villains*. I am well trained in observing everything that's going on around me and spotting Taliban snipers during my tour of duty in Afghanistan has served me well since. Are you going to be at the office tomorrow?' Martin answered in the affirmative and told him he would be returning to Australia by the end of the week.

He decided to remain in his suite and work on the Houston Art Chronicles report. He ordered dinner from room service and switched on his laptop while he waited for the food. There were a number of emails waiting for his response so attended to those until his dinner arrived. Later he called Isabella and told her he should be back in Melbourne by the weekend. He didn't mention *The Villains* and told her he intended to visit Bilbao soon to see her and check on whether his Spanish office was coping OK or possibly needed an increase in staff.

One of the emails was from Ron Stephens the FBI detective. Their investigations into the paintings that had been sold to owners throughout the USA had so far turned up one in San Francisco and one in Las Vegas that had concealed drugs. In both cases, there appeared to be no connection between the new owners and the Mexican drug baron. They are still tracking down the other paintings on the list. There are three paintings that were bought by a mystery person in Ontario they hadn't been able to locate yet. The Canadian Mounties were assisting them and believe that the buyer had given a false name to the auctioneers which immediately raised suspicions. The paintings were delivered to a self-storage warehouse in an outer suburb of Toronto and the Mounties are going to carry out a raid as soon as a judge gives them permission to break into this private storage facility. Martin thanked him for the update and promised to keep in touch.

He switched off his laptop just before midnight and watched a late night interview show on TV before retiring for the night.

CHAPTER 13

HITTING THE HOME RUN.

Next morning after a heavy workout in the gym, he swam fifty laps, showered and ate a hearty breakfast before setting off for the Houston Chronicle headquarters. Glancing in his rear-view mirror every now and then and seeing nothing out of the ordinary, he believed the event yesterday evening must have been nothing but some sort of warning. About halfway to his destination, he noticed four motor cyclists riding side by side spread across the same lane he was in but with a couple of cars between them and Martin. Keeping an eye on them for the remainder of the journey, he saw that they kept straight on the freeway after he turned off at the exit near the Houston Chronicle. He parked in the secure staff parking lot and after signing in at reception went straight to the fourth floor stopping first to see Neville Montgomery.

'Good morning Neville, do you have a moment?'

'Of course Martin, how can I help?'

'I am planning to complete my contractual obligations in regards to the art purchases and the magazine article interviews by Thursday so I can fly home Friday. To this end and for security reasons I am putting in as much time as I can at night in my suite at the hotel to finish the *Houston Art Chronicles Report*. Because I am being followed by a group of *The Villains* motorcycle thugs to the Chronicle and again when I return to the hotel, I won't tempt fate by venturing out at night. As I have enjoyed my time working with you and Robert, I wish to thank you personally by inviting you both with your wives to have a farewell dinner at my hotel on

Thursday evening. I will also be inviting Lonnie Macpherson and his wife if they can arrange for a baby sitter.'

'That would be great Martin I'll call Estelle right away and tell her. As I mentioned previously, she took a real shine to you and will more than happy to have a night out. Is there anything you'd like us to do regarding this motorcycle gang?'

'No thanks Neville, when I found myself surrounded by a mob yesterday evening, I called Daniel Gunn and moments later a Highway Patrol car appeared on the scene and chased them away. Today they just followed me from a distance and didn't try anything stupid.'

Martin then walked down to Robert's office and offered the same farewell dinner invitation. 'By the way Robert, the cost of this party will not appear on our invoice! This is my personal thanks to you, Neville and Lonnie for the way I have been welcomed into your organization and the friendships that have resulted from my time here.' Back in his office, he tracked Lonnie down and invited them to the dinner party. 'Thanks Martin, my parents will be happy to look after the kids for the evening and Margaret will jump at the chance for a night out without the children.'

He next called Janita and told her that he was free all afternoon if she would like to continue with her interview. She told him that Mr. Mason had instructed her to concentrate on the magazine story as Thursday was to be Martin's last day at the office so this afternoon at 1.30 would be convenient.

Settling down to reading through the almost complete *Houston Art Chronicles* report he spent the rest of the morning correcting and improving the document. Lonnie called to suggest they meet in the canteen for a chat over lunch and as it was then after midday, Martin said he would go there right now.

When they were seated with their food at a small table at the back of the room, Lonnie whispered to Martin that he was followed to work today. 'I have been watching out for *The Villains* since you told me of your experience last night. This morning as I drove here there were four of them riding so close to the rear of my truck I thought that if I had to brake suddenly they would crash into me. Fortunately nothing happened but they certainly wanted me to know they were watching my movements. These critters obviously don't know anything about me and will soon find that I am a force to be reckoned with should they try any funny business.'

'I'm sorry that you have found yourself caught up in this cat-and-mouse game because of my snooping around Mexican drug entities and suspect that the situation will cool down after I depart for Australia. I also know you can take care of yourself having seen you in action under difficult conditions. Please keep Daniel Gunn informed of *The Villains* actions as he has them under investigation regarding their possible involvement in the murder of Miguel de Cristobal.'

Lonnie had to cut short their lunch date when he received a call that there were two visitors from the Hearst New York office needing to be driven to the airport in fifteen minutes. 'That's OK Lonnie as I have a meeting with Janita that will keep me on my toes for most of the afternoon. See you tomorrow.'

He had just settled down at his desk when she arrived and greeted him saying she had heard that he was being pursued by a group of motorcycle thugs. 'Martin, your story grows daily and I have my hands full keeping up with what's going on. You'll need to sit quietly on a beach somewhere and let things settle down so I can finalize the magazine article.'

For the next two hours they discussed the case of the sacred objects stolen from the Maltese cathedral which had brought Martin to New York. This was a very complicated case and she kept firing questions throughout the interview. Finally she switched off her recorder and collected her notes saying, 'We'd like to get some photos of your fiancée in Spain and have arranged for a professional photographer in Bilbao to take these on our behalf. Please clear this with her and let me know tomorrow if she is OK with this.'

Martin told her he would discuss this with Isabella this evening and provide contact details tomorrow before flying out Friday to Melbourne. He then called the company travel agent. 'Hi Jane, this is Martin Taylor, please book me on a flight to Los Angeles Friday to connect with one of the daily flights to Melbourne with Qantas. I have an open ticket which was originally with Qantas to fly from New York to Melbourne via Los Angeles and can give you that booking number if that will help. I know it will be a difficult mess to sort out but if there are any issues please get back to me on this extension number.' She told him it will probably take a while to sort out and it might be tomorrow morning before she has the tickets. 'That will be fine thanks, I will be here tomorrow as it will be my last day working in this office. Any additional costs for the flight will be covered by the Houston Chronicle and Robert Mason will authorise the expense.'

Martin read through the *Houston Art Chronicles* for a final review and then saved the complete document on a USB. He called Robert to tell him he would bring the USB to his office now if he was free. 'I certainly am Martin, come along now.' Shortly after Martin sat down in the office with him and handed him the USB. He told him that Jane in the travel department was working on his flights back to Australia and she would probably need authorization for any additional charges related to changing his original ticket. 'As for the magazine article, Janita will carry out my final interview tomorrow and any questions that arise after I am home can be answered by email. After the article goes to print will you please have copies sent to my office address?'

'That goes without saying Martin, it will be our pleasure to forward copies to you. As I have yet to see the final draft that Janita is working on I can't estimate how many weekends it will run to but my guess is two or three. I have arranged for a small farewell function at lunchtime tomorrow in the canteen so the reporting team who haven't met you can say hello. The ones you have worked with will also be there of course. My wife Barbara is looking forward to chatting with you again at dinner tomorrow night.'

Martin then asked, 'Do you think I should have invited other senior personnel such as the company president, Matthew McBride, and the executive editor, Emma Johnson plus their partners?' He replied, 'On one hand they might feel somewhat left out, but on the other hand they have had very little input into your contract with us and would understand that you are just having an intimate dinner with those who have been closest to you over the past two weeks. In any case they will be at the lunchtime function tomorrow.'

Martin returned to his office and immediately telephoned the Marriott Marquis Hotel and reserved a table in the main dining room for seven people tomorrow night at 8pm. He said goodnight to Neville as he passed his office on his way to the elevator.

The traffic was particularly heavy on the freeway as he drove to the city with vehicles bumper to bumper all the way. If the motorcycle boys were around they must have given up trying to harass Martin this evening.

He nonetheless kept his eyes peeled for any sign of them but he entered the hotel car park free of the roar of the Harleys. Once again he decided to dine in his suite and catch up on correspondence with his Melbourne office and his accountant.

With no Houston Chronicle work to do at night now he sat down and watched TV until it was a suitable time to call Isabella and assure her that all was well here. 'That a relief,' she told him, 'I was very concerned for your welfare these past few days. There's no question that I'll feel better when you are back in Melbourne.' Martin told her that he would settle his business affairs promptly on his return home and after catching up with his mother and sister would arrange a visit to Bilbao ASAP. 'By the way, the Houston Chronicle has appointed a professional photographer in Bilbao to meet with you and take some photos for the magazine article. If you are OK with that I will pass on your contact details so the photographer can make arrangements to meet you. Ensure that he doesn't use your house or office for backgrounds.' She answered that she had no issues with being photographed and would suggest they meet at the Guggenheim Museum which would be a great backdrop for the photos.

After a leisurely breakfast the following morning, he advised the clerk at the front desk that he would be checking out Friday morning. 'Please make up my account for my accommodation and all the meals that I've had during my stay but do not include for the farewell dinner for seven people I will be having in the dining room tonight. I will pay that bill separately after we finish the meal. One other thing, please contact Hertz and tell them they can collect the rental car from the hotel this evening around 6 o'clock. I will be here to hand back the keys and show them that the car looks as good as it did when they delivered it to me.'

The drive to the Houston Chronicle was uneventful until he headed down the exit ramp from the freeway and found himself suddenly surrounded by *The Villains* gang again. Once he was on the side road leading to the newspaper's office he gunned the motor and the car took off like one of Elon Musk's SpaceX rocket ships! He narrowly avoided hitting one of the motorcycles as they quickly parted to allow him through and when he turned into the company parking lot the gang continued past at breakneck speed. He decided not to call the police as the gang had not broken any laws and were only putting on a show of strength.

When he arrived at his office, there was a note on his desk to go to Robert Mason's office as soon as he arrived. He plugged in his laptop and then wandered down to the senior editor's office. Robert waved him in and asked him to take a seat. 'Good morning Martin, I thought you'd like to hear our latest bit of bragging news. The exclusive front page story of the events in Mexico City has been given an internal Hearst Publishing Group award for the best written and presented news article of the year. I haven't told the team yet but will announce it at the farewell lunch today.' Martin smiled and said, 'At least there has been some reward for what Lonnie and I experienced at the hands of those criminals. I must remember to pack a copy of that newspaper to take home with me tomorrow.

I think there may be a copy in my office but if the cleaners have disposed of it where can I get a replacement?' Robert walked over to the storage unit against the wall and opened a wide drawer that was filled with recent copies of the newspaper. He withdrew the one Martin wanted and handed it to him at the same time telling him that Matthew McBride and Emma Johnson were both attending a business function this evening so wouldn't have been able to come to Martin's dinner. 'Thanks Robert, I'll see you later at lunch.'

Back at his desk, he called Janita to inform her that he was ready for their final interview. Within minutes she appeared at his doorway and he pulled out a chair for her. This session covered the visit to Mexico City and added some details that were missed in the newspaper article. Martin told her that his fiancée Isabella had agreed to being photographed for the magazine story and is going to suggest that the photographer meet her at the Guggenheim Museum. He provided her with her cell phone number and her full name to pass on to the photographer. They were so engrossed in what they were doing that they didn't notice the time until Neville came by and told them they were wanted in the canteen.

When they arrived they were met with applause from the crowd who were milling around holding cans of Doctor Pepper and Seven Up. Martin spotted Lonnie standing nearby and went over to join him. Robert was playing the role of MC and began by asking for some hush in the room. 'Welcome everyone to this farewell to our guest Martin Taylor whom many of you have met previously. As you all know by now, Martin was already in the news following his involvement in assisting the NYPD following a major robbery that had occurred in Manhattan. We had covered that case from its inception and culminated in a murder trial at which Martin was a witness for the prosecution. We had found his background in art with the Melbourne police of particular interest and managed to contact him whilst he was still in New York and I asked to meet with him here in Houston. He acted on our behalf in the acquisition of some paintings which are now hanging in the boardroom and some offices on the fourth floor. As some of these pictures turned out to be copies produced by an art forger in Mexico City, Martin and the company chauffeur Lonnie Macpherson visited the forger to follow up on our pictures. Events occurred whilst they were there which have been well documented in our newspaper and today I can announce that we have won a Hearst award for the way we presented that front page news. Congratulations to our great team…. well done everyone. We are preparing a series of articles about this super-sleuth for our weekend magazine and this is being managed by our senior reporter Janita Sullivan. Martin will be departing for Melbourne tomorrow and we all wish him well for the future. Enough of my rambling… please enjoy the snacks that are spread around the room and then back to work everyone!'

Martin found himself shaking hands with a number of people he hadn't met before and they all fired a barrage of questions at him. A lot of selfies were taken with him as if he was a Hollywood star or a sporting legend and he was somewhat embarrassed by all this attention. One of those was the travel officer Jane, and she handed him an envelope saying that she had succeeded in sorting out his flights and the e-tickets were enclosed.

He thanked her for all the help she had provided while he was here. Janita Sullivan appeared with the photographer Sammy Gollings who took some photos of Martin shaking hands. The party broke up soon after and the crowd dispersed to their various destinations throughout the building. Janita informed him that she was getting close to completing the magazine article and that she would be presenting it to Robert Mason for his editorial input early next week. Once he has finished with it, she will send it via Cloud to his email address for his approval. Hopefully, this would be by the middle of next week.

Back in his office he opened the travel envelope and noted that the American Airlines flight out of Houston to Los Angeles tomorrow departed at 11.15am and check in was 45 minutes before boarding. He should be at the airport by 10.15am.

There would be three hours change over time at L.A. airport for the Qantas flight to Melbourne as this was necessary for him to walk to a different terminal and then be processed through Customs and Immigration. If the flight home was on time, he should arrive in Melbourne Saturday evening local time.

His phone rang and Robert asked him to come by for a short discussion on the *Houston Art Chronicles*. He went straight there and spent about an hour as they read through the report together. No major changes were required but some layout modifications were suggested and these would be made by the editing team prior to printing. Martin remembered to tell him that dinner was reserved for 8.00pm in the main dining room of the Marriott Marquis. On his way back to his office he called by Neville and told him the time for tonight's dinner also. He sent a text to Lonnie on his cell phone with the same information. Lonnie immediately called him back. 'By the way Martin, Robert Mason has instructed me to take you to the airport tomorrow. What is your check-in time?' Martin told him 10.15am and Lonnie said he would be out the front of the hotel by 9.00am.

He then cleared out his personal items from the office and went down to reception to sign out for the last time. As he drove away from the company parking lot onto the side road to get to the on-ramp to the freeway, he looked around for *The Villains*. Seeing none, he hit the accelerator and joined the constant throng of vehicles heading towards the city. Setting the cruise control to the posted speed limit, he sat back to enjoy the now familiar scenery. A highway patrol car zoomed past and a moment later a second siren sounded and another highway patrol vehicle sped by. A mile or so later he could see flashing lights ahead and vehicles in all lanes of the freeway were slowing down. As he got closer to the flashing lights, traffic was moving from two of the left lanes into the right lanes. He was in the second right-hand lane and had to allow cars to move to the right ahead of him. As he slowly moved past the flashing lights he got a glimpse of a crumpled Harley Davidson and the large SUV that had collided with it. An ambulance was nearby and a gurney was being loaded through the rear doors. Once past the accident site, the traffic quickly reverted to the speed limit. Martin wondered if it was one of *The Villains* motorcycle gang that was being placed into the ambulance but then decided that was ridiculous as not everyone who rode Harleys belonged to gangs. The rest of the drive to the hotel was uneventful and he parked the car in the driveway at the front of the hotel.

He removed his personal items from the car and walked into the lobby. He handed the car keys to the clerk at the front desk clerk and requested he call Hertz to collect the car. 'Please tell them I enjoyed driving the Tesla and ask them to delete my phone log from the control panel as I don't know how to do that.'

If they wanted to speak to him or had a document needing his signature, he would be in his suite. The clerk confirmed his instructions saying, 'Thank you Mr. Taylor, we'll make up your final account tonight as requested and include for the buffet breakfast tomorrow morning. Should you take anything from the mini-fridge tonight you can pay for that separately before you leave in the morning.'

Martin went up to his suite to pack everything he didn't need for this evening and left out what he would wear for the flight home. He emailed the limousine service in Melbourne with his flight details so they could have one of their drivers waiting for him on his arrival at Melbourne

Airport. He then showered and dressed in his suit and went down to the lobby to wait for his dinner guests.

The first to show up was Lonnie with his wife Margaret, and five minutes later Robert and Barbara arrived together with Neville and Estelle. They had another driver from the company bring them in the Houston Chronicle Cadillac SUV. Martin greeted everyone then escorted them to the main dining room where the *maître d'* led them to a large table decorated with a beautiful floral arrangement.

Once they were all comfortably seated, a waiter appeared to take their pre-dinner drink orders. Lonnie opted for a Doctor Pepper as he was the only one at the table that had to drive home! Martin started the conversation by thanking them all for coming tonight and for the Texas welcome they had given him. 'I have really appreciated your warmness and cooperation during my short stay in Houston and it will no doubt remain with me for a long time.'

The menu was studied and after the meal orders were placed, bottles of red and white wine were requested. The conversation briefly touched on the recent events in Mexico City but soon changed to questions about Martin's personal life and how he manages having a fiancée on the other side of the world. 'Of course it's not an ideal situation,' he told them, 'but fortunately our careers enable us to get together relatively often and sometimes in great locations such as with her visit here last week.' The conversation continued in a pleasant manner for the next two hours as a delightful dinner was consumed. The meal was completed with liqueurs and eventually the guests made their farewells. As Lonnie departed with Margaret he told Martin he would see him out front in the morning to take him to the airport.

After they had all gone, Martin went over to the front desk to settle the bill for the dinner as this had to be kept separate from his accommodation account which was reimbursable. He also checked with the front desk that Hertz had collected the Tesla. The clerk told him that and as there were no issues such as damage, or having to top up the fuel tank as he would have done with a conventional car, they had taken the car back to their depot.

As promised, Neville had arranged for the Hertz account to be sent directly to the Houston Chronicle by email which would save Martin having to pay it and then pass on the costs.

Satisfied with the way the dinner had gone, he went up to his suite and was able to do some more packing before calling Isabella for a last chat from Houston. 'We had my farewell dinner tonight at the hotel and it went very well,' he told her, 'they are such a friendly group of people. Unfortunately there were an uneven number of people at the table because the most important person was missing!'

Isabella told him that the photos for the magazine article were planned for tomorrow and the photographer sounded nice on the telephone. 'Have a good trip back to Melbourne,' and then finished up with, 'we'll next talk when you've got over your jetlag my love.'

Martin then confirmed his flight details with Jessica Wainwright and completed the email by asking her not to call him over the weekend as he would probably sleep most of Sunday. Before he shut down his laptop, he sent an email to Michelle Robinson thanking her for her advice when he visited the Houston Museum of Fine Arts but unfortunately he hadn't been able to find time to revisit for a more comprehensive look at their collection as he was returning to Australia the next day.

CHAPTER 14

MANY HAPPY RETURNS BRINGS
AN UNWANTED BIRTHDAY PRESENT.

Lonnie was waiting out front when Martin appeared wheeling his suitcase. 'Thanks for a great dinner last night Martin, we thoroughly enjoyed it. I picked up today's Houston Chronicle for you to read on the plane. You'll definitely be interested in an article on page two about a motorcyclist who was seriously injured on the Southwest Freeway yesterday evening. He is reported to be a member of *The Villains*.' Martin then expressed his concern that he was close to that event when he was driving back to the hotel yesterday evening. 'I did wonder if the rider was part of the group that had been harassing me on the freeway. As I drove slowly past I saw the injured person being put into the ambulance and a totally wrecked motorbike nearby. Because the traffic was in a mess around the accident scene, I didn't notice if there were any other motorcyclists nearby. It may have been just a coincidence but being a realist and as a result of my years in the police force, I normally don't subscribe to coincidences. I didn't want to mention my concerns at the dinner last night as it would have put a dampener on the mood at the table.'

Lonnie stopped at the entrance to the American Airlines departure terminal where they shook hands and promised to stay in touch. Martin checked his bag right through to Melbourne at an electronic check-in station and moved on through security to the Club Lounge to wait for the announcement of his flight to Los Angeles. Grabbing a coffee and sitting by a window where he could watch the planes landing and taking off, he read the article about the injured motorcyclist. The name didn't mean anything to Martin other than it was obviously Spanish and therefore the man was possibly Mexican. Another coincidence he wondered? The flight was called and he boarded via the front sky bridge to the business class section at the front. An hour and ten minutes after take-off the plane landed at Dallas where more passengers joined the flight and business class now had all seats filled. The rest of the journey was non-stop and took about three and a half hours. Martin spent the time reading the American Airline's inflight magazine. The guy next to him slept the whole way. Martin decided he must have had a big night out.

After arriving at the Los Angeles airport, Martin asked one of the crew standing by the door into the terminal how he should get to the international terminal from where they were now. She told him to go down to ground level and exit to the street out front. 'We are at terminal number 4, turn right and follow the signs to the Tom Bradley International Terminal. It will take you about 15 minutes.' He thanked her and started walking. Arriving at the correct location he headed straight to the Qantas desk and was directed to the security area. Once through the screening he then passed through immigration and on to the duty-free shops. He bought presents for his mother, sister and her husband Fred, as well as for his office manager. He had more than an hour and a half before departure so elected to wait in the Qantas lounge. He called Charlie Watson to tell him he was on his way back to Melbourne and would stay in touch. His flight was announced and he boarded the Airbus 380 for the fourteen hour trek across the Pacific Ocean. The service on this flight was superb and Martin managed to relax and watch a couple of movies between meals.

He had dosed off late in the flight and was awakened by an announcement that they were about to land at Melbourne's Tullamarine Airport.

He passed quickly through Customs and Immigration, picked up his suitcase from the carousel and saw the limo chauffeur holding up an iPad with his name on. He followed the driver out to his car and a few minutes later they were on the freeway to the city. It was night-time and the city buildings were lit up and presented a welcoming sight to a very tired traveller. Twenty minutes later they arrived at his Brighton apartment and he thanked the driver who handed him his suitcase and said goodnight.

Grabbing letters from his mailbox at the entrance, he unlocked his front door and turned on the lights. Everything looked ship-shape so after unpacking his bag, he made a mug of coffee and settled down to look through his mail. A few items were bills and some were advertising junk mail but one large envelope caught his eye. It was postmarked Melbourne and his address was handwritten in an almost illegible manner. He studied it for a few moments before deciding not to open it. He set it aside to look at more carefully tomorrow as his instinct told him that something about it was definitely not kosher.

Deciding it was too late to telephone any of his family or friends to tell them he was home, he headed to the bathroom for a shower and then retired to his bedroom. He shot off a brief email from his phone to Isabella to say he was back home and then hit the sack. He was deep in sleep within minutes.

Around 11.00am Sunday he was awakened by his landline telephone ringing and it took him some moments to open his eyes and grab the phone. 'Hi dear, it's your mother calling to wish you a happy birthday. I hope I haven't disturbed you too early.' He swallowed a mouthful of water before answering. 'What's this about my birthday Mum?' She answered, 'I never miss your birthday dear, don't tell me that you hadn't remembered what day it is today?' He told her he would call her back shortly after he had shaken off some of his jetlag. Opening the calendar on his iPhone he saw that indeed it was his birthday but with everything else that had been going on these past weeks he hadn't given it a thought. He went into the kitchen and set the machine into action to make himself a double strength black coffee. While he was sitting there his mobile phone started ringing. This time it was his sister Barbara to wish him happy birthday and welcome home. 'Hi Barb, Mum just called with the same greeting. I have had so much happening recently that my birthday was not on my mind.' She invited him to come for dinner tonight and to please pick up Mum on the way. He thanked her and she said to come about 6.30.

Now that his plan to sleep all day had been thwarted, he decided to shower and dress and take the suspicious envelope to the Bayside area police headquarters in nearby Moorabbin. There were a number of duty officers working there that Martin knew from when he was with Victoria Police and he would telephone first to see if any of his old colleagues happened to be there on a Sunday. Around midday he made contact with Sergeant Toby Smith whom he had worked with on a case at the Melbourne headquarters back in 2019.

'Toby, I returned last night from Houston, Texas where I was working for the main newspaper in that city. I found a suspicious package in my mail box and would like to have it checked out before I open it.' Toby told him to come at 2.30 and they would do what they could to help, although it might be somewhat limited considering it was a Sunday. 'There is one of our forensic experts on duty today and I'll see if he will take a look at it before anyone opens it. What were you up to over there that might lead to someone wanting to harm you?'

'I found myself up against a Mexican drug baron and his motorcycle gang cohorts so there might be a connection there although I didn't expect they would follow me halfway around the world. I'll see you this afternoon and tell you more about it then.'

He called his mother to arrange to pick her up to go to Barbara's for dinner. 'Sorry if I was a bit short with you earlier but I am somewhat jetlagged after almost twenty four hours of flights and hanging around airports. I'll make sure I'm in a better mood when I see you later.'

He then went to the supermarket just up the road from his office and filled the cart with fresh food and groceries. After a light lunch he gingerly picked up the thick envelope and drove to the police complex on the Nepean Highway, Moorabbin. Toby Smith greeted him and took him through to an interview room where he was introduced to Inspector Barney O'Brien. Martin gave them a run through on the events surrounding the visit to Mexico City including his kidnapping and the threats made by a drug baron. 'Following my return to Houston I was harassed whilst driving on the freeway by members of *The Villains* outlaw motorcycle gang who I suspect was on the Mexican drug baron's payroll. I know that *The Villains* have a branch here in Melbourne and it wouldn't be unreasonable to consider they might have something to do with this envelope.'

Barney put on surgical gloves and picked it up and held it to the light and said there appears to be a small packet of some sort inside. He excused himself for a moment and left the room briefly before returning with a device that looked like some kind of microscope. 'I can look inside packages with this clever gadget,' he told them, 'so let's see if I can ascertain what kind of gift someone has sent you.' Placing the envelope on the bed of the device he flicked a switch and studied the enlarged view he was getting of the packet inside the envelope. After a minute or so, he turned to Martin and said, 'It contains a very fine powder which in my opinion is not an explosive product as there is nothing else there such as a fuse or any kind of electrical circuit that would be required to set it off when you opened the envelope. It is more likely to be a toxic powder that would render you very ill, or worse, when it was exposed and you either touched or inhaled it. I will send it to our lab and hope to have a report back in a couple of days.'

Toby Smith then added, 'We'll see if we can pick up any finger prints on the envelope apart from yours and on the packet after it has been removed from the envelope. No doubt your fingerprints will be in our system from when you were a member of the Force so we'll be able to eliminate yours.

You mentioned *The Villains* gang earlier… well we have quite a number of their member's fingerprints on record as they have been on our watch list for a long time.'

Martin thanked Barney, and Toby escorted him back to the front entrance where he had to sign a register of his visit. He shook hands with Toby and walked to his car. Feeling somewhat paranoid, he searched the passing traffic looking for motorcyclists riding Harley Davidsons. Seeing none, he got in his car and drove home.

He spent the evening with his family and had lots to tell them about the contract with the Houston Chronicle. His brother-in-law Fred had lots of questions especially regarding the magazine article. Barbara had baked a birthday cake which they washed down with champagne. He had brought a copy of the newspaper which had the events of the Mexico City kidnapping filling the front page. Martin watered down the dangerous aspects of that experience with a comment that newspapers often like to blow things up out of proportion.

He also told them that he had spent a couple of wonderful days with Isabella who had taken time off to be with him in Houston. They then handed him their birthday gifts which included an Italian leather wallet, a couple of Gazman shirts and a cashmere jumper. He passed them the gifts he had brought back and all in all it was great homecoming. No mention was made of the strange unwanted *birthday* gift he had received in the post! Later at home, his phone rang and it was Isabella to wish him happy birthday and to see how he was settling back into things. He did not mention the envelope which was now in the hands of the local police because he did not want to add to the issues that had arisen in Mexico. 'Depending on what is waiting for me at the office here, I am hoping I can fly to Bilbao later this week.' She said that she was very busy with court appearances this week but after Friday it should be quieter.

The following day, he managed to drag himself out of bed early and drove to the office in Bay Street, Brighton. Jessica was at her desk when he came in. She got up and gave him a big hug. 'Welcome back Boss, it's great to see you are looking so well.' He asked her to come into his office so they could catch up on everything that's been going on both here and in Houston. She presented the projects that were in progress at this office and then told him which of their team was working on each job. Martin then reviewed the contracts that had been completed and if any issues had arisen. It was obvious that Jessica had managed everything extremely well and this confirmed his decision to make her a partner in the firm had been a worthwhile step.

He then told her in detail about his work for the Houston Chronicle and concluded with showing her the infamous newspaper headline article. 'Wow Martin, you certainly appeared to have jumped into the deep end of the pool.' Martin smiled as he suggested with tongue in cheek, 'Some pundits say that all publicity is good publicity, although I'm not sure that in this case that is true!'

After reviewing the contracts on hand at the Bilbao office, Martin told her that he is planning to visit there in the next week or so. Jessica printed out a list of the work that was in progress there and pointed out that the job for the client in San Sebastian had reached a stalemate. 'The guy in Biarritz flatly refuses to pay our client for the painting he bought from him and our man there, Juan Lopez, has tried all his powers of persuasion without success. I advised our client to hold off taking court action until you had returned as I was certain you would like to get involved once you were aware of the situation.' Martin nodded and asked her to send an urgent message to the client and tell him that I'll be there next week and I will arrange to meet with him at his gallery once flights had been finalised.

His mobile phone rang and it was Barney O'Brien at the Moorabbin police station. 'Martin, our lab has tested the powder that was sent to you and reported that it is an extremely toxic chemical that would have made you very sick if you had so much as touched it or breathed a small amount of it in. The results have been recorded and the powder destroyed in a laboratory furnace. Our department is still working on the envelope looking for clues as to its origin. Whoever is behind this attempt to harm you may well try again once they realise that you have escaped this time, so please be alert and keep us advised of anything out of the ordinary.' Martin thanked him for the update and told him that he was setting off for Spain later in the week and would stay in touch.

He told Jessica that he was off to see the accountant Paul Cohen now to go through all the last minute charges to be invoiced to the Houston Chronicle. 'I will then go to see my friend Aart van den Haag at his gallery in Armadale. I expect to be back at the office later in the day and meanwhile could you please speak with the agent that handles our travel arrangements and book flights for me to Bilbao departing Melbourne Thursday. I'll also require a rental car at Bilbao airport, preferably an electric vehicle if they have any there.'

Arriving at Paul's home in Caulfield, he was greeted by his wife Doreen who gave him a big hug as she and Paul are old friends. She led him through to Paul's office and left them alone to talk business. Together they reviewed the income and expenditure figures in the bookkeeping ledger and compared the numbers with the recent bank statements. Martin was pleased to see that they were in a healthy financial position and if things continued this way until the end of June, which is the end of the tax year in Australia, it looked possible they would make a healthy profit. They were fortunate that their clients paid their invoices promptly and this was an enormous boost to their cash flow situation. 'That reminds me,' Martin said, as he handed Paul the last of the expense receipts from the Houston assignment, 'Please prepare the final invoice for the Houston Chronicle.' He then related some of the events of his time in Texas and Mexico. 'Despite the issues that arose when I was in Mexico City, the overall experience was fantastic Paul, and it has resulted in opening up a whole new world for me and the business. Some security issues remain and I am working to resolve these with the police here.' Paul expressed concern over this last statement but figured Martin knew what he was doing.... after all he had been in the Victoria police force for some years and this must have taught him how to take care of himself. As he was leaving, Doreen invited him to come for Sunday lunch. 'I'll roast a side of beef and you can tell me all about your gorgeous fiancée Isabella. Have you settled on a wedding date yet?'

He shook his head and thanked her for the invitation to lunch but told her he was off to Spain before the weekend. 'We can discuss Isabella after I return....I may have some more definite news following my visit.'

He called Aart from his car to check that he was at his gallery this afternoon and told him that he would be there in about ten minutes. Parking in the private lot behind the gallery, he pressed the bell on the rear door and Aart opened up to greet his friend with a big smile. 'Hi Martin, I heard from Jessica that you had been getting up to mischief while you were in Houston!'   Martin smiled and replied, 'Calling it mischief is an understatement Aart but in hindsight, I can compare it to the fun you and I had in Holland a couple of years ago retrieving the stolen Belgian diamonds. Anyway, how are your family and were you affected by the Corona virus?'

'Everyone is well thanks Martin and none of us actually tested positive during the pandemic although some of our friends caught it and had to isolate. The gallery actually managed to sell a lot of paintings during the protracted Melbourne lockdowns as people working at home spent some of the government handouts on new furniture and accessories. Because we had to keep the gallery closed for long periods, customers were looking at our paintings on-line and buying them without seeing them close up. We offered to take them back if they weren't happy with their selection after they were delivered. Out of the dozens we sold that way, only two were returned and both customers selected other paintings which they then kept.

I have to say it has been one of our busiest periods. Incidentally, I sent those close-up photos to Sheila Black and she confirmed that it was possible the painting at the auction was genuine.' Martin smiled as he reported that they had actually succeeded in their bid for the Robin Black and it is now hanging in the newspaper's boardroom. 'If it a genuine Black then we got it at a bargain price.' Before he left the gallery, he informed Aart that he was flying to Bilbao later this week and suggested that they go out for dinner tomorrow night if they are free. Aart replied, 'Helena will be pleased to see you and I suggest we go to our favourite Greek restaurant in High Street, Prahran called Lemnos Taverna. If you agree, I'll call and reserve a table for 7 o'clock. You can tell us all about your recent adventures over dinner.'

Back at his office in Brighton, he asked Jessica for the case file on the assignment in San Sebastian. As she handed him the file she told him that the travel agent had been able to book flights with Emirates Airlines from Melbourne to Dubai for a change of aircraft to Madrid and then with Iberia to Bilbao. She'll have the tickets for you tomorrow. There will be a Europcar waiting for you on arrival in Bilbao but apparently they don't have any electric vehicles there. 'Would you like her to try another car rental company to enquire if they have an EV available?' He shook his head and told her it was just an idea as he had driven a Tesla in Houston and it was a great experience.

He familiarised himself with the San Sebastian versus Biarritz case before reading the reports from Juan Lopez who despite his best efforts to achieve a compromise solution to the issue could not get the man in Biarritz to hand over any money or return the painting.

Martin decided he would have to pull a rabbit out of the hat to sort this one out. The businessman in Biarritz is behaving like a bully and therefore is unlikely to react favourably if handled gently.

He concluded that tough talk is probably the only language people like that understand. He emailed the Bilbao office manager, Dario Montoya, to tell him that he will be arriving in Bilbao Friday and will be at the office Monday to discuss current assignments. Juan is to be there also to discuss the case and then on Tuesday will go together with Martin to see the client in San Sebastian before proceeding to confront the trouble-maker in Biarritz.

Jessica popped in to say goodnight and Martin told her he'd like to speak with their two field investigators tomorrow if they could come in to the office around midday. 'We'll order pizzas to be delivered and chat with them over lunch.'

He had a quiet night and began sorting out the clothes he'd need for the upcoming visit to Bilbao. He needed to take some clothes to Oscar's in Church Street for dry cleaning in the morning to make sure they'd be back by Thursday. Isabella emailed asking if he had flight details yet and he answered that he would have these tomorrow.

He watched an episode of a madcap program called *HARD QUIZ* and found it somewhat amusing then read a few chapters of a book he had picked up at L.A. airport between flights. Jetlag finally caught up with him and he fell asleep with the book in his hands and the light on. He woke up some time during the night and turned off the light then rolled over and fell into a deep sleep.

CHAPTER 15

IT'S A SMALL, SMALL, WORLD.

The following day, Martin dropped by the Moorabbin police headquarters to speak with Sergeant Toby Smith. 'No doubt Barney has informed you of the result of the lab test on the powder I was sent, and I was wondering if you have had any luck in tracing the origin of the envelope.' They were standing at the front reception desk when Toby explained that the postmark on the envelope revealed that it had been mailed at the main post office in Dandenong. 'You had mentioned having had a run-in with the outlaw motorcycle club, *The Villains*....well they have club rooms in Doveton which is close to Dandenong. This doesn't prove anything but it is enough of a coincidence for us to investigate further. There were some faint fingerprints on the envelope and we are checking those against our data base of criminals amongst which are a number of *The Villains* members. There have been many instances of arrests of gang members over the years following shootings and bombings so we'll soon know if they are involved with this attempt to harm you. By the way, you might be interested to know what *The Villains* motto is.... OUR PARENTS WARNED US ABOUT PEOPLE LIKE US! That about sums up the quality they look for in members.'

'Thanks Toby, your assistance in this matter is much appreciated. I am leaving for Spain on business Thursday but will stay in touch with you via email. Here is my card with all my contact details so please send me an update when you have some news and I will respond from wherever I am at that time.'

As he was driving to his office he received a call from Jessica saying that a photographer had turned up to take some photos for the Houston Chronicle magazine article. He told her to give the person a cuppa and he would be there in five minutes. As he turned into Bay Street from the Nepean Highway he noticed a motor cyclist following close behind. It looked like a Harley Davidson but he couldn't be sure so decided to continue past his office and turned left into New Street then immediately left into Barkly Street and on past the Firbank Girls Grammar School. The motorcycle had stayed with him up to this point so he suddenly gunned the motor and swung right into Inner Crescent and along Wilson Street. The streets in this area are quite confusing for those not familiar with them and the motorcyclist became muddled and Martin momentarily lost him. He took advantage of the situation and zoomed back to Bay Street and into the underground parking garage of the building where his office was located. He took the elevator up to the second floor and met Jessica at reception. 'Sorry Jess, it took a little longer than expected and I'll explain later…is the photographer still here?' She answered that he was having a coffee in the amenities room. 'His name is Roger Jones and I'll bring him to your office once you settle down.' A few minutes later, he was introduced and a series of photos were taken in various poses both sitting and standing in his office. Martin instructed him not to take any photographs of the outside of the office building for security reasons. After the photographer had departed, Martin called Jessica in and told her of his stalker on a motorbike.

'I seem to have shaken him off but have no idea if he knows this address so will be watching for him when I leave later. Who of our investigators have advised that they will be here for lunch?' Jessica replied, 'You'll be pleased to know that both Heather Mountford and Simon Matthews will be here shortly. I inquired what pizzas they prefer and have ordered four different toppings to be delivered at 12.30. Hopefully you'll be happy with what I chose for you Martin!'

While he was waiting, he telephoned Toby Smith and told him about the motorcyclist who had followed him earlier. 'Unfortunately as motor cycles don't have registration plates on the front, and the helmets hide the faces completely I can't give you any descriptions.' Toby responded that they had found a match for the fingerprint on the envelope. 'It belongs to one of *The Villains* who has been before the courts a number of times on serious charges. His name is Jack *'The Ripper'* Danielson. He earned his nickname from attacking people with knives. At least three rival gang members have been hospitalised over the past few years following fights outside nightclubs. He has served time for knife attacks, drug and firearm offences. I have put out an alert to our cruising officers and once again I suggest that you watch your back and if you see anything suspicious call me on my direct number that is shown on the card I gave you Sunday.'

There was an email from Daniel Gunn at Houston police saying that the injured motorcyclist was a member of *The Villains* and had been identified as Reinaldo *"The Lion"* Martinez, a Mexican immigrant who had been in and out of prison a number of times. He was still in hospital in intensive care and meanwhile a search of his smashed motorbike revealed a gun hidden in one of the saddle bags. Forensics has proved it was the weapon used to shoot Miguel de Cristobal and Martinez will now be charged with first degree murder. Martin's work for the Houston Chronicle stirred up a hornet's nest which has resulted in the solving of an open murder case. He ended the email by wishing him well.

Martin replied describing the mystery envelope and its contents, and the subsequent investigation leading to involvement by the Melbourne chapter of *The Villains*. Obviously the instructions from the drug baron in Mexico City had spread to Australia via Houston which means his brush with the outlaw motorcycle gang was far from over. Modern technology has shrunk long distances and in doing so, has made it *a small, small world* he wrote.

Jessica came by to say that their two investigators had arrived and were seated in the amenities room. Martin greeted them whilst Jessica put the coffee machine into action. 'I wanted to take this opportunity to meet with you and tell you about my recent work in Houston and the outcome of the project. After that, lunch will arrive and while we enjoy our pizzas, I'd like to hear from you about the assignments you are currently involved with, and if there is anything I can help you with.' He related the story of the art auction and how he had bid on a number of paintings on behalf of the Houston Chronicle newspaper. The discovery of drugs hidden in two of the art works resulted in the Houston police and the FBI getting involved.

'Although the majority of items sold at the auction were listed as being attributed to well-known artists, it was suspected that they were actually painted by a talented art forger. I went to Mexico City to meet with one such person to confirm that he had produced most, if not all of the pictures I had successfully bid for. The rest of the story is featured on this newspaper's exclusive front page that I have here for you to read whilst you are here in the office.'

During lunch Heather talked about her assignment which was to track down paintings by the late great indigenous artist, Albert Namatjira that may possibly be owned by private collectors. The client is the stunning new art museum in Shepparton which is intending to have a Namatjira retrospective shortly. She had only commenced the search at the start of the week and so far has found two owned by a businessman living in a mansion on the *Golden Mile* beachfront in Brighton not far from the office. He had bought these paintings many years ago whilst on an outback tour when it passed through Hermannsburg in the Northern Territory where the artist lived. Back then, many paintings were sold by the artist directly to tourists so there were no records of the buyers. Heather had been knocking on doors of known collectors of indigenous paintings and one such person had pointed her in the direction of the family in Brighton. Martin suggested Heather contact Elizabeth Hall who is the director of the National Gallery of Victoria, and his good friend Aart van den Haag at his Armadale gallery. 'Both these people have a huge list of contacts in the art world and may be able to assist in the search. Jessica can give you their contact details,' Martin told her.

Simon was close to wrapping up an assignment assisting the Victoria Police in a multi-million dollar fraud case. 'Who is your contact at the Victoria police?' Martin inquired. 'Senior Sergeant Carl Dockendorff,' he answered. 'Well, he's a top guy,' Martin told him, 'he was my second-in-command when I was there. Please give him my regards when you next speak.' The meeting ended with Martin thanking them for their attendance and wishing them well.

Jessica brought Martin his airline tickets for his flights Thursday to Bilbao. 'The travel agent sent them by courier while you were holding your meeting. Your flight to Madrid doesn't leave until late afternoon but due to left-over issues from the pandemic, particularly staff shortages, getting through immigration and customs is slower than usual so you are requested to arrive at least three hours prior to departure.' He thanked her and said he was heading home to pack as he had a dinner date with Aart and his wife tonight. On the way home he called the limousine service and booked a car to take him to the airport tomorrow afternoon.

As he was turning into the underground car park at his apartment complex he noticed a motorcyclist sitting on his bike on the other side of the road. He drove into the car park and waited until the electrically operated gate had closed to ensure he hadn't been followed inside. He parked in his designated spot, locked the car and took the lift up to his floor. Once in the apartment he called Toby Smith and told him about the guy waiting outside. 'I'll despatch one of our patrol cars immediately and if the guy is still there when they arrive they can get his name and question him as to what he is doing there. He's not committing a crime just sitting on his bike in the street….but we can move him on.'

Martin thanked him and started tidying up his apartment. Later on, he called a taxi to take him to the restaurant in Prahran. When he stepped out the front of the apartment complex, he looked up and down the street and there was no sign of the motorcyclist. As the taxi drove off, his phone rang and it was Toby to report that his officers had confronted the guy and when asked what he was doing there he answered that he was waiting for a mate.

Toby continued, 'They took down his details and told him to wait for his mate somewhere else. It was the same member of *The Villains*, Jack *"The Ripper"* Danielson. We'll be keeping a watch on his movements and make sure he's aware that we are not far away every time he's on the move.' Martin told him he was in a taxi going to meet friends at the Lemnos Taverna in High Street, Prahran. 'We're almost there and I have been looking out for any motorcyclists but there hasn't been any sign of anyone following us here. As I mentioned previously, I'll be leaving for Spain Thursday and use a limousine service to take me to the airport. I'll open up the underground car park for the driver to come in so I can get into the limo without anyone outside looking for my car actually seeing me leave. I'll be away for a week but will keep in touch by email.'

Martin had a most enjoyable evening with Aart and Helena van den Haag at the Greek restaurant. He briefly outlined what had taken place in Houston and Mexico City deciding not to go into much detail, and ending his story on a positive note. 'The Houston Chronicle is writing a series of articles about me for their weekend magazine which will provide me with a lot of publicity. They have one of the largest circulations amongst American newspapers and being part of the huge Hearst group it will no doubt be read by a lot of people. They will send me copies of the magazine after it has been published and I'll make sure I keep a copy for you. I know you met the reporter, Janita Sullivan, when she was in Melbourne Aart, and you kindly showed her your gallery. I believe she took some photos so no doubt at least one of those will appear in the article about the stolen diamonds case.' Aart replied that he had enjoyed meeting her and looked forward to reading the article. Helena asked about Martin's trip to Bilbao tomorrow and wondered if there were any marriage plans on the agenda? 'Everyone asks me that question Helena, you'll be one of the first to know when we make that decision,' he replied.

He was about to call for a taxi but Aart told him he would drive him home so they could continue their conversation on the way to Brighton. Martin was certain that *The Villains* weren't aware of his dinner date at the Lemnos Taverna and in any case they wouldn't recognize Aart's Mercedes. He kept looking out the rear window but there was no sign of anyone following them. As they approached Martin's apartment block in Wilson Street, they spotted two men on Harleys sitting waiting on the opposite side of the street. Martin ducked down so anyone watching would only see a man and a woman sitting in the front. He pressed the remote on his key ring and the security gate swung open. Aart drove straight in and stopped by the elevator. There was one free visitor's spot vacant and Martin suggested parking there and coming up for a quick cup of coffee while he called the police. Once they were in the apartment, Martin phoned Toby Smith who was at home watching a football night match on TV.

'Sorry to disturb you again Toby but my friend has just driven me back from the restaurant and there are two motorcyclists waiting out front. They are probably waiting for me to arrive in my own car so they wouldn't have seen me crouched down in the back of my friend's Mercedes as we drove into the underground car park. If you can get someone to move those nuisances away ASAP I'd appreciate it so my friends can go home.' Toby told him that the police helicopter was on its way back to Moorabbin airport from covering a disturbance that had taken place this evening outside the State Parliament building. 'As they will be passing right over Brighton on their way I'll have them to fly low over Wilson Street and shine their spotlights on the motorcyclists. That will no doubt scare the pants off them.'

A few minutes later the familiar *thrump thrump thrump* of the chopper could be clearly heard and this was soon followed by the distinctive sound of Harley Davidson exhausts as the motor cycles roared off at great speed.

Martin wasn't going to tell Aart and Helena about the harassment by *The Villains* outlaw motorcycle gang that had followed him here from Houston, but now he had no choice. He made coffees for them all and related the story of the suspect envelope that was waiting for him when he arrived back a few days ago and the connection to *The Villains*. 'I'm fortunate that my police associates here are treating this situation seriously and have acted immediately each time I have contacted them as you've witnessed just now.' As they were leaving, Aart suddenly remembered to tell Martin that Heather had called this afternoon asking for some help in tracking down Albert Namatjira paintings held in private collections in Melbourne. 'I know two families here that have some of his earliest paintings so I told her that I would contact them first to check that they agree to speak to her about lending them to the Shepparton Art Museum. Some people are shy about this sort of thing so it's better for me to check before I give her their details.' Martin walked down with them to the car park and Helena gave him a kiss on the cheek whispering for him to take special care. He thanked Aart for helping Heather and said goodnight.

Back in his apartment, he decided to call Isabella to confirm his flights and tell her how much he was looking forward to seeing her Friday evening Bilbao time. He put the cups and saucers in the dishwasher then checked his emails. There was one from Lonnie Macpherson in Houston inquiring how things were, which he answered by telling him about the local *The Villains* and how he could make good use of a bodyguard. He ended up by saying, WANT A JOB?

Janita Sullivan had sent a list of questions she needed to fill in some gaps in a couple of the case stories and he easily answered those. She said that the final draft of the article about him was close to being presented to

Robert Mason for editing. They had set a date for releasing part one on the first Saturday of next month.

Neville Montgomery sent a message that he and his wife Estelle have planned for them to come to Australia for a two week vacation next month. They would fly first to Melbourne for five days to see the sights and catch up with Martin, then head to the Queensland Gold Coast to enjoy some sunshine for the rest of the time.

Martin replied that he would look forward to showing them around Melbourne as there are some great things to do within a few hours' drive from the city.

Before switching off his laptop, he sent an email to Robert Mason telling him of the events that occurred since he arrived home in Melbourne. He emphasized that the local police are aware of what has been going on and are keeping an eye out for suspicious activities. The key to everything is the involvement of *The Villains* that has spread from Houston to Melbourne and is of major concern. He then advised Robert that he was flying to Spain Thursday and would be based in Bilbao for a week.

He watched a couple of episodes of a new series on Netflix before turning off the bedside lamp.

CHAPTER 16

BIENVENIDO MARTIN!

Wednesday morning, Martin was up bright and early and looked through the fridge to check for any food that might not keep until he returned. He had a free day and decided he would take the train into the city and go to the National Gallery of Victoria to look at the *blockbuster* exhibition that was on right now. He also wanted to catch up with the gallery director, Elizabeth Hall, if she was available. When he telephoned, he was told she was in a meeting but would call back as soon as she was through. In the meantime, he called his office and spoke with Jessica. He told her of his plans for the day and she was welcome to come over and take any food items she could use at home while he was away. 'You've got a spare key to my apartment,' he said, 'and you know the security code so come by whenever you can and help yourself.' He followed up with a call to his accountant and they discussed commercial matters for over an hour. 'Don't forget,' Paul reminded him, 'Doreen wants you to come for our Sunday roast after you return from Spain.' He had just finished the call when the phone rang and it was Elizabeth Hall. They spoke briefly and arranged to meet in the NGV Members Lounge at 1 o'clock.

Martin walked to the nearby North Brighton railway station and sat back enjoying the view through the train's large windows of people's backyards as it whizzed him through to Flinders Street station in just over a quarter of an hour. He was disgusted at the amount of graffiti sprayed on almost every wall and boundary fence along the railway track. Even houses weren't immune from this senseless activity. It was only a short walk across Princes Bridge to the gallery where he joined the queue to get a ticket for the special exhibition which was called *The Picasso Century*. The exhibition had been curated with 70 works by Picasso and 100 pieces by his contemporaries. Most of the items on display had come from the Centre Pompidou and the Musée National Picasso-Paris. Martin was so engrossed with the exhibition that it was only when his phone beeped indicating an incoming SMS that he noticed the time….ten minutes past one! He looked and saw it was from Elizabeth checking where he was. Hurrying along to the Members Lounge, he found her waiting by the door. They sat together drinking coffee for a while, talking about families and how they had fared during the Pandemic and the world record number of lockdowns experienced in the state of Victoria. 'Two years when almost everything was at a standstill,' Elizabeth groaned, 'the NGV was closed for more days than it was open and we had to lay off staff as it dragged on for so long. At long last we are operating at close to pre-Covid numbers but there appears to still be a large number of patrons who do not want to be in an enclosed crowded environment. I regularly speak to the hierarchy in the Arts Centre next door and they are still struggling to fill the large Concert Hall and the State Theatre.'

They decided to go to the delightful café on level one to continue their get-together over a light lunch. Elizabeth wanted to know more about what Martin was doing in Houston so he gave her a brief rundown on the Houston Chronicle assignment and the subsequent visit to Mexico City.

She was particularly interested to hear about the auction of the drug baron's art collection. Martin finished up telling her of his upcoming trip to Bilbao and raised the subject of Heather's assignment regarding Albert Namatjira paintings in private collections. Elizabeth said she would be happy to assist in any way she could. They parted soon after with Elizabeth returning to her office and Martin continuing his tour of the gallery.

There was a separate exhibition called Women of Design featuring the architectural work by a woman whose name Tatiana Bilbao caught his eye. When he read the background story on the wall at the start of the exhibition, he was fascinated to see that she wasn't from Bilbao as he had assumed, but from Mexico City! Apparently she was famous for her building designs in many countries and had put together a large scale installation of scale models and textiles. He found the work absolutely fascinating and was surprised that he hadn't heard about her before considering she was so famous. He took some photos on his phone to show Isabella.

He took the train back to North Brighton and walked to his apartment with no sign of any motorcyclists in his street. Once inside, he telephoned the limousine service and left instructions for the driver to arrive at precisely midday tomorrow and Martin would open the car park gate for him to drive straight in. He was to park near the lift and Martin would be waiting for him there.

After a good night's sleep he arose late and checked everything was neat and tidy in the apartment before picking up his suitcase and carry-on bag. He set the alarm and double dead-locked the front door. He rode the lift down to the basement level at precisely twelve noon. He could see the limo sitting in front of the security gate and pressed the remote. The car came in and the driver spotted Martin standing by the lift. Five minutes later they drove back out and were soon on the Nepean Highway heading towards the city. The driver was one of the usual ones he had met a few times previously. They chatted about the weather, the football and the forthcoming State Government election. The driver said he was so disillusioned with both the major parties he would probably vote for an independent as a protest. He definitely wouldn't vote for the Greens as he couldn't abide the person who was standing in his electorate. He went on to complain about the Federal Election held earlier in the year and the upstart party which didn't win any seats despite the tens of million dollars spent on advertising. The Tullamarine freeway was very busy and it took longer than usual to get to the airport. Martin had plenty of time before the flight so was not concerned. He was looking out for motorcycles between the cars and trucks but saw nothing suspicious. He was dropped right at the front of the international terminal and thanked the driver for his superb driving skills and his lecture on Australian politics!

He went straight to the Emirates Business Class check-in and handed over his suitcase. He walked through the swing doors to Customs and Immigration where there were numerous queues of passengers shuffling slowly forward. There was a special line for First and Business Class passengers which had fewer people lined up, but it was still very slow moving. Eventually he was through and found himself amongst the duty-free stores.

He stopped and bought a bottle of Coco Chanel perfume for Isabella then went on to the Emirates Lounge. He settled down to read today's Age newspaper which was filled with articles on the forthcoming state election.

Finding the election stories particularly boring, he walked over to the magazine rack and selected an architectural issue which featured outstanding homes in Australia. He picked up a bottle of James Squire light beer and found a comfortable lounge chair to sit and wait for the flight to be called.

The departure status board on the wall showed that his flight was scheduled to leave right on time and it wasn't long before passengers were called to go to the departure gate. Once on board he found himself in a single window seat with ample legroom for tall passengers. He lifted his carry-on bag into the overhead locker and sat back watching the activity on the tarmac outside as the last of the bags were stowed away in the hold and the doors were closed. The stewardess handed him a glass of champagne and a dish with pretzels and nuts.

They were soon moving out onto the main runway and after waiting a few minutes were given the all-clear for take-off. The Airbus A380 is a marvellous plane for long-haul travel and before long they were up and passing through the clouds. After a great dinner, he wandered down to the Business Class bar and sat chatting to a fellow passenger from country

Victoria who was on his way to Amsterdam for an agricultural convention. They would be parting company at Dubai where almost all Emirates flights to Europe from Australia require a change of planes. Martin had a two hour wait for his onwards flight to Madrid and spent some of the time browsing through the huge duty free area and settled on a bottle of Veuve Clicquot French champagne. He had decided that they should settle on a wedding date whilst he was staying with Isabella in Bilbao and they could celebrate with a glass or two of bubbly.

The flight to Madrid was from the same terminal but at the opposite end from where he had disembarked from the Melbourne flight and he had quite a walk to get to the departure area. As he was wandering along thinking about Isabella and not taking much notice of the people around him, someone called out his name. He looked up and recognized the man who had been the Chief Commissioner of Victoria Police when Martin had been a senior officer in the force. Sir Charles MacPherson had been a high ranking member of the London Metropolitan police force before accepting the top job in Melbourne. Martin had heard that he had recently retired and had moved back to the UK. As they walked along together they chatted amiably about what they had been doing since leaving the force. 'Although I am supposed to be retired,' Sir Charles said, 'I give lectures at the London police training college one or two days a week and thoroughly enjoy the interaction with the recruits. It keeps my mind active and alert, in fact, I have just spent a week here in Dubai as a guest speaker at a police training convention which was very enlightening.' Martin congratulated his old chief and briefly related how he had fared running his own private detective agency. There wasn't enough time to go into much detail as they had arrived at the departure gate where Sir Charles' flight was to leave for London. They shook hands and said goodbye. Ten minutes later Martin was at the departure gate for his flight just as they were commencing to board.

Despite constant attention during the flight to Madrid with offers of food and drink, Martin decided he would get some sleep on this long leg of his journey and in fact had to be woken up by the stewardess as they were preparing for landing. First he had to pass through Spanish Customs and Immigration and then find his way from the international to the domestic terminal to catch the Iberia flight to Bilbao. This relatively short flight was uneventful and they landed at the architecturally eye-popping airport building right on time.

Martin collected his suitcase from the carousel and went straight to the Europcar desk to pick up the rental car which had been reserved for him. After completing the formalities, he was given the keys to a bright red Seat Ibiza and given a map showing where the rental cars were parked.

What a surprise it was to find that the car had a manual gearbox….he hadn't changed gears manually since he first learned to drive. When he was settled into the driver's seat, he typed Isabella's home address into the GPS and found it had a function where a number of languages including English could be selected. It was early evening when he drove away from the airport and headed towards the city. The road led him over some hills and it wasn't long before the Guggenheim Museum came into view. The titanium cladding was literally glowing as it reflected the colours of the setting sun. Although he had been here previously, he hadn't experienced the sight of this amazing building from this vantage point at sunset. Following the directions of a very British sounding woman on the GPS, he soon found himself parked outside Isabella's modern house in a newly developed suburb. The lights were on so he assumed she was at home. Grabbing his bags, he walked up and rang the doorbell. The door swung open and she rushed forward to embrace him. They went inside and he put the bags down and kissed her long and lovingly.

'Bienvenido Martin,' she greeted him in Spanish, 'it seems so long since we were in Houston together but it's actually only been a couple of weeks hasn't it?' He nodded and asked if it was alright if he took a shower as it had been a long time since he departed from his apartment back in

Melbourne. 'I would like to freshen up before we sit down together.' As he hadn't been to her new house before, she had to show him the way to the bathroom. 'There is plenty of space in my walk-in closet for you to hang up your clothes Martin and I'll be in the kitchen while you shower. Just call out if you need anything.'

Half an hour later, a revived young man appeared on the other side of the kitchen bench to watch Isabella as she chopped up parsley. 'I'm sure you have been well fed whilst travelling halfway around the world in Business Class so I'm preparing a pasta dish for this evening, if that's to your liking my good sir?' He opened the duty free carry-bag with the bottle of champagne he had bought in Dubai and asked her to put it in the fridge for another night. She finished chopping the parsley and set a pot of spaghetti on the stove to boil. She came around to the other side of the bench, took his hand and led him to a big leather sofa in the adjoining family room. They sat down together and she cuddled up and kissed him on the cheek. 'That smells better my love, what is the name of your deodorant? It's really cool.' He had to think for a moment before answering, 'It's called Brut although I doubt the name has anything to do with the kind of brutes I have run into lately!'

From the same bag he produced a small gift-wrapped package saying, 'I hope this is to your liking Isabella as it was a first for me to purchase something like this and I had to rely on the recommendation from the sales person.' She peeled away the wrapping and was delighted at the choice of perfume. 'It's one of my favourites Martin, and I'll wear it when we go out tomorrow night to somewhere special I have in mind.' She gave him another long kiss then jumped up to stir the pasta. While she was busy in the kitchen he went back into the bedroom and finished unpacking. It was only then that he came across the other gift he had bought for her.

It had been beautifully gift-wrapped by the woman in the jewellery shop at his hotel in Mexico City and he remembered how the silver choker necklace shone under the lights in the shop. He would give it to her after dinner.

When he returned to the kitchen, he saw she had set the table with Rosenthal dishes and Georg Jensen cutlery and there were candles lit at each end of the table. She had placed a bottle of Pinot Grigio on the table and asked Martin to open it and pour two glasses. 'Is this a local wine?' he asked. 'No, it's actually from Argentina and was recommended by the wine merchant in my local shopping centre. I'm serving the pasta now Martin so please be seated.' She brought two steaming dishes of spaghetti bolognaise to the table and a large bowl of mixed salad. They clinked glasses and smiled at each other. Later, they finished the meal with raspberries and lemon gelato. After they had cleared the table and set the dishwasher in motion, they moved to the lounge so they could talk without the whir of the dishwasher disturbing them.

When they had settled down, Martin produced the other gift he had brought for her from Mexico. When she opened the box and saw the beautiful necklace, she gave him a big hug and asked him to place it around her neck so she could look at it in the mirror in the bedroom. Five minutes later she returned carrying a large package. 'Martin, as this has turned into gift giving time, I have something here for your birthday. I was going to wait until tomorrow after you had rested but it seems an appropriate time now.' He opened the package and took out a brown leather jacket and a smaller cardboard box. Inside was a matching pair of leather boots. 'When I was with you in Houston I took note of the sizes shown on the labels in your suit coat and in your shoes. I had them custom made here in Bilbao so if they need any alterations it can easily be arranged. The leather is of the finest Spanish quality.' Martin stood up and tried on the jacket and it fitted perfectly. He then tried on the boots which he told her were superbly comfortable. 'What a *bienvenido* this has turned out to be…thanks a million my love. That's one of the few Spanish words I recognise as I have seen it on big signs everywhere in this lovely country welcoming travellers at airports and train stations and of course, it was your greeting when I arrived tonight.'

'By the way Martin, I have reserved a table for six at a lovely restaurant tomorrow night and you will meet my parents who have moved back to Bilbao recently now that my father has retired. He was one of the Presidents of the Chambers at the National Court of Spain in Madrid. This is the highest court in the country and has jurisdiction over all of Spain.

My mother and father are looking forward to finally getting to meet you and I know they'll have lots of questions for you! The other couple who will join us will be my Uncle José and Aunt Marianna who invited you to their home for dinner when you were assisting the police following the murder of a man on the Funicular here. Thanks to them for also inviting me to dinner that *fateful* night, we met and as they say in the classics….the rest is history! As you know, my uncle is the chief inspector of the Bilbao police and when I called him to say you were arriving today he told me he wants to hear all about your adventures since you were here three years ago. It looks like I'm not going to have much time alone with you this weekend!' Martin replied he was looking forward to meeting her parents and to renew his acquaintance with her uncle and aunt.

'Why did you describe our meeting at your uncle and aunt's home as that *fateful* night?' She smiled and told him that he would get his answer when they turned out the lights shortly!

The next morning, Martin awakened to the sound of birds singing outside the bedroom window and immediately noticed that Isabella was not there. He looked at the clock and saw that it was 10.30 and wandered down to the kitchen where he saw his lovely lady standing at the stove cooking an omelette. He walked up and gave her a hug from behind and kissed her neck. 'Buenos dias', he whispered in her ear. 'Buen dias', she replied. 'Didn't I say it correctly,' he asked. 'Yes, that is the more formal version of good morning but in modern Spanish we prefer to use the shorter version.' He asked, 'What have you planned for us to do today?' She placed the dishes on the table and answered, 'I am taking you to the Guggenheim Museum as there are some great exhibitions on there at the moment. Apart from displaying many of their own collection of masterpieces which had not been out on show for many years, they have a special exhibition of cars and their connection with architecture. This has been jointly curated with the famous British architect Norman Foster and it has been receiving rave reviews from the public. The promotion for this exhibition states that many of the vehicles on display belong to private collectors and have not been shown to the public before.'

Before they left to go to the museum, Isabella showed Martin the proof photos taken by the local photographer for the Houston Chronicle. There were a couple of nice shots of her standing in front of a non-descript city building and one of her at her desk. None revealed the location which is precisely what Martin had requested.

They spent about three hours at the Guggenheim looking at the *Masterpieces from their Collection* which included huge canvases painted by some of the most famous of the well-known artists. They agreed that it certainly was a most impressive collection and well suited to the environment where they were hanging. They had stopped by a huge painting by Andy Warhol called *One hundred and fifty multicolored Marilyns* that was over ten metres wide when Martin remarked, 'Earlier this year, another of his paintings of Marilyn Monroe sold at auction for one hundred and ninety five million dollars. It was the highest figure ever paid for a painting by an American artist.' After a short break for coffee, they went to look at the display of automobiles which was called *Motion – Autos, Art, Architecture.*

Martin counted forty vehicles which were displayed in the centre of the gallery exhibition hall. On the surrounding walls were paintings and architectural drawings related to the automobile industry. 'There are some amazing looking vehicles here most of which I have never seen before, and some which I had seen in a huge car museum just outside Shepparton, a town north of Melbourne near the border with New South Wales. I stopped to look at the cars and other vehicles on display as I drove into the town to see the new Shepparton Art Museum, better known as SAM, just before I left for New York to give evidence in the murder trial.'

Returning to Isabella's home late afternoon, they sat and discussed the exhibition with a glass of the Pinot Grigio they had opened the night before. Isabella told him about the restaurant they were going to tonight. 'It is a fabulous old building that had once been a market and is now called *Casa Victor Montes*. According to a framed notice on the wall near the entrance, on October 3, 1997, it hosted the signing of the Guggenheim Museum project. The event was attended by local government officials and the architect Frank Gehry himself. Since then, I have been informed that many famous people from around the world have dined there. So tonight they can add Martin Taylor to their list of *famous people* who have expanded their fine dining experience at this restaurant!'

They then dressed for the big night out and Isabella looked resplendent in a gorgeous cocktail dress topped off with the silver necklace Martin had given her. He asked her if he should wear the Texan necktie that she had bought for him when they were together in San Antonio and she nodded saying, 'It will be a standout dear…I'm sure you'll be the only man there attired that way!'

She volunteered to drive as she knew the way and would be easier than having to direct him….besides that means he could have a drink or two! 'Uncle José is picking up my parents so we can go straight there. I have reserved the table for 8 o'clock which gives us plenty of time to talk and for you to get to know everyone better before ordering our meals. As you may well remember, eating dinner out at night is a late affair in Spain and usually not starting before 9 o'clock.'

Martin recalled his first night in Madrid for the police convention three years ago when he wandered into a restaurant opposite his hotel around 7 o'clock and discovered that meals weren't served until much later. 'That was when I met two American police officers who were also there for the convention one of whom remains a friend. His name is Charlie Watson and it was he who introduced me to his cousin in the New York Police Department. He was also instrumental in helping us get away from our kidnappers in Mexico City two weeks ago.'

Isabella asked Martin what he would like to do tomorrow and he told her he'd really like to ride the funicular to the top of the mountain overlooking the city as this for him had very sentimental memories.

'After all, my first ride on this train is what brought the two of us together.'

'The forecast is for a lovely warm sunny day tomorrow,' she told him, 'so that will be a nice touristy thing for us to do.'

He then told her he would like for the two of them to discuss their future together and kick around some ideas how we can best work things out. 'Let's not complicate this evening's celebratory dinner with your family but wait until we are alone tomorrow.'

'I agree,' Isabella replied.... 'tonight I just want to have a good time with you and my family.' She looked at the clock on the wall and announced it was time to go. 'Parking can be difficult in that part of town, especially on a Saturday night, so I'll need to find a parking garage as close as I can to the restaurant.' They set off around 7.30 and Martin sat back and enjoyed looking at the lovely old buildings which lined the streets of the old city. 'It's pleasing to see that developers haven't torn down these buildings and replaced them with modern concrete and glass edifices which would have ruined the character of the place,' he commented. 'The centre of Bilbao is protected by strict heritage regulations and these have succeeded in maintaining the beauty of our city,' Isabella told him.

As she cruised slowly along the Plaza Nueva, Martin pointed to a large blue sign with a white P and said, 'Let's see if they have a vacant spot for you to park Isabella.' She followed the sign into a laneway that opened up to a small parking lot. There was a machine at the entrance that required swiping a credit card which lifted the boom gate. There was a fixed charge for Saturday night of ten Euros. They found a spot just large enough for her Peugeot SUV and they walked back to the restaurant. Martin had brought along his SLR camera and took a photo of Isabella standing on the steps at the imposing looking entrance.

The front of the building had the appearance of a very attractive old delicatessen shop with lots of marble in the façade and old fashioned sign-writing proclaiming wines and liqueurs of the best brands and select groceries. Isabella explained that it had originally been a large food and drink market and the restaurant owners wanted to retain that image. 'In fact,' she continued, 'you will see as we pass through the front bar area, that the walls and counters are covered with all kinds of delicious culinary goodies which are for sale.' Martin had never seen anything like the interior of this restaurant before and snapped a number of photos as he followed Isabella into the main dining room. Every centimetre of shelf space had bottles of wines, spirits and liqueurs as well as boxes of crackers, cheeses and all kinds of delicatessen items.

A waiter greeted them at the front of the dining room and Isabella gave him her name under which the reservation had been made. He consulted his iPad and then led them to a table for six which was set along the side wall. They sat down on a padded bench with their backs against the wall so they would spot the family when they arrived. The waiter poured glasses of sparkling water then moved away. 'This is certainly an amazing place you chose for tonight my love, and the atmosphere is electric.' He had just leant closer and given her a kiss when a voice shattered the intimacy of the moment. 'Lucky we came when we did Martin….there's no telling what might have happened next if we had arrived a little later!' Isabella chided her Uncle José as Martin stood up and shook the hand of the Chief Inspector. He said hello to Marianna Segueras and then turned to greet Isabella's parents. 'This is my mother Rosetta, and my father Victor,' she informed Martin. They all sat down and within seconds the waiter reappeared and poured glasses of sparkling water for the new arrivals.

Pre-dinner drinks were ordered and the waiter passed around the menus before moving away to the bar. As the chats got under way, Martin studied the faces of Isabella's parents. He could immediately see that Isabella had inherited her mother's good looks as she was a fine looking woman. Her father was somewhat handsome although Martin could see a measure of sternness in his facial expression. Probably a result of sitting on the bench in court and having to bring down heavy sentences on desperate criminals he decided. The talking subsided while menus were consulted and orders placed.

José was anxious to hear about Martin's exploits since they had last met but his wife cut in and said, 'Let's give the poor man some time to enjoy himself tonight José. Isabella told me on the phone yesterday that Martin will be here for a week so I'd like to invite him to visit us when he has some free time and he can tell us all about it then.' Marianna also said she would like Martin to come to dinner so they get to know him under quieter conditions than in a crowded restaurant. Martin thanked them and said he would make sure he made time to spend with all of them.

As Isabella expected, the dishes started arriving around 9 o'clock and talk was reduced considerably as the party began to consume an absolutely delicious meal. Some fine Spanish and French wines were enjoyed with each course and the repast ended with a huge cheese platter complimented by an excellent Portuguese port. Martin asked the waiter to take a photo of the whole group at the table before they left the restaurant. He then requested the bill and the waiter told him that it had already been taken care of by the gentleman with the moustache….. Isabella's father.

As José had parked in the same parking lot as Isabella, they all walked together to their cars and said goodnight there in the car park promising to speak again in the next day or so. On the drive back, Martin told Isabella how much he enjoyed the company of her family which prompted her to say, 'I knew that you'd like my parents and I could tell that they felt the same about you. I was also pleased that they didn't start quizzing us about wedding plans although I'm sure they would have liked to.'

Once back at Isabella's, they decided to relax in a hot tub and allow the big meal to settle before going to bed. 'I feel really revitalized after that,' said Martin. 'That is what I was hoping for,' Isabella informed him!

CHAPTER 17

DECISION TIME.

They slept late Sunday morning, and the two bleary eyed lovers sat opposite each other in their night attire drinking freshly squeezed orange juice. Neither was hungry after the huge dinner they had consumed the previous night which hadn't finished until almost midnight. 'Wow,' exclaimed Martin, 'that was some feast we had and thanks for arranging it Isabella, but I am embarrassed that your father paid the bill as I had intended to take care of it myself.' She smiled and told him, 'My father insisted, telling me it was his way of welcoming you into the family.' Then she added, 'Judges are very well paid you know, and he can well afford it!'

Later in the morning when they were dressed ready to go out, she asked Martin if he wanted to go to the funicular then or have their serious talk first. 'Let's do the tourist thing and we can relax back here afterwards for our chat.' Martin decided to drive as he was keen to get used to finding his way around Bilbao because he was certain that he would be spending more and more of his time in this city. Isabella directed him to the old area of town where the funicular station is located at the bottom of Mount Artxanda. They found a parking spot in a nearby street and walked to the Plaza del Funicular. 'I remember the entrance to the station,' he told Isabella, 'it's kind of hidden at the end of the plaza and I almost missed it the time I was here before.' They purchased return tokens and waited for the train that was on its way down.

When it docked, the driver got out and walked to the other end to take the carriage back up to the top. As he passed them, he turned and stared at Martin for a moment then stopped. He spoke in Spanish and Isabella translated. 'He asked if you are the English man who witnessed a murder on the funicular about three years ago. If it's OK with you Martin I'll tell him you are that person.' He answered by nodding his head and walked over to shake the driver's hand. Smiling, the driver told Isabella that he couldn't stay there any longer as he needed to get the train moving and enable the one at the top to start its decent. They boarded the old carriage and away it rumbled upwards at a leisurely pace.

Halfway up the steep slope, the other train went by at the passing loop. Martin looked into the train as it passed expecting to see some action but of course nothing happened. 'That was an eerie experience,' he said to Isabella, 'I don't know what I was expecting but it was like I had stepped back three years into another time.' At the top, the driver approached and said he had a couple of minutes to talk before he had to head back down. Isabella quickly mentioned that she and Martin were now engaged to marry and that he wasn't British but Australian. They shook hands again and Martin dug deep to remember the Spanish word for goodbye. 'Adios Señor,' he managed to say. The driver grinned and waved as he hurried off to the front of the train.

Isabella and Martin walked to the nearby lookout to admire the best view of the Guggenheim Museum. They wandered about for an hour or so looking at the quaint old houses that lined the road.

Isabella told him that a lot of the residents living up here worked and shopped in the city so the funicular was the quickest form of transport to use to ascend and descend to the CBD.

Later, down in the plaza below, they sat at a café and enjoyed cups of strong coffee with a plate of Churros, the favourite Spanish delicacy, served with a choice of hot chocolate or butterscotch sauce. Afterwards, they walked slowly hand-in-hand back to where the car was parked and as they passed a noisy bar Martin noticed some men sitting with their backs to the open window. They were wearing the leather jackets proudly displaying the name and logo of *The Villains*. Isabella followed his gaze and frowned. They kept walking and when they were sitting in her car, she told Martin that *The Villains* had been branded as an outlaw motorcycle club last year following arrests in towns along the Mediterranean coast. In a very concerned voice she added, 'The police had charged club leaders with possessing and dealing massive quantities of drugs. There have also been a number of shootings between them and rival motorcycle gangs in San Sebastian. Fortunately our law practice is only involved with commercial cases but I know some lawyers who have taken on work defending gangsters on drug charges and they finish up nervous wrecks.'

As they drove to Isabella's home, Martin kept his eyes peeled for any signs of them being followed but as there were none he decided once again that he was having a bout of paranoia. He drove the car into her garage and parked alongside Isabella's SUV. They entered the house directly from the garage and settled themselves down in the lounge. Martin straightaway broached the subject of a wedding date and where it should be held. 'The first problem as I see it,' he said, 'is that whichever of our countries is decided upon, it will mean either your family and friends or mine would have to travel to the other side of the world to attend. Choosing an alternative location somewhere, say approximately halfway between our two countries could be a solution but both options would be costly for anyone wishing to attend.'

Isabella excused herself for a minute, got up and went to the kitchen. She returned with a bottle of wine and a bowl of potato crisps. While Martin poured the wine, she told him she had thought hard and long about this issue. 'I believe we can keep things simple by proposing the following. We'll have a small formal wedding either here or in Melbourne with just close family attending. For instance if we have it in Bilbao, my parents plus Uncle José and Aunt Marianna and their two children would attend. You could bring your mother, sister, brother-in-law and their children. If we chose to marry in Melbourne, the reverse would be easy to arrange. As for timing, I would like our wedding to take place in spring so the month would depend on which place we settle on. After the wedding, we could honeymoon in or close to the country where we married and afterwards have a party for all our friends in that city. Soon after we would visit the other country and throw another party for our friends there.'

Martin thought about this for some time before responding. 'What you suggest makes perfect sense and I'd like to add the following: As my business is located in both our countries and your law partnership is here, I propose that we wed in Bilbao in the northern spring which is only a couple of months away, then shortly after our honeymoon fly to Melbourne for a week.

My office manager, Jessica Wainwright has shown to be extremely competent each time I have been travelling overseas and I have absolute trust in her. For that reason, before I left to go to New York for the murder trial, I offered her a junior partnership in the business.

One more thing Isabella: as we are of different religions, I would like our wedding to be performed by a marriage celebrant. You have never mentioned whether your parents are particularly religious or not so I hope this wouldn't upset them.' Isabella smiled as she informed him that people in the Basque region were generally somewhat less religious than in other parts of Spain. 'This may be a throwback from the civil war of 1936 to 1939 when that evil General Franco tried to wipe out the entire Basque population with the help of the Nazis. So, to allay your fears be assured that my parents will graciously accept that we are having a non-religious wedding.'

Isabella opened up the calendar on her phone and selected two Sunday dates in May and two in June. 'I'll look into celebrants and ask amongst friends for a recommendation of a small intimate venue. Let's run through who would be at the actual wedding.' By the time they had counted up the immediate family members and included themselves, it numbered thirteen. 'I'm not superstitious,' Martin told her, 'what about you?' Before she could answer, they both heard the noise of motorbikes roaring up and down the street outside. Martin drew aside the curtain on the lounge room window just enough to peer out. 'Damn,' he exclaimed, 'there are four of them riding slowly passed and then turning around and coming back again. Assuming the instruction to keep harassing me has filtered down from Mexico to Houston, then to Melbourne and on to Bilbao, how the hell did they find me at your address?' Isabella immediately wanted to call her Uncle José and tell him what was going on outside. 'Hold on dear, let me go out and confront them first so I can try to establish what their intentions are before you drag your uncle and the entire Bilbao police force out on a quiet Sunday afternoon. Maybe all they have been instructed to do is make life uncomfortable for me wherever I am.' Isabella was dead set against this idea and told him, 'These men have a well-earned reputation for being ruthless and you would be heavily outnumbered confronting them in the street. I need my husband-to-be staying in one piece for the wedding.' Before she had finished talking, Martin had stood up and was heading to the front door.

She followed him, and realising he was determined to stand up to these thugs, she asked him to wait one moment before opening the door. She disappeared into one of the spare bedrooms and a couple of minutes later reappeared with a rifle. 'Don't look so shocked Martin, I am a lot tougher than you ever imagined! My dad used to take me deer hunting in the National Park a few hours from here. I have a license for the gun and if I may so, I'm not a bad shot. Anyway, it's not loaded but might scare them off just staring down the barrel.' He smiled as he took the rifle, kissed her and went out to face the mob. As soon as they saw him walk out onto the road carrying the weapon, they spun around and roared off down the street at such a speed that their tyres left skid marks for about 30 metres on the tarmac.

As he was walking back to the house, a neighbour appeared and called out something in Spanish which Martin didn't understand. Fortunately Isabella had followed him out the front door at that moment and answered the man. He came over and she introduced Martin as her fiancée from Australia. 'Pleased to meet you Martin,' he said as he shook hands, Isabella has told me a little about you. My name is Antonio Lopez and my son Juan works for your Bilbao office. Isabella had suggested that he submit his CV when you were establishing your branch here. What was going on with those motorcyclists just now?' Martin briefly explained that he had a run in with members of the same gang in other countries and they appeared to be following him wherever he goes. 'I apologize for being responsible for upsetting the peacefulness of this neighbourhood. Hopefully brandishing Isabella's unloaded hunting rifle in their faces earlier will make them realise it will be in their best interests not to mess with us. Incidentally, I congratulate you on speaking such good English as I have yet to take Spanish lessons. I will be meeting Juan tomorrow morning at the office and later we are going to San Sebastian to follow up on an assignment we are working on.' They said goodbye, and moved inside to continue the important discussions regarding the wedding plans. The rifle was once again locked away in its special storage cupboard.

Isabella firstly told Martin that she was blessed with marvellous neighbours who looked out for her and Antonio and his wife Marta were especially close. 'You'll like Juan too when you meet him tomorrow. He is definitely a chip off his father's block. If you are wondering how it is Antonio speaks such excellent English, it's because he has a very successful corporate travel agency that specializes in arranging travel for government departments and large businesses. He handles all our firm's travel arrangements as well as mine when I've been to Australia to spend time with you and more recently when I travelled to Houston.'

After dinner, they sat down to design the wedding invitation which they decided to produce themselves on a computer. It wasn't worth getting them professionally printed for such a small number of guests. Besides as Martin pointed out, Isabella has such a good eye for design, he was confident that the finished invitation would be quite unique. 'I'll design it in such a way that with a little modification we'll turn it into the *after wedding party* invitation,' she suggested. Deciding that they'd had enough excitement for one day and were about to get ready for bed when the telephone rang. She was surprised to hear the voice of her uncle at this time on a Sunday night. 'Is something wrong Uncle José?'

'I had a call earlier from your neighbour Antonio Lopez, who as you know is also my good friend, to tell me that you have been stalked by a bunch of motorcyclists. He said that Martin confronted them waving an unloaded rifle and the group then high-tailed it out of there in a hurry. We've had problems with outlaw motorcycle gangs for some years but this is the first time an issue has arisen that affects someone from my family and this concerns me greatly. I would like Martin to call me tomorrow and tell me what has prompted this form of harassment so I can ensure neither of you find yourselves in a dangerous situation.' She thanked him and told him that Martin would call from his office tomorrow.

After she related her uncle's conversation to Martin, he apologized for dragging her family into his problems, 'I didn't want to involve others in my war with *The Villains* but following my run-in with the mob today, I guess I can be thankful that your uncle is the Bilbao chief of police.'

'I am his only niece and he treats me like a daughter. He has been my protector since I was a small child and especially while my Dad was on the bench in Madrid for years. Uncle José was always there looking out for my wellbeing so you can appreciate his concern when he was told of the *fun and games* that took place outside my house this afternoon.'

Martin smiled and took her hand as he led her to the bedroom.

CHAPTER 18

GROWING PAINS IN SPAIN.

Isabella suggested that as his office was only two blocks from hers, he could follow her Monday morning and when he arrived at *Taylored Investigations S.A.* she would continue on to her office. Martin's company leased a small office in a modern building on the edge of the CBD. He didn't know how many spaces they had in the building's car park so he parked the rental car in the street and pressed the buzzer by the front door to announce his arrival. The door clicked open and he took the elevator to the second floor. The office manager, Dario Montoya was standing by the open door and greeted Martin with a cheery smile. 'Welcome Mr. Taylor, I trust you are well after your long journey?' Shaking his hand, Martin followed Dario into the office. It was a reasonably sized open plan layout with four desks each set up with a large screen computer monitor and telephone. Along one wall were filing cabinets and a free-standing colour printer. There were some framed tourist posters hanging on the walls which helped to dispel the austere atmosphere of the office and Martin was pleased to note that it was also very clean. In one corner there was a table with an automatic coffee machine and a row of mugs.

'I've only been here once before Dario, when I came to sign the lease and interviewed you. You've done an excellent job setting it up and thank you for that. As you know I will assist Juan to clear up the outstanding issues with his San Sebastian assignment and had asked him to meet me here this morning. Do you know where he is?' Dario answered that Juan had come in early to meet Martin and was in the utility room making coffee for them. 'He should be here any minute Mr. Taylor.' Martin held back from asking Dario to call him by his first name suspecting that it was probably customary in Spain to address one's superior in a formal manner. He would check with Isabella this evening.

They reviewed current assignments as well as ones recently completed and Martin was suitably impressed with Dario's record keeping. They have three new inquiries for work in the Basque region and two requiring someone in Madrid. An on-line ad has been posted looking for people in both Bilbao and Madrid with a background in art. Applicants should be conversant with European languages and English. Dario is expecting submissions this week. As Martin will be back in Bilbao from San Sebastian in a couple of days, Dario suggested they review the applicants for the new assignments together on his return.

Juan arrived carrying a coffee for Martin and shook his hand as he greeted him. For the rest of the morning, they studied the reports on the San Sebastian case together. They began with his initial visit to the art gallery in San Sebastian where Señor Garcia Sanchez, the owner, described in detail his negotiations with the buyer of an expensive painting by the late 19th–early 20th century Basque artist Adolfo Guiard. The sale price included replacing the original picture frame with a more modern design which the gallery was to organise. A 50% deposit was paid and it was agreed that the remainder of the price would be paid on delivery to the buyer's home in Biarritz, which is just over the border in France. The painting was taken to a renowned framing company in Bilbao.

When Señor Sanchez returned to inspect the painting in the new frame, he was pleased to see they had carried out the work satisfactorily. He had them pack it securely and send it by courier to the buyer's address in Biarritz. An invoice was then sent for the outstanding 50%. After many weeks had passed and the invoice remained unpaid, Señor Sanchez tried to contact the buyer by telephone but his calls went unanswered. A debt collection agency was sent to the buyer's home but he wouldn't speak with them when they appeared on his doorstep. As the amount owing was seventy five thousand Euros, Señor Sanchez asked around other art gallery owners he knew if they could recommend a private detective agency that specialized in art crime.

Juan elaborated, 'This resulted in us being contracted and as you know I met with him in San Sebastian, then drove to Biarritz to see the buyer whose name is Pierre Beaumont. I telephoned him first and explained our role making sure that I was friendly and not confronting which paid off as he agreed to meet with me. He suggested one of the bars along the beautiful Biarritz beachfront. He first confirmed that he had received the painting but in his opinion the new frame was not to his liking and he believed that there was now some damage to the painting due to the framing company's negligence. In a conciliatory tone he then offered to pay a further 10% of the outstanding amount and said that in his opinion it was a reasonable offer. He told me to pass this on to Señor Sanchez and to emphasize that it was a *take it or leave it gesture* with no further negotiations. He then got up and left the bar without saying anything further.' Martin considered everything Juan had reported and instructed him to spend the afternoon checking with the authorities in Biarritz if Monsieur Beaumont had ever been before the courts for fraud. 'Meanwhile, please contact Señor Sanchez and tell him we'll be at his gallery by 11 o'clock tomorrow morning to assure him that we'll be doing everything we can to see he is fully compensated for the painting.'

Dario told Martin that turning on refreshments for the visiting company CEO was a must, and besides he said, 'We wanted to make you feel quite at home here.' Coffee and pastries were then distributed and Martin sat at an empty desk to call Chief Inspector José Segueras at the Bilbao police headquarters. He was connected to him immediately when he telephoned and described in full what had occurred in Mexico City and the subsequent harassment by *The Villains* thugs, first in Houston then again in Melbourne and now here. The Police Chief proposed that CCTV cameras should be installed on Isabella's house not only at the front but on each side and at the rear as well. 'I have exclusive arrangements with a company here that specialises in that industry and they will do the job immediately and at a good price. I will make sure they are installed tomorrow as I know you are going to the coast for a couple of days and I want my niece properly protected while you are away. I will have them program the system so I am able to look at what is going on at any time of the day or night. Please inform Isabella of my intentions when you see her later and assure her that it will be a worthwhile investment. She'll probably protest that it sounds like over-kill but I'll rely on you Martin to convince her.' Martin agreed and thanked him.

He spent the rest of the afternoon reading through the new inquiries with Dario and helped establish the quotations to be sent to new clients. He walked over to Juan who was working at his desk and asked him if he resided with his parents.

'Yes Mr. Taylor, I recently moved back home after ending a relationship in which I was living at my girlfriend's place.' Martin then proposed that Juan ring Isabella's doorbell at 8 o'clock in the morning and they would set off in Juan's car. 'You know exactly where we're going and your travel costs are included in our charges to the client. Bring an overnight bag as we'll be staying somewhere in Biarritz for the night.'

He then went out to his car, set the GPS to Isabella's saved address and drove there feeling that he had achieved a lot today. Isabella had given him a spare remote to the garage and the alarm code to enter the house from the side door. He decided that as he was home first he would prepare dinner tonight and give Isabella a break. Opening the fridge he found that she had stocked up with plenty of food in preparation for his visit. He put together a bowl of salad to have with a mushroom omelette. He whipped up the eggs and then set them aside to wait for her to arrive before cooking. Opening and closing all the kitchen cupboards and drawers until he found the dishes and cutlery, he then set the table.

He had just sat down and was reading the Channel 9 Melbourne news on his phone when he heard the garage door opening and soon after Isabella came in. He got up and welcomed her with a hug and a kiss. She looked tired so he told her that after she had freshened up to come back and relax while he cooked their dinner. He found a tub of olives in the fridge and put them out with a glass of sauvignon blanc. She came back having changed into a smart casual outfit and gave him a grateful smile as she sat down with the glass of wine. 'So how did things work out at your office today?' He sat down beside her and clinked their glasses of wine as he answered. 'It went very well and I am pleased with the way Dario is managing the business, 'We are having growing pains now as our name spreads around the country and inquiries are pouring in. Dario has to be selective in which ones he follows up as he and Juan are limited to how many assignments they can handle until we take on additional staff. He has advertised for people and we'll review candidates together when I return from Biarritz.'

'How long do you expect to be away?'

'Just tomorrow night.... Juan and I will go to see the client in San Sebastian tomorrow then drive to Biarritz and look for a hotel for the night. We'll meet with the guy who is refusing to pay the remainder of his account the next morning and then return to Bilbao that evening. That reminds me Isabella, your uncle has arranged to have CCTV cameras installed here tomorrow so that you can see what's going on outside particularly when you are here alone. He will also have it programmed so he can check on you from his phone as well. If you are not happy with this arrangement, you should call him tonight at home.'

'I'll think about it over dinner and then call Uncle José later to give him my decision. What do you think of the idea of me being monitored 24/7 Martin?' His immediate response was, 'To be quite honest Isabella, I think it's a great idea and I'll feel more relaxed knowing you are being looked after especially when I'm not in Bilbao.'

He moved back into the kitchen to cook the omelette and finish preparing the salad. Later when he was clearing away the dishes, Isabella called her uncle and after a few minutes of discussion about how the CCTV system would operate, she agreed to have it installed. Martin told her that he was happy that she had accepted his advice.... particularly as José had already arranged for the contractor's people to be there at 7 o'clock in the morning!

Whilst she was on the phone speaking to her mother, Martin packed a few clothes into his small carry-on bag for tomorrow and then came back to the living room just as she hung up the phone. They talked some more about their marriage plans and Martin brought up the subject again on who they should actually invite to the wedding in Bilbao. 'I thought about this while I was preparing our dinner earlier and came to the opinion that there are some other people I would like to be here for the actual wedding ceremony apart from our close families. For example I would add to the list my closest friends Aart and Helena van den Haag and Paul and Doreen Cohen. These friends would not have a problem with the cost of travelling here.' Isabella agreed that this was a good idea and added her thoughts on the matter.

'That would solve any superstitious concerns we may have had when the number of attendees was thirteen! If we do add to the list I would include my wonderful neighbours Antonio and Marta Lopez and this would also please my uncle as they are such close friends. I thought about inviting my partners at our law firm but that would have swollen the number by another eight when you include their husbands and wives. We'll invite them to the after party.'

'That's my feeling also about the employees at my two offices. They'll also be invited to the parties we'll have later. If my maths is correct, that makes a total of nineteen, including us, at the wedding which sounds like a manageable number. That reminds me....what is the protocol regarding how employees should address their management? In Australia it is not

225

uncommon for staff to be on first-name basis with their superiors but I have a feeling that may not be the case here.'

'We would normally expect our employees to address us by our surname preceded by our title. Europeans are usually far more formal in their ways than Australians and we feel this is particularly important in maintaining the status quo in business relations.'

Isabella told Martin that she had to attend court in the morning for a pre-trial hearing for a new case she was now working on. 'My client is suing the owner of a large commercial building developer because the shop she purchased is nothing like the property she had chosen from the plan prior to construction starting. It has ended up smaller and not facing the main street which is what she wanted for her business. The developer is claiming that the council forced him to change the plans and has offered the woman a small refund but money is not the key to the issue…..the shop's size and orientation is of paramount importance.

Anyway as the court doesn't open until 10 o'clock I'll be here to show the CCTV people around before I leave. Fortunately they won't need access inside the house until the following day and I can be here then.'

CHAPTER 19

MARTIN'S MINI-WAR BETWEEN SPAIN AND FRANCE.

Juan was waiting kerbside at precisely 8 o'clock when Martin came out the front door. Isabella was outside discussing placement of the CCTV cameras with the contractor sent by her uncle. She turned and waved to Martin as he tossed his overnight bag into the back of Juan's late model Peugeot 308. Martin strapped himself into the passenger seat and greeted Juan.

'Thanks for being so punctual, I believe it's important that we arrive on time at the gallery in San Sebastian. What reaction did you get from Señor Sanchez when you told him that I would be coming with you?'

"He seemed surprised that the owner of the company had come from the other side of the world to fight for justice on his behalf. I assured him that the company treated all their clients with utmost care and attention. I also explained that you had combined this visit with other business to attend to whilst you were in Bilbao.'

'Well done Juan, you replied to his comment in a suitably diplomatic way. Now, what have you found out about the guy in Biarritz…Monsieur Pierre Beaumont?'

'It appears that he has been declared bankrupt twice over the past ten years and somehow managed to bounce back each time following mysterious injections of cash into his bank account to pay off his business debts. He runs an importing business specializing in farm machinery most of which is manufactured in Asia. He has been under investigation by the French National Police but so far no charges have been laid. Interpol has also been investigating him.'

'Sounds like a nice character that we'll be dealing with tomorrow Juan. Did you by any chance think to inquire with Inspector Segueras in case he knows something about this character?'

'I did consider it but ran out of time yesterday Mr. Taylor'

'Never mind Juan, I'll call him myself later.'

By now they were passing through verdant countryside towards the coast and whilst Juan was concentrating on his driving Martin was sitting back enjoying being a tourist. They arrived at the outskirts of San Sebastian around 10.30 and twenty minutes later pulled up outside a smart looking art gallery. Martin followed Juan to the front door which was locked. Pushing the security button and announcing who they were, a buzz sounded and Juan pushed open the front door. Garcia Sanchez greeted them and waved them inside. Martin studied their client and guessed his age would be around sixty. He was of a tall slim build with a mop of jet black hair and a fine black moustache. They were led past walls covered with many large impressionist style paintings to an office at the rear of the gallery. Juan explained that Martin did not speak Spanish so it would be better to hold their meeting in English. 'That's no problem as I have had a lot of American and British customers passing through San Sebastian so have polished up my knowledge of English over the past decade or so.'

'Thank you Señor Sanchez, I apologize that I only know a few words of Spanish but I will be taking lessons soon as it is my intention to spend more time in my Bilbao office in the near future. Now I would like to discuss the question of how best to deal with Monsieur Pierre Beaumont? Juan has discovered that this person appears to be a rogue businessman who might be involved in illegal dealings through his import company. We also heard that he has a large art collection. Had you dealt with him prior to the painting you sold him recently?'

'No, but I have checked with other private gallery owners along the Basque coast and learnt that he had cheated two others out of the agreed-upon full price. One was paid only 60% and the other 70% and agreed to accept his offer as they did not want to pursue the outstanding amounts by hiring expensive lawyers. I on the other hand do not want him to get away with his fraudulent ways and unlike my colleagues I have no qualms in pursuing him by all the means available to me.'

'Rest assured, Señor Sanchez, Juan and I will use all our powers of persuasion to ensure we don't leave Biarritz without the money you are rightfully owed. Please give me a copy of the invoice showing the agreed purchase price minus the 50% deposit and highlight the balance owing. Juan probably didn't mention it before but I was a senior detective in Melbourne starting my own agency specializing in art fraud cases. I tracked down and subsequently brought to justice numerous criminals like Monsieur Pierre Beaumont so my goal will be to stop him cheating innocent business people such as you once and for all.'

Señor Sanchez prepared the invoice and handed Juan a copy for them to take to the meeting tomorrow in Biarritz. He then wanted to show his gratitude by inviting them to have lunch at a small café a few doors along the street. Martin had wanted to leave immediately for Biarritz as he assumed it would take a few hours but Juan told him that they would be there in an hour or so as it wasn't very far. They accepted the invitation as they did not want to appear rude.

'Thanks Señor Sanchez, we'll just have a snack and then hit the road as soon as we can. Can you recommend a hotel in Biarritz?'

'I certainly can Mr. Taylor, it is called *Le Bayonne* and is centrally located and unlike most of the older hotels it has secure parking. It has 4 star rating and I have found it to be spotlessly clean each time I have stayed there. I'll give you the address and phone number when we are in the café as I have it in my phone.'

During their casual lunch, Martin advised Señor Sanchez that they will telephone him after they had concluded their meeting with Monsieur Beaumont tomorrow and hopefully they would be returning to San Sebastian with his money! When they were back in the car, Juan called the hotel and reserved two rooms for the night. It was off season and they had plenty of vacancies at the moment.

Juan programmed the car's GPS with the hotel's address and headed out of town. They were soon on the coastal highway heading towards Biarritz. Martin was deep in thought gathering ideas for tackling the crook tomorrow. He told Juan that it was imperative that they took the upper hand right from the start in the morning. 'We'll finalize our strategy over dinner at the hotel this evening. In the meantime, you watch the road and I'll watch the scenery!'

About an hour later they arrived at the outskirts of Biarritz and followed the GPS instructions directly to the hotel which is located on Avenue Jean Rostano. They checked in and were given instructions where to park the car. They agreed to meet in the public lounge in half an hour after they had taken their bags to their rooms and refreshed themselves. Martin took the opportunity to telephone Isabella and pass on the details of their accommodation.

'How was your day in court for the pre-trial hearing?'

"It went well and the magistrate has set a date for the case which will be in two weeks. The defence lawyer wanted more time to prepare but was told that they had already had two months to prepare and their request to delay was denied. How did you enjoy your day travelling through the northern Basque country?'

'It was most pleasant and I liked the look of San Sebastian during our short time there. I'm looking forward to when we can spend time together there and you can be my tour guide. By the way, did the CCTV firm get the cameras installed?'

'They certainly did and I have to say they were a competent bunch of people. As well as completing the installation of the cameras, the wiring has been run inside the roof space. They apparently managed that by lifting some roof tiles. When they return tomorrow, they'll install the monitor on a wall in the kitchen and program my mobile phone so I can check on my security at anytime from anywhere, even when I am abroad. Uncle José will pop in during the morning so they can program his phone at the same time they do mine.'

'That's great Isabella, I certainly feel happier that by tomorrow afternoon you'll be that much better protected. If all goes well in the morning and we achieve our goal, we should be back in Bilbao mid to late afternoon. Goodnight my love.'

'Buenas noches my darling.'

Later in the lounge, Juan told Martin that he had researched the painter who is the subject of this assignment. 'He was known as Adolfo Guiard but his full name was Adolfo Guiard Larrauri and he was born in Bilbao in the mid 1900's. He was one of 15 children whose father was a French photographer. In 1900 he participated in the first exhibition of modern art in Bilbao. His paintings are rarely seen on the market and are sought after by serious collectors. Consequently they can command high prices.'

Next morning, Martin and Juan checked out of the hotel straight after breakfast and drove to the same bar on the beachfront where Juan had met with Pierre Beaumont previously. The bar had not long opened for the day and there weren't many patrons there at this time in the morning. They looked around the dimly lit room and just when they thought they had been stood up, Juan pointed to a solitary figure sitting in the far corner. He led Martin over and greeted Monsieur Beaumont in French. A grunted response was received, 'Bonjour, asseyez-vous.' They sat down and Martin immediately took charge of the meeting.

'Mr. Beaumont, I understand that you do not intend to honour the contract you have with Señor Sanchez in San Sebastian for a painting you purchased from his gallery. We have checked into your business activities and have no doubt that you fully understand the legalities involved when one of the parties to a contract decides to break the contract? Because you have a machinery import business I assume you can speak English, but if there is anything you don't understand, please hold up your hand and I'll have Juan translate it into French.' Giving him time to digest what he had just said, Martin waved to the barman and asked for three coffees.

Monsieur Beaumont mumbled in heavily accented English that he had understood. 'Señor Sanchez wants too much money for the painting,' he began, 'and the new frame isn't exactly what I expected. The frame maker also appears to have damaged the painting as well. That is why I have made a generous offer to pay another 10%.'

'When you signed the contract of sale Mr. Beaumont, you had agreed to the price at that time and as I understand it you selected the new frame from a sample shown to you at the gallery. As for damage to the painting this is definitely unlikely because Señor Sanchez inspected the finished job at the framer's workshop and watched it being wrapped for transport and it was unmarked at that time.'

Mr. Beaumont started to mumble a reply but Martin cut him short. 'I put it to you that your behaviour in this matter is a prime example of how you carry out your business dealings. We have evidence that you have short-changed other art dealers in the Basque region and you treat it as a kind of game. Well let me assure you, Señor Sanchez is not going to play along with your game. I propose the following way to resolve this issue:

We will follow you to the address where the painting is currently located, inspect it for any damage and then we will follow you to the bank where your accounts are kept. You will have the bank prepare a teller's cheque made out in the name of Señor Sanchez for the full amount owing and we'll sign a receipt for it. Should you not accept my proposal then we will return to Bilbao and immediately commence legal proceedings against you. The outcome is certain that you not only will have to pay the amount owing but all legal costs as well and you will be a lot more out of pocket. We will make sure that if a trial ensues, it will no doubt draw a lot of unwanted publicity to you and your business ventures.' Just then the barman arrived with the coffees and they drank them in silence whilst Monsieur Beaumont considered his limited options.

With a very grim look on his face, he agreed to Martin's proposal and asked them to walk with him to his car which was parked in the same street as Juan had also parked. They then followed Monsieur Beaumont's black Mercedes 250 through the quiet streets of Biarritz to a somewhat large mansion in very pleasant surroundings. He led them inside and along a wide hallway with a number of impressive paintings lining the walls. In the lounge room he pointed to the painting that had brought on the mini-war between Spain and France and stood back to let them examine it.

Juan produced a small magnifying glass which he mentioned that he found a useful tool in inspection work and proceeded to examine the surface of the painting. After a while he turned to the Frenchman and asked him to point out the so-called damage. After a few moments, he mumbled that he couldn't see it at this moment. 'I did say that it was only slightly damaged didn't I?'

'What don't you like about the frame,' Martin asked.

"It doesn't look the same as what I had chosen from the sample book.'

Juan then opened his file folder and drew out a sheet showing the design of the selected frame which he received from Señor Sanchez. Holding the picture up next to the frame, he asked how it was different. 'Looks exactly the same to me you'll have to agree.'

Martin announced firmly, 'Monsieur Beaumont, there is no difference between that picture and the actual frame so we have proved that your claims are all nonsense. We will now follow you to the bank and wait whilst you have the cheque drawn up.'

Two hours later they were on the road back to San Sebastian carrying the bank teller's cheque for seventy five thousand euros. Juan had telephoned a delighted Señor Sanchez with the good news before they left Biarritz.

When they handed the bank cheque to Garcia Sanchez he complimented them on the success of the mission and promised to pay their account within a week after he received it. He also intended to tell all his colleagues about *Taylored Investigations S.A.* which prompted Martin to remark to Juan on the way back to Bilbao, that the sooner they increased the staff numbers the better.

It was dark when they arrived outside Isabella's home and Martin told Juan he would see him at the office tomorrow. As he walked up the path to the front door he looked up and saw the CCTV cameras under the eaves at each side of the front of the house. He unlocked the door and turned on the lights as he entered and looked around but there were no signs that Isabella had arrived home yet. He called her mobile phone number but it went to voice mail. He left a message for her to call him ASAP. Half an hour passed and there was still no response from Isabella so he tried calling her office to see if she was working late but they were closed and a recorded message in Spanish which he understood meant to call back during office hours tomorrow. He was by now becoming quite concerned and made a call to her parents but they had not spoken with her today.

Her father said that she may have stopped off at a shopping mall on her way home and probably had her phone switched off. 'If you still haven't heard from her in another hour I suggest you call José and let him start a search.'

Martin tried calling her again but her phone still seemed to be switched off. He paced up and down for a while and then decided not to wait any longer and called her uncle. Once he had explained the reason for his call, the police chief told him he would check the CCTV footage on his phone and call Martin straight back.

'There appears to be no activity recorded apart from Isabella driving off to her office early this morning and the rest of the day showed people walking their dogs and cars and delivery vans driving past. The last activity was of you getting out of Juan's car and walking up to the front door. This means that whatever happened to Isabella has taken place elsewhere during the day. I have the home number of one of her partners and will call him right now to check that she was at the office today. Stay there and I'll call you back in a few minutes.' Martin started pacing up and down again while waiting for the call.

'I have spoken with her partner Raimondo Velasco and he told me that she was in court most of the day and returned to the office around 4.30. She was still working at her desk when he left the office at 5.30. Unfortunately there are no CCTV cameras on their building but I'm certain there are others in that street as there are a number of modern city-centre apartment buildings which are likely to have cameras. I will pick you up in half an hour and we'll go together to headquarters where I will assemble a team to start the search. Should she miraculously turn up in the meantime please call me immediately otherwise I'll see you shortly.'

As expected, she did not arrive home and Martin was picked up by José thirty minutes later. At headquarters, a small team of uniformed officers were already at work checking locations of CCTV cameras along the street where Isabella's law office was situated. José had started the ball rolling with a couple of phone calls before he had left home to pick up Martin.

Martin was introduced to Sergeant Manuel Oliverez who was heading up the team and he asked if Martin had any photos of Isabella in his phone. 'I certainly do,' he answered, and opened up his mobile phone's photo gallery to show the sergeant. The phone was plugged into a computer and a couple of the photos were downloaded.

Shortly after, one of the officers reported that he had located a camera that was on the front of an apartment building diagonally opposite Isabella's office. He had tracked down the concierge and arranged for an on-line link to be sent which would enable the police to view the day's footage. Fifteen minutes later the officer opened the link and started reviewing the video which for a change was of reasonably clear quality. There was nothing untoward for the first nine hours until around 5.30 when Isabella's car was spotted emerging from the underground car park. She had just turned into the street when two motorcycles came screaming by and merged in front of her car. A couple of minutes later another two motorcycles moved into position behind her.

The *convoy* then proceeded along the street out of range of the CCTV camera. Although the video sequence did not last long, it was sufficient for Martin to speak up. 'I saw enough to recognise the jackets were those of *The Villains*.'

Chief Inspector Joseba Segueras addressed the team…. 'Does *The Villains* club have a chapter in Bilbao?' Sergeant Oliverez answered, 'As far as I know chief, this outlaw motorcycle gang has its main chapter in Barcelona but is quite small in the Basque region. We'll check, but I suspect that the local chapter will be in San Sebastian, certainly not in Bilbao or we would know about it.'

Just then, Martin's phone rang and when he answered, a gruff voice started babbling in Spanish. He switched to speaker mode and calmly asked the caller what they wanted. There was silence for a moment then Isabella came on the line saying that she was being held hostage somewhere in the countryside. While she was speaking, one of the officers moved closer to Martin's phone with a recording device and microphone. Everything being said was now being recorded. 'Are you OK Isabella?' Martin asked. Before she could answer the phone must have been snatched away by one of her captors.

The gruff voice came back on and this time he spoke in broken English.

'Your lady will entertain us until you put together two million euros in cash which we want in exchange for her release. We call you in half hour with instructions.' One of the officers took Martin's phone and called the IT specialist who was on duty this evening. 'Please track the location that the last call came from and make it quick please…we've got a hostage situation and every minute counts.'

A video projector was switched on and a large map of the Bilbao region was then displayed on a screen. The Chief had returned to his office to take a call and he came back to tell Martin that it was Isabella's father wanting to know what was going on. 'I told him where we were at right now and he understands how serious the situation is….after all, my brother was a judge for many years and no doubt has seen plenty of similar cases brought before his court.'

The officer who had requested the mobile phone location came over with the information. 'The call came from a small country village called Durango which is about halfway between Bilbao and San Sebastian.' The Chief jumped immediately into action, 'That village is only fifteen or twenty minutes from here and I want three unmarked cars each with two officers on board to leave for Durango in the next few minutes. I am sure they made the call using Isabella's mobile phone as it would have Martin's number programmed in it. They would also know that he would recognise her number and be keen to answer it straight away. You are to take tracking devices which can hone in on her frequency which we'll obtain whilst you are on your way there. Do not use sirens and as you get close to the place where Isabella is being held hostage, it is imperative that you do not announce your presence. We'll follow a little after you as I want to take charge of the actual operation to release Isabella from her captors.

This must be carried out in the safest possible way to prevent any harm coming to my niece. Lo entiendes camaradas?' 'Si, Si, we understand,' they answered in unison as the six officers departed.

The rest of the team waited with Martin for the next call from the kidnappers. Strong cups of coffee were distributed whilst Martin sat in the Chief's office. Shortly after an officer came in to report that they had the frequency information for Isabella's phone and had passed it on to the others that were on their way to Durango.

Martin's phone rang and *Señor gruff* started by saying they had checked out their captive's financial situation and were sure that her family should not have any problem raising the funds.

'Have you agreed to get the cash we asked for?'

Martin replied, 'I can get the money but it would be easier to pay by electronic bank transfer.'

'No, no, no! Cash only will we be accepting…no messing around with banks.'

'OK, but it might take a while to gather so much cash together. Have you worked out how we would make the exchange? I need to be certain that *my lady* as you called her, is unharmed and being well cared for before handing over such a large amount of money.'

'You no worry about what we have to do, but worry about getting money for us pronto. Entendido?'

'Understood! Now that I have agreed to your terms, I would like a word with *my lady* to ensure she is in good health.'

'Martin is that you? Please do what they ask so I can come home as soon as possible.'

'Isabella, I've agreed to your captor's demands and José says he's also looking forward to seeing you soon.'

The line went dead and a few minutes later one of the officers on their way to Durango called in to report that they had tracked the phone call to a farmhouse just outside the village. He gave the coordinates which when they checked on the map projected on the wall, gave them the name of the road. Apparently there was only one building along this unpaved farm road. The Chief and the others were to travel quietly to the place and park 100 metres short of the farmhouse.

Martin rode in the police car with José and the others followed. At this time of the night there was not much traffic and they arrived at the rendezvous in no time at all. With all the team assembled, the Chief instructed half the group to approach the front of the building and wait five minutes before knocking on the front door. This would give him and his group time to sneak around the back as he suspected the kidnappers would storm out from the rear of the building once they knew police were out front.

When they crept around the rear of the farmhouse they found four Harley Davidsons and Isabella's car parked close to the back door. Two of the officers quietly walked over to the motorcycles and removed the leads of the ignition lines to the spark plugs. The Chief and the officers drew their guns and waited. The group at the front of the building banged loudly on the door and called out OPEN UP, THIS IS THE POLICE! This was followed by loud swearing and the sound of heavy boots running on the bare floorboards. As the Chief suspected, the rear door was suddenly flung open and out came the four men dragging Isabella along with them. Following them were two young women also wearing *The Villains* leather jackets. They all stopped dead in their tracks when they realised there was a *welcoming committee* waiting for them with guns drawn. One tried to drag

Isabella in front as a shield but the officers who had come in the front door were right behind them and he let go of her when he felt the cold muzzle of a gun at his back. As the police were attaching handcuffs to the gang members, Martin ran over and put his arms around Isabella. He led her to her car and opened the door.

He was surprised to see the key in the ignition and then realised the gang must have left it there in case they needed to make a quick getaway. The Chief approached and told them to go home as they would be here for quite a while going over the place for evidence they will need when the case makes it to court. 'I also have to wait until a prison van gets here to take this mob to the lock-up tonight.'

Martin and Isabella both thanked him for the manner in which he had managed the operation against Isabella's kidnappers and the bloodless way it had ended. She could only guess what had transpired since she had been nabbed leaving her office but Martin promised to fill in the details when they back home and she was more relaxed. 'No doubt a soak in a hot bath is what you need right now,' he told her. As he drove her car back towards Bilbao, she nodded and said, 'Actually, what I need is your arms around me for comfort so we'll heat up the spa bath which is large enough for the two of us!'

CHAPTER 20

PEACE IN OUR TIME? MOST UNLIKELY!

Martin was preparing breakfast mid-morning when a bleary eyed Isabella appeared and gave him a peck on the cheek before flopping onto a chair. She called Raimondo, her fellow senior partner at the law firm to tell him she was OK but would stay home and rest today following the exhausting and traumatic time she had experienced yesterday. 'I'll tell you the details when I see you tomorrow but if I never see another motorcyclist riding a Harley Davidson it will still be too soon!'

She then received a call from her parents to check if she was feeling alright this morning as Martin had telephoned them as soon as he was up to tell them she was back home and sleeping late. They wanted to come see her but she said it would be better if they left it until the afternoon as she couldn't face visitors right now.

Martin served her breakfast and had just sat down when his phone rang. It was the Chief Inspector to say that all four men had been charged with kidnapping and taken before a magistrate first thing this morning. Due to the seriousness of the crime, they will be held in custody until they face trial later in the year. The two women were charged as accessories to the kidnapping and released on bail. Their passports have been revoked and they are to report to their local police station twice a week until they are called to appear in court. 'I'm certain Martin that you and Isabella will not be harassed by these thugs again. My colleagues in San Sebastian will be keeping a close watch on the other members of the club and will come down on them like a ton of bricks if they step out of line. Now, before I forget, Marianna would like you and Isabella to come for dinner tomorrow night if she is feeling up to it. She can phone Marianna later today to let her know if you will be coming.'

After he hung up, he passed the invitation on to Isabella and then excused himself to go into the spare bedroom and set up his laptop on the desk there. 'I have a few calls to make and some emails to prepare and once these are out the way we can sit and talk quietly. Meanwhile I'd like you to try and relax and think about our wedding plans and where we'll go for our honeymoon.' She smiled and said, 'Aye, aye Capitán Taylor!'

He spent some time on the phone with Dario Montoya, his local office manager, telling him about Isabella's kidnapping which had taken place while he was away with Juan in Biarritz. It had ended well thanks to the timely intervention of the Bilbao police. 'Please have Juan submit his final report to Señor Sanchez and put together our invoice which the client insists he will pay immediately on receipt. On another note, have you received any résumés from investigators in Madrid and for your office as well?'

'Yes, I have and if you aren't coming in to the office today, I'll forward them to you by email and you can call me to discuss after you've read them Mr. Taylor. I had requested applicants to submit their applications in English so you'll have no trouble understanding them. By the way, congratulations on bringing the San Sebastian case to a satisfactory conclusion.' Martin replied that Juan had performed well and was a key factor in the success of the assignment.

Jessica Wainwright had forwarded an update on assignments in progress in Australia and he would go through them later and respond accordingly.

Martin then composed a long email to Robert Mason at the Houston Chronicle describing in detail the events that had taken place from the time he arrived in Bilbao until today. He finished up by repeating the words of the British Prime Minister Neville Chamberlain who after meeting Hitler in 1939, famously said 'PEACE IN OUR TIME' and within a week world war two had commenced!

He looked into the lounge room and saw that Isabella was stretched out on the sofa fast asleep. He found a blanket in a closet in the hall and carefully covered her with it making sure not to wake her up.

Returning to his laptop, he found that Dario had sent through the résumés for his review. The first two were for the position in Madrid. One was from a man who had only a little experience in investigative work and none of the assignments he had listed were related to art. The second was from a woman who had a university degree in the arts and had worked for a number of galleries in and around Madrid including the Prado for some years before branching out as an independent contractor. In this role she had advised private galleries on how to improve their security.

There were three other résumés from applicants who resided in the Bilbao district. Two of these were of interest and Martin wrote down their names on his notepad then telephoned Dario.

'I have reviewed all the résumés and have decided on the following:

For the Madrid assignment I would select the woman whose first name was Lisa because of her education and experience in the art world, and for the additional investigator needed here in Bilbao my choice is between Antonio and Raul. I'd like you to contact those two and bring them in for face-to-face interviews. If they can come in before I depart for Australia at the weekend I'll sit in while you question thm otherwise I'll wait to hear from you how it went and respect your choice.'

He had just hit the SEND key when the doorbell chimed and he looked at the screen on the wall and saw that it was Isabella's parents. He opened the front door and as they came in Isabella appeared from the lounge obviously awakened by the bell. They all went to the family room and settled in whilst Martin busied himself taking coffee and tea orders. Isabella assured them that other than being extremely tired, she was OK. "Despite the rough treatment I received from those thugs, I was otherwise physically unharmed.'

Rosetta told them that Marianna had also invited them for dinner this evening so they would come by and pick them up so they can all go together. 'This is assuming you are feeling up to it Isabella?' Martin appeared from the kitchen with a tray of tea and coffee cups. He surprised them all by producing two packs of Tim Tam chocolate biscuits that he had brought from home for Isabella. 'I introduced your daughter to these Aussie favourites when she visited Melbourne for the first time.

They are a hit whenever I give them to people for the first time. There are two types…dark and milk chocolate, so take your pick and enjoy.'

In between sipping his tea and munching on a Tim Tam, Victor asked the couple if they had made any decision on when they might get married. 'I hope this is not too presumptuous of us but Mother and I are anxious to see you two tie the knot. We know that this is the first time we have actually met you Martin, but we have heard so much about you from Isabella these past few years that we already consider you a part of our family.'

Martin thanked them for accepting him into the family and Isabella took over to explain what they had decided so far. 'The date has not been fixed yet but we intend to be married by a wedding celebrant here in Bilbao this coming spring. We want to keep it small and will only invite close family and a small number of our best friends….a total of 20 including us and the celebrant. We'll honeymoon in Europe then have a party of close friends and business associates in Bilbao. Later on we'll do the same thing in Melbourne.'

'I'm excited already,' remarked Victor, 'I had a feeling that Martin's visit here this week was for something more important than just business! Can we mention your plans to **Uncle José this evening Isabella?** We know how much he likes Martin so he'll be as *pleased as Punch* also.'

Isabella said that she would have told the others this evening but as Dad is so excited about it, she was OK with him announcing their news when they're having pre-dinner drinks with **Uncle José** and Aunt Marianna. 'What time will you pick us up Dad?' Victor replied that they were to be there around 8 o'clock so they would come by at 7.30. 'We'll head off home now and see you both later.'

Isabella was tidying up the afternoon tea dishes and Martin went back to the desk in the spare room to work. There was an email from Robert Mason commenting on the events that had taken place since Martin arrived in Bilbao. He was clearly upset that the harassment that started in Houston on his return from Mexico City had crossed the Pacific Ocean to Melbourne and then raised its ugly head again in Bilbao. The email was full of apologies as he felt responsible being the person that had drawn Martin into a world where gangsters prevailed. Martin replied assuring him that he was also partly responsible as it was his idea to go to Mexico City in the knowledge that he would be entering a lions' den.

Robert sent a further email in which he was pleased to announce that the next weekend magazine has been printed and includes part one of the Martin Taylor story. It was clear now that the serial would extend to three episodes and the third and final one would now be amended to include the events that have just taken place.

Isabella came to see what Martin was up to and to ask his advice on which outfit she should wear this evening. She held up two smart pants suits, one pale green and the other beige. He chose the pale green suit and she said, 'That's perfect as I will wear the emerald necklace that my parents gave me for my twenty first.'

He then told her about Robert Mason's email and how upset he was that *The Villains* harassment had followed him all the way to Bilbao. 'I've written back just now that we are tough and have come away from the bullying in better shape than the thugs who are now locked away and will remain that way for a long time.'

They were ready and waiting in the front room for Isabella's parents when they heard the car pull into the driveway. They switched off the lights and turned on the alarm and got into Victor's luxurious Audi sedan. As they drove away Martin was struck by how quiet it was and remarked to Victor how earlier models were usually noisy diesels. 'It's the latest Audi electric vehicle Martin, they call it e-Tron whatever that means.'

Martin recognised the house as soon as they pulled up and turned to Isabella saying, 'What a wonderful feeling this gives me returning to the place where we first met.' She took his hand as they got out of the car and walked to the front door. They were welcomed by the oldest of their three children, Maria, who told Martin that she was now 16 and in her final year at high school. 'I remember you Mister Taylor when you came here for dinner and told us about Australia. I am hoping to visit your country after I graduate and take a gap year before going to university. My two brothers are upstairs doing homework and will be down when dinner is being served.' She led them into the lounge where José was behind his bar preparing drinks. 'Good evening everyone, I know what my brother and sister-in-law enjoy for pre-dinner drinks but am now ready to take orders from Isabella and Martin.'

Marianna appeared from the kitchen and once they were all settled with their drinks in hand, Victor stood up to propose a toast to Isabella and Martin. 'Rosetta and I are pleased to announce that plans are under way for Isabella and Martin to marry in the spring and we wish them every happiness for their future together.' Hugs and kisses followed and Isabella was bombarded with questions about when and where the wedding was to take place.

José took Martin aside and wanted to know more about the events that culminated in the kidnapping of Isabella. This discussion took quite some time as Martin needed to explain how it all began with leaving the Victoria Police and starting his own private investigation company. He tried to be brief but there was so much to relate and José kept asking questions along the way. Finally, Marianna interrupted and invited everybody to move to the dining room as dinner was about to be served. Their other two children, André who was 13, and Marcus who was 10, appeared and shook hands with Martin.

It was close to midnight when the wonderful meal was topped off with crêpes and liqueurs. The children headed to bed and the visitors thanked their hosts and departed. On the way home Martin told Victor and Rosetta that he was leaving Saturday to return to Melbourne and how much he had enjoyed their company this week. 'I apologize for the trauma that I have been responsible for these past few days and promise that I will do everything in my power to keep your daughter safe.'

As the car pulled up outside Isabella's home her father turned to Martin and said, 'We understand fully what took place and the responsibility falls squarely on the Mexican drug baron and the thugs he employed to make life difficult for you.' Martin thanked him and Victor continued, 'I have come across these types of crooks many times during my long career in courtrooms and believe that people involved in trafficking drugs are the lowest of low amongst the world's humanity.' Rosetta said she would telephone tomorrow to say goodbye to Martin. They said goodnight and Isabella and Martin went inside and straight to bed feeling quite exhausted.

Next morning Isabella announced that she was feeling well enough to go to work and would drive Martin to his office if he wished. 'I shouldn't need the car today,' he replied, 'so that would be nice thanks.'

His phone beeped an incoming text which was from Dario saying both the applicants were available for interview today. The first was coming at 11 o'clock and the other at 2 o'clock. Martin replied that he would be there shortly.

On the way to the office, Martin suggested they have a quiet night together as it has been such a busy week. 'Fortunately my flight to Madrid tomorrow is not till late morning and then I have a couple of hours there waiting for the ongoing flight to Dubai.' Isabella nodded agreement as she turned into the street where Martin's office was located. She pecked him on the cheek and said she'd be back around 5.30 to pick him up.

Martin ran into Juan Lopez as he entered the office. 'Good morning Juan, are you about to go out?' Juan nodded and told him he was about to meet with management at the Bilbao Fine Arts Museum to discuss a new assignment. Martin told him that he had visited that museum when he was here previously and remembered what a wonderful collection of Basque paintings they had. Juan departed and Dario took him through to the room where they would interview the applicants. 'How is Señora Segueras?' Martin thanked him for asking and told him that she was OK and back at work. 'In fact she drove me here today so I wouldn't have to worry about where to park my rental car.'

The two men then went through the current inquiries and decided that hiring one new investigator would suffice for the moment. At precisely 11 o'clock the buzzer sounded and Dario asked who was there via the security intercom. 'I'm Antonio Arozenta, and have come for the interview.' Dario pressed the button to unlock the front door and went to greet the man. A fine looking young man entered and Martin guessed his age at around thirty five. He was well dressed and had taken care to present himself in a neat and tidy fashion.

He was seated in the interview room and given a cup of coffee to relax before being questioned. He had graduated from Toledo University with degrees in Ancient Spanish History and Curatorial Studies. This led to a number of curating positions at public and private art galleries. He handed over the most recent reference letters from his employers. Each gave glowing statements concerning his knowledge of art, especially from the

15th and 16th centuries. They each spoke of his honesty and zeal for the job.

Martin allowed Dario to manage the interview which was carried out mostly in English and showed Antonio had an excellent ability to switch from Spanish to English effortlessly. When asked what he did for relaxation he answered that he played tennis and also spent a lot of his free time swimming. He was thanked for attending today and promised that a decision would be made by this weekend and he would be notified on Monday if he was successful or not. After he departed, it was agreed that he seemed to have the kind of qualities they were looking for,

At 1 o'clock, Dario locked the office and they walked across the street to a small café for a light lunch. Back in the office, Dario translated the full text of Antonio's reference letters which were all in Spanish as during the interview he had only read out the highlights.

When the second applicant arrived just after 2 o'clock, the first thing Martin noticed was that the fellow was wearing a black leather jacket. In his mind he decided that his paranoia was getting the better of him but then looked down and saw that he was wearing big heavy boots. When he was seated in the interview room, Martin looked at the application form then spoke first. 'Your name is Raul d'Aragon, is that correct?' He replied, 'Si Señor.' Martin continued as Dario sat silently witnessing this interrogation. 'Do you like riding motorcycles? Please answer in English as it is a requirement for all our employees that applicants have the ability to speak languages other than Spanish, and English is a must.' Raul spluttered and mumbled his response. 'I do not have a car but travel everywhere on my motorbike which suits me best as it is easier to find somewhere to park in the city.'

Martin nodded to Dario to take over the questioning. When pinned down to specifics of what was written in the résumé, Raul stumbled and it was clear that someone else had written the document. The two reference letters he offered were obviously forgeries because according to Dario one of the galleries purported to have been his employer had closed down in the early 2000's! Martin then stepped in again and asked straight out if Raul had heard of *The Villains*. The guy burst into tears and admitted that he was forced into this charade by someone he had met in a bar one night. He had been offered payment to submit the application for the job and as he was actually unemployed he grabbed the chance to make some easy money. 'Raul d'Aragon is not your real name is it?' asked Dario. He shook his head. Martin asked him to write down his real name and address and get out before the police were called in. 'Don't mess us around anymore by giving us any false information as you will be hunted down and face the full force of the Bilbao police.'

After he had rushed out the door, Martin ran to the window and looked down on the street below just in time to see the guy jump on his motorbike. He snapped a couple of close-up photos of the license plate as it raced away. Dario turned to Martin and said, 'The surname d'Aragon is something from the dim, dark ages and it's unlikely anyone living today would have that name. Do you wish me to follow up with the third application we received or go with Antonio whom we interviewed earlier?' 'I'm satisfied that Antonio will be an asset for the company so please notify him and negotiate a starting salary and fix a date when he can join us.'

Martin selected the best photo of the motorbike and texted it to the police chief with a message describing the interview. He also attached the guy's supposed real name and address and suggested that they keep a watch on him. He might be just an innocent fool but one never knows.

He spent the remainder of the afternoon composing emails to his Melbourne office and the limo service with his flight details. Just before 5.30 his phone rang and it was Isabella to say she would be out front in five minutes. Martin packed up his things, shook hands with Dario and went down to wait in the street. He had just walked out when Isabella pulled up. On the way home he related what had occurred with the interviews. 'Wow,' she exclaimed, 'those people don't want to let up it seems. Just like the world in general, peace seems to be eternally elusive!'

CHAPTER 21

A SURPRISE ENDING.

Back at Isabella's house, Martin had started sorting out his clothes for the long flights ahead to Melbourne when Isabella brought him a glass of Bourbon. I can't be bothered cooking tonight so will order pizzas to be delivered later. He followed her into the living room where they both sat sipping their drinks. Isabella had poured herself a Portuguese sherry and switched on the radio for some classical music. They were both silently engrossed in Edward Elgar's Violin Concerto in B minor when the sublime moment was shattered with the ringing of the doorbell. Martin jumped up and went straight to the CCTV screen to see who was at the door and called out to Isabella, 'It's OK love, wait till you see who's here.' He swung open the front door with a flourish and welcomed Robert and Barbara Mason!

'I can't believe my eyes,' he exclaimed as Isabella joined him in the front hallway. Handshakes and hugs all round, they took their guests into the formal lounge and sat them down. 'Why didn't you let us know you were coming to Bilbao?' Martin asked. Robert replied that they had planned a two week vacation in Italy and had reserved all their flights and accommodation. When the weekend magazine with the first episode of Martin's story was ready for this week, Barbara suggested that they could deliver it personally to Martin and Isabella. As Martin had mentioned in a recent email that he would be leaving Bilbao this Saturday, they had their travel agent pull out all strings to get flights organised that would get them here today. 'So here we are,' they exclaimed in unison! Isabella immediately offered to put them up at her house. 'Thank you but we have already checked into a suite in a beautiful modern hotel right opposite the Guggenheim Museum,' Robert told them. 'What's the name of the hotel?' Martin asked. Robert looked at their room key and read out, '*Gran Hotel Domine.*' 'That's the same hotel I stayed in three years ago,' Martin said. 'It's a gorgeous place and the suites have a glass wall between the bathroom and the bedroom so at night you can luxuriate in the bath as you gaze out at the floodlit Guggenheim. It's an absolutely stunning never-to-be-forgotten view.' Barbara remarked that they have the same sort of suite and have yet to experience the view at night.

Martin asked, 'How did you get this address?' Robert replied that he had read in Martin's story that Isabella's uncle was the Bilbao chief of police and it was easy to track him down. 'I called him and we had a pleasant chat during which I explained our relationship and he agreed to provide me with Isabella's address. I told him that we wanted to surprise you and he agreed not to tell you we were coming today. Before we departed Houston, I was asked to pass on regards from Neville Montgomery who told me that he and Estelle will be seeing you in Melbourne shortly when they take an extended vacation *Down Under.*'

Robert then opened the bag he had brought with him. Out came two bottles of Dom Perrier champagne and four copies of the Houston Chronicle Weekend Magazine. Isabella then insisted that they stay and have pizzas with them.

She had a copy of the local pizza restaurant's menu in the kitchen and asked them to choose what she should order for home delivery.

After she had telephoned the order through, they sat in the lounge and discussed the places they were visiting in Italy. Barbara said she can best give the details as she'd made all the arrangements, Robert being too busy at the Houston Chronicle.

'We are going to spend a few days in Florence visiting all the grand sights including the Uffizi Gallery, the Pitti Palace and because I'm a mad gardener we're also going to see the Boboli Gardens which I have been told are magnificent.' Isabella remarked that Barbara's selections were excellent choices as she had visited Florence a couple of times and taken in those same sites. Barbara continued, 'We are then travelling by train to the Cinque Terre and will spend five days there.

From the brochures I picked up from our travel agent, it appears that these five towns are amongst the most picturesque places to visit in Italy and we're really looking forward to our stay there.' Isabella told them she hadn't been there herself but her parents had been there twice on vacation and raved about it. 'We then complete our tour with three days in Rome,' Barbara said.

The doorbell chimed and Martin collected the pizzas from the young delivery guy handing him a tip. He took them to the kitchen so Isabella could put them onto her best dishes and set them on the dining room table. Martin popped the cork on the champagne and filled four flutes. As they were eating, Robert asked if they had made wedding plans. 'Having read your story in detail for the magazine article Martin, I finished up with a feeling that maybe this could be the right time for you both to make plans…. am I correct?'

Isabella decided to answer this question. 'Robert, you must be psychic, as we have made some crucial decisions concerning our wedding and just today I finalized a date with a marriage celebrant. I hadn't got around to telling Martin yet and was about to give him the news earlier when our doorbell rang and we received the surprise of our life when you arrived. It's going to be on Sunday July 24 here in Bilbao and will be attended only by my closest family members and my neighbours who happen to be my family's best friends.' Martin stepped in to provide his input to the wedding party. 'I'll bring out my mother, sister, brother-in-law and their children for the actual wedding plus two couples who happen to be my closest friends.'

Before he could continue, Robert stood up and on behalf of his wife and himself wished them all the best for their future together. Martin thanked them and explained that following their honeymoon they would have a large party here for Isabella's extended family and friends plus her law-firm colleagues and friends. 'Later on Isabella will fly to Melbourne and we'll have another party for my far-flung relatives, business associates and close friends in my home town.'

After the pizzas had been consumed, Isabella served up bowls of berries and ice cream which was washed down with the second bottle of champagne.

The weekend magazine was then opened up on the coffee table and as Martin flicked through the pages, he and Isabella commented on the high quality of the reproductions which is not always the case when photographs are transferred into newsprint. They would read the text later….. Isabella after Martin had left for Australia, and he when he had hours to spare during the long flights.

It was getting late when the Mason's said they'd like to return to their hotel as they were still somewhat jetlagged, Martin offered to drive them, but Isabella warned he had consumed a lot of champagne and it wasn't a good idea.

Robert then told them that they had arranged to call the same taxi driver that had brought them there earlier and he would come to take them back to the hotel. 'I had the driver's business card and I had called him fifteen minutes ago when I went to the bathroom.' Sure enough, the doorbell rang and the driver was standing outside. As they were leaving, Barbara promised to stay in touch and suggested that should they receive an invitation to attend the after-party in Melbourne, she would make sure Robert takes the time off so the two of them could make the trip across the Pacific for the first time. The Mason's then departed in the taxi and Isabella tidied up whilst Martin finished packing ready for tomorrow.

Later in bed, Martin told Isabella that the evening had turned into a wonderful surprise and she responded saying, 'The surprises aren't over yet my darling!'

THE END

(or is it?)

www.ingramcontent.com/pod-product-compliance
Lightning Source LLC
LaVergne TN
LVHW091535060526
838200LV00036B/618